reflections at the window

Michael Manosca

edited by
Regena Slater

Copyright © 2025 by Michael Manosca

Visit the author's website at www.michaelmanosca.com

All rights reserved.

Edited by: Regena Slater

ISBN:

979-8-9998773-5-2 (paperback)

979-8-9998773-7-6 (electronic)

979-8-9998773-6-9 (hardcover)

Library of Congress Control Number: 2025919055

First Edition.

Los Angeles, California, United State of America

The story, all names, characters, and incidents portrayed in this production are fictitious. No identification with actual persons (living or deceased), places, buildings, and products is intended or should be inferred.

For the searchers and the welcomers—those finding their way home and those who open their doors

Sometimes the heart recognizes
what the mind cannot yet understand.

preface

For years, I worked in the entertainment industry in Los Angeles, culminating in my time at 20th Century Fox studios in Century City. Many days, I would take a lunch walk across the lot and exit onto Pico Boulevard—getting my steps in and, more importantly, clearing my mind. The street bustled with life: cyclists traveling across town, shoppers heading to and from the nearby mall, and unfortunately, people who were clearly homeless.

I say unfortunately not because I didn't want to see them, but because they were in that position at all, especially the younger ones. I'd wonder how they got there and what, if anything, I could do.

One day, I caught sight of a kid, perhaps sixteen or seventeen, sitting at a bus stop across the street. He looked like he came from the suburbs somewhere, but the streets had already hardened him. When our eyes met, it felt as if I could sense his entire life story—all the short years he'd been old enough to craft it. He stepped aboard the bus as I stood watching, and I wondered what would become of him.

I spent fifteen years thinking about that encounter, writing fragments of this story with his image in mind, but nothing ever materialized. Then something clicked—I can't say what exactly—but the words began to flow and the result was *Reflections at the Window*.

My hope was to explore the idea that finding our way home, whatever that means for each of us, is life's most important journey. And just when it seems impossible, another sojourner appears, willing to help us get there. This is a story about connection across the spaces that divide us and the recognition that sometimes the heart sees what the mind cannot yet understand. It's about choosing who to let in and the courage to trust again, about opening our doors to strangers who might not be strangers after all.

For all the searchers still walking Pico Boulevard and streets like it everywhere, and for all the welcomers watching from windows, wondering how they might help—this story is for you.

one
the executive

DAVID HARMON ADJUSTED his tie in the reflection of his office window, the sprawling Los Angeles basin stretching endlessly beyond the glass. Twenty-six floors above the Miracle Mile, his corner office at Meridian Pictures commanded a view that still occasionally caught him off guard—not because of its beauty, but because of how far he'd traveled from the small Indiana town where he'd learned to keep his head down and his thoughts to himself.

The morning ritual was always the same: coffee black, emails triaged by priority, calendar reviewed for potential conflicts. By seven-thirty, he'd absorbed the overnight box office reports, the international tracking numbers, and three trade publications. His assistant wouldn't arrive for another hour, but David preferred these quiet moments when the building hummed with possibility rather than the controlled chaos that would follow.

His phone buzzed. A text from his counterpart in London: *Preliminary numbers look strong. Well done on the campaign.*

David typed back a brief acknowledgment, then set the phone aside. Success felt different at fifty-three than it had at thirty-five—less intoxicating, more like a well-tailored suit that fit perfectly but had lost its novelty. He'd climbed every rung he'd set out to climb, earned respect from colleagues and competitors alike, built a reputation for steady judgment and innovative thinking. The trades quoted him regularly. Industry panels sought his expertise. Yet most mornings, he felt like an actor playing a role he'd perfected but never quite believed in.

The irony wasn't lost on him that he'd built his career in an industry dedicated to storytelling while keeping his own story carefully edited, essential scenes left on the cutting room floor.

A knock interrupted his thoughts. Tom Richter peered around the door, coffee in hand and expression bright with the kind of enthusiasm that made David feel simultaneously grateful and exhausted.

"Morning, David. Got a minute to talk about the Jacobson project?"

David gestured to the chair across from his desk. Tom was good at his job—thorough, creative, reliable—and at thirty-eight had the hungry energy David remembered having once, before success had taught him that every victory was temporary and every relationship in this business came with invisible expiration dates.

"The director's pushing back on the marketing approach," Tom continued, settling into the chair. "Wants to emphasize the romance angle over the thriller elements. I think he's wrong, but..."

As Tom spoke, David found his attention drifting not to the content of the conversation but to something else entirely. Tom's wedding ring caught the morning light, and David noticed how the younger man's voice softened almost imperceptibly when he mentioned discussing the project with his wife the night before. There was something in that soft- ness—a quality of being truly known by another person, of having someone who genuinely cared about the small defeats and victories of his workday.

The observation came without warning or invitation, the way these moments always did. David felt himself pulled, as if viewing Tom's life through glass that suddenly became permeable. He could sense the warm kitchen where Tom had discussed the project over dinner, could almost taste the wine they'd shared, could feel the comfort of being heard and understood by someone who chose to care about your professional frus- trations simply because they cared about you.

The sensation lasted only seconds, but it left David hollow in its wake. He forced himself back to the conversation, offered the strategic advice Tom needed, made the executive decision about the marketing approach. But the echo of that inadvertent glimpse into Tom's life lingered like a song you couldn't quite get out of your head.

After Tom left, David stood again at his window. The empathic episodes—for lack of a better term—had been part of his life for as long as he could remember. As a child, caring for his cousin Danny, he'd first noticed his ability to slip inside another person's experience, to feel their confusion or fear, or simple contentment as if it were his own. His aunt had called it sensitivity, his mother had worried it was unhealthy, and David had learned early to keep these moments to himself.

Over the years, he'd developed strategies. In restaurants, he kept his gaze focused on his companion rather than scanning the room. At the theater, he chose aisle seats where he could look toward the stage rather than at the faces around him. The episodes were unpredictable—sometimes months would pass without incident, and then he'd be blindsided by someone's grief or joy or loneliness in a grocery store checkout line.

The ability had shaped his career choices more than he liked to admit. Films were stories about other people's lives, experiences he could explore safely from behind a camera, through scripts and performances that maintained the necessary distance. In marketing and distribution, he could analyze emotional responses without risking the uncontrolled immersion that happened when his empathic radar activated unexpectedly.

It had also shaped his personal life, though he tried not to think about that too much.

His assistant's voice came through the intercom. "David? Your ten o'clock is here."

The day proceeded with its familiar rhythm: meetings, phone calls, decisions that would affect the careers of people whose names he knew but whose lives remained safely distant. Lunch was a working meal with two executives from a competing studio—professional pleasantries masquerading as friendship, the kind of relationship that served everyone's interests while requiring nothing more vulnerable than shared opinions about market trends and talent packages.

By evening, David's office had emptied except for the cleaning crew. He stayed late not because the work demanded it, but because the alternative—returning to his beautifully appointed house in the hills—felt more like an obligation than a refuge. The house was everything a successful executive should own: four bedrooms, three and a half baths, a kitchen that had been featured in Architectural Digest, a pool he rarely used, and a view of the city that suggested both achievement and isolation.

He finally gathered his things and headed for the elevator, nodding to Jerry, the security guard who'd worked the building for fifteen years. In the parking garage, his BMW started with its usual quiet precision. The drive home took twenty-five minutes in light traffic, winding through neighborhoods that grew progressively more vibrant and eclectic as he entered West Hollywood.

The house greeted him with silence. Motion sensors activated lights as he moved from room to room, creating the illusion of life without its substance. He poured himself a glass of wine—a bottle he'd brought back from a vineyard in Sonoma—and stood on his terrace, looking down at the grid of lights that marked other people's lives.

Somewhere down there, Tom Richter was probably helping his kids with homework or discussing the day with his wife. Somewhere, Jerry was heading home to whatever family awaited him. Somewhere, people were arguing and laughing and making love and making up, living the messy, complicated, connected lives that David observed from a distance, like a film he could analyze but never quite enter.

His phone buzzed with a text from Elena: *How was your day?*

He considered several responses before typing back: *The usual. Yours?*

Exhausting. Aiden's been moody all week. Teenage hormones or something deeper—hard to tell.

David stared at the message, remembering Elena's eldest son, whom he'd met twice during his infrequent visits to Boston. Seventeen now, if he remembered correctly. The age when everything felt impossibly urgent and adults seemed to speak a foreign language.

Growing up is complicated, he typed back. *Especially when you're figuring out who you are.*

Speaking from experience?

He almost smiled at that. Elena had known him long enough to read between the lines of his carefully neutral responses. She'd been Michael's best friend first, then had somehow become David's anchor after Michael died, one of the few people who remembered the version of himself that had existed when he'd been half of something larger.

Ancient experience, he replied. *Give him time.*

Thanks. Get some sleep. You work too much.

David set the phone aside and finished his wine. Elena was probably right about the work, but she didn't understand that work was easier than the alternative—sitting in this beautiful house, surrounded by the evidence of his success, trying to remember what it felt like to be necessary to another person.

He turned off the terrace lights and headed inside, past the guest rooms that never hosted guests, past the home office where he sometimes worked weekends just to fill the silence. In his bedroom, he changed into comfortable clothes and picked up the novel he'd been reading—a story about a man who inherits his father's bookstore and discovers family secrets that change everything he thought he knew about his own life.

Twenty pages in, David set the book aside. Fiction required a kind of emotional investment he wasn't sure he still possessed. The characters loved and lost and found each other again with a passion that felt simultaneously familiar and foreign, like a language he'd once spoken fluently but had somehow forgotten.

He turned off the light and lay in the dark, listening to the distant hum of the city below. Tomorrow would bring another day of meetings and decisions, professional accomplishments that would add to his reputation and his portfolio but leave him essentially unchanged. He'd built a life that looked perfect from the outside—successful, independent, comfortable—and most days, that was enough.

But sometimes, in the space between sleeping and waking, he remembered what it felt like to matter to someone else, to be part of a story larger than his individual ambitions. Sometimes he missed that feeling so intensely it took his breath away.

Tonight was one of those nights.

two
through glass

DAVID HAD BEEN COMING to Mel's Diner for three years, ever since discovering it during a particularly long day when the studio commissary had felt too claustrophobic and the trendy restaurants near the office too performative. The place had the comfortable anonymity of a 1950s time capsule—red vinyl booths, black and white checkered floors, and waitresses who called everyone "hon" without irony. Most importantly, it was the kind of place where a man could sit alone with a book and a cup of coffee without attracting attention or pity.

Thursday evenings had become his routine. Leave the office by six-thirty, drive the fifteen minutes to the diner, claim the corner booth that faced the window but kept his back to most of the restaurant. Order the same thing: coffee, black, and whatever soup they had that wasn't too adventurous. Read for an hour, sometimes two if the book was good and the booth stayed available. It wasn't much of a social life, but it felt more honest than the industry events where conversation never moved beyond the superficial.

Tonight, he'd brought a biography of Akira Kurosawa, hoping the filmmaker's insights into visual storytelling might spark something useful for the project that had been consuming his thoughts all week. The diner was busier than usual—a few families finishing early dinners, a couple of students bent over laptops, an elderly man working a crossword puzzle with the focused intensity of someone for whom this was serious business.

David was forty pages into a chapter about the making of "Seven Samurai" when something shifted in his peripheral vision. Not movement, exactly, but a quality of stillness that drew his attention despite his better judgment. He glanced up from his book and found himself looking across the diner at a young man sitting alone in a booth near the far window.

The kid—he couldn't have been more than eighteen or nineteen—sat with his shoulders hunched slightly forward, staring down at a cup of coffee that appeared to have gone cold long ago. There was something in his posture that suggested he was trying to make himself smaller, less noticeable. His clothes were clean but worn, jeans that had seen better days and a sweater that looked like it might have come from a thrift store. Dark hair fell across his forehead, partially obscuring his face, but David could see enough to recognize the particular kind of exhaustion that came from carrying too much weight for too young a pair of shoulders.

David tried to return his attention to the book, but the words seemed to blur on the page. Something about the young man's stillness felt magnetic, like a film frame that demanded closer examination. Without quite meaning to, David found himself looking up again.

That's when it happened.

The sensation was immediate and overwhelming—like being pulled through water, or through glass that had suddenly become permeable. One moment David was sitting safely in his own booth, and the next he was drowning in someone else's experience.

Fear. Raw, animal fear that made his hands shake and his stomach clench. The constant awareness of being watched, judged, found wanting. The exhausting effort of trying to appear normal when nothing felt normal anymore. Hunger—not just for food, though that was real enough, but for safety, for belonging, for someone to see him as more than a problem to be solved or a threat to be avoided.

Underneath it all, a grief so profound it took David's breath away. The grief of a child who had lost everything familiar, who woke up each morning to the fresh shock of remembering that home was no longer a place he could return to. The particular ache of missing a mother's voice, a father's approval, even when those voices had become sources of pain.

David gripped the edge of the table, fighting the disorientation that always accompanied these episodes. He could taste the bitter coffee the young man had been drinking, could feel the worn vinyl of the booth seat beneath him, could sense the way his eyes kept darting toward the door— always aware of exit routes, always ready to run.

But there was something else, something that made this episode different from the usual involuntary glimpses into strangers' lives. Beneath the fear and grief, David sensed a core of strength that hadn't been broken, a fundamental goodness that refused to be extinguished despite everything that had tried to crush it. This wasn't just survival—it was a daily choice to remain human in circumstances that made humanity feel like a luxury he couldn't afford.

The connection lasted perhaps thirty seconds, though it felt much longer. When David finally managed to break free, pulling himself back into his own body and his own booth, he was shaking. His coffee had grown cold, and his book lay forgotten beside his plate.

He looked up again, expecting to find the young man staring back at him, somehow aware of the intrusion. But the kid was reaching into his pocket, pulling out a few crumpled bills and counting them with the careful attention of someone for whom every dollar mattered. David watched him place exact change on the table—enough for the coffee and a modest tip—then slide out of the booth and head for the door.

David's first instinct was to follow, but his legs felt unsteady, and by the time he'd gathered himself enough to stand, the young man had disappeared into the evening foot traffic along Pico Boulevard. David remained standing beside his table for a moment, uncertain what to do with the emotional residue of what he'd just experienced.

"You okay, hon?" The waitress—Dolores, according to her name tag —appeared at his elbow with a concerned expression. "You look like you've seen a ghost."

"I'm fine," David managed, though his voice sounded strange to his own ears. "Just... thought I recognized someone."

Dolores followed his gaze toward the now-empty booth. "The kid? Sweet boy. Been coming in a couple times a week for the past month or so. Always orders just coffee, sometimes a piece of pie if he's feeling flush. Polite as can be, never causes any trouble."

David nodded, not trusting himself to speak. He left money for his own check and headed for the parking lot, his mind racing. In all the years he'd been experiencing these empathic episodes, he'd never felt anything quite so intense, so complete. Usually, the connections were fragments—a flash of someone's joy or sorrow, a brief glimpse into their emotional landscape. This had been different. This had felt like stepping completely into another person's life.

The drive home passed in a blur. David found himself taking a longer route, driving slowly past bus stops and late-night diners, though he couldn't have said what he was looking for. Or perhaps he could—he was looking for a young man with dark hair and worn clothes who carried himself like someone trying to disappear while simultaneously fighting to survive.

Back in his West Hollywood house, David poured himself a larger glass of wine than usual and stood on his terrace, looking out over the city lights. Somewhere out there, that young man was spending another night in circumstances David could only imagine. The thought made him feel simultaneously helpless and compelled to act, though he had no idea what action might be appropriate or even possible.

He thought about calling Elena, but what would he say? That he'd had another empathic episode, this one stronger than usual? That he'd glimpsed into the life of a homeless teenager and couldn't stop thinking about it? Elena would listen—she always did—but she lived three thousand miles away with teenage problems of her own.

David finished his wine and headed inside, but sleep proved elusive. He lay in his comfortable bed in his expensive house, surrounded by all the evidence of his successful life, and couldn't shake the memory of that profound loneliness he'd felt in the diner. Not just the young man's loneliness, but his own—the isolation he'd become so good at managing that he'd almost convinced himself it was a choice rather than a wound.

For the first time in years, David found himself wondering what it would be like to matter to someone again, to be necessary rather than merely successful. The thought was as frightening as it was appealing.

Outside his window, Los Angeles hummed with its endless energy, eight million people living their separate lives in the sprawling grid of lights. Most nights, that vastness felt comforting in its anonymity. Tonight, it felt like a sea of missed connections, of people who might need each other but would never find a way to bridge the space between.

David closed his eyes and tried to sleep, but every time he began to drift off, he found himself back in that diner booth, experiencing someone else's fear and grief and stubborn hope. It occurred to him that this might be the first time his empathic ability had shown him someone whose need he might actually be able to address—if he could figure out how, and if he had the courage to try.

The question was whether he was brave enough to let himself care about a stranger, or whether thirty years of careful emotional distance had made him too cautious to take such a risk.

Only time would tell.

three
second sighting

THREE DAYS PASSED before David returned to Mel's Diner. He'd told himself he was simply maintaining his routine, that Thursday evening dinners at the familiar booth had nothing to do with the young man he'd encountered there. But as he scanned the restaurant from the doorway, his eyes automatically sought the booth where the kid had been sitting, and the disappointment he felt at finding it occupied by a family with two small children revealed the lie he'd been telling himself.

The weekend had been restless. David had attended a gallery opening in Beverly Hills on Friday night—the kind of professional obligation that filled his calendar but left him feeling more isolated than if he'd stayed home. Saturday brought a tennis game with his neighbor Craig, followed by dinner at a restaurant where the food was excellent and the conversation safely superficial. Sunday, he'd driven to Malibu and walked the beach for two hours, trying to shake the persistent memory of that overwhelming empathic connection.

But the young man's presence lingered in his thoughts like an echo that wouldn't fade. David found himself wondering where he'd slept those three nights, whether he'd had enough to eat, whether anyone else had noticed the quiet dignity with which he carried his obvious hardship. The questions felt intrusive, even unasked, but he couldn't seem to dismiss them.

Monday morning brought its usual rhythm of meetings and decisions, but David's concentration felt fractured. During a presentation about international distribution strategies, he caught himself staring out the window, scanning the street below for a figure that wouldn't be there. Tuesday was better, but Wednesday found him leaving work early—something he almost never did—and driving aimlessly through West Hollywood and Santa Monica, as if the BMW might somehow carry him to answers he couldn't articulate.

Thursday evening, he was back at Mel's Diner.

The booth he preferred was available, and David settled in with the same Kurosawa biography, though he'd made little progress since the previous week. Dolores appeared with coffee almost immediately, her smile warmer than strictly professional.

"Back again, hon? You're becoming quite the regular."

"Creature of habit, I suppose," David replied, grateful that she didn't mention the previous week's odd behavior.

"Nothing wrong with that. Creature of habit myself—been working here twelve years come November." She poured his coffee with practiced efficiency. "You want the usual? We've got a nice mushroom barley tonight."

David nodded, though he hadn't really heard the menu options. His attention was already drifting toward the other booths, scanning faces with the kind of casual surveillance he'd trained himself to avoid. The young man wasn't there—he knew that within thirty seconds of sitting down—but David found himself checking periodically anyway, as if sustained observation might somehow conjure the presence he was seeking.

The soup arrived, along with the crusty bread that Mel's served with everything. David ate mechanically, turning pages without absorbing their content. The evening crowd was lighter than the previous week: a few college students, an elderly couple sharing a piece of pie, a middle-aged woman reading what appeared to be legal documents while nursing a cup of tea.

By eight o'clock, David had accepted that this was simply going to be a normal Thursday evening—no empathic episodes, no mysterious young men, no disruption to the careful equilibrium he'd spent years constructing. He was almost relieved. The intensity of the previous week's experience had unsettled him more than he'd wanted to admit, and perhaps it was better to let sleeping dogs lie.

He paid his check and headed for the parking lot, keys already in hand. The evening air carried the familiar scents of Los Angeles twilight —car exhaust and blooming jasmine, fast food and possibility. Traffic on Pico Boulevard moved in its usual stop-and-go rhythm, commuters heading home to families and obligations David could only imagine.

That's when he saw him.

The young man was sitting on the bus bench directly across the street from the diner, hunched slightly forward in the same posture David remembered from their first encounter. Even at this distance, there was no mistaking the particular quality of stillness that surrounded him, the way he seemed to occupy space while simultaneously trying to disappear within it.

David stopped walking. His hand tightened around his car keys as his mind raced through possibilities. Should he cross the street? Approach the bench? What would he say? The kid hadn't noticed him yet—seemed entirely focused on something in the distance, perhaps watching for a bus that might not come for another twenty minutes.

Before David could decide on a course of action, his empathic radar activated without warning.

This time, the connection was briefer but no less intense. Exhaustion, profound and bone-deep, the kind that came from weeks of poor sleep and constant vigilance. The metallic taste of anxiety, sharp and familiar. And underneath it all, a growing desperation that the young man was fighting to keep under control—the recognition that his current situation couldn't continue indefinitely, that something would have to change soon, one way or another.

David gripped the door handle of his BMW, using the physical anchor to pull himself back to his own consciousness. When he looked up again, the young man was standing, peering down Pico Boulevard with the focused attention of someone waiting for salvation in the form of public transportation.

This was David's chance. The street wasn't particularly busy at this hour—he could cross safely, maybe sit down at the other end of the bench, strike up a casual conversation about bus schedules or the weather. It would be natural, unstaged, the kind of encounter that happened between strangers in a city full of strangers.

David took a step toward the crosswalk, then stopped. What was his plan, exactly? To offer help to someone who hadn't asked for it? To insert himself into a situation he understood only through involuntary psychic eavesdropping? The young man might be perfectly fine, might have resources and support that weren't immediately visible. David's assumption that he needed rescuing could be nothing more than projection, his own loneliness making him see isolation where none existed.

While David hesitated, paralyzed by uncertainty and second-guessing, the bus arrived.

It was one of the newer Metro buses, blue and white and efficient in its anonymity. The young man stood as it approached, checking his pockets for what David assumed was exact change. The bus doors opened with a hydraulic sigh, and after a brief exchange with the driver, the young man climbed aboard.

David remained standing beside his car, watching through the bus windows as his mystery passenger found a seat near the back. For a moment, their eyes met through the glass—the young man looking out, David looking in—and David felt a jolt of recognition that seemed to travel both directions. Then the bus pulled away from the curb, carrying its passenger toward destinations unknown, leaving David alone in the parking lot with nothing but questions and the growing certainty that he'd just missed something important.

The drive home felt interminable. David found himself taking the same route the bus had taken, as if he might catch up with it at a red light or bus stop, though he had no idea what he would do if such an opportunity presented itself. The bus disappeared into the evening traffic, and David continued west toward his empty house, accompanied by a frustration that felt disproportionate to the circumstances.

Back in West Hollywood, he poured himself a scotch instead of wine —something stronger seemed necessary for the evening's emotional residue. He stood on his terrace, looking out over the city that had swallowed the young man as completely as if he'd never existed at all.

David's phone rang. Elena's name appeared on the screen, and for a moment he considered letting it go to voicemail. But Elena had an uncanny ability to call when he most needed to hear a friendly voice, even if he hadn't realized it himself.

"Hey," he answered, settling into one of the terrace chairs.

"Hey yourself. You sound weird. Everything okay?"

David almost smiled at her directness. Elena had never been one for polite small talk, a quality that had served her well as Michael's best friend and had made her invaluable during the darkest period of David's life.

"Just thinking," he said. "How are the boys?"

"Noah's fine—obsessed with some video game I don't understand. Aiden's still being moody, but I think it's more than teenage hormones. I'm wondering if he's struggling with something he doesn't know how to talk about."

David took a sip of his scotch. "What makes you say that?"

"Mother's intuition, mostly. He's withdrawn, spends a lot of time alone in his room. Gets defensive when I ask how school's going. I remember being that age and feeling like the whole world was waiting for me to figure out something I didn't have the vocabulary for yet."

David thought about the young man on the bus, carrying burdens that seemed too heavy for eighteen-year-old shoulders. "Maybe he just needs time to work through whatever it is."

"Maybe. Or maybe he needs to know he's not alone with it, whatever 'it' turns out to be." Elena's voice carried the particular weariness of a single parent trying to navigate uncharted territory. "Sometimes I wish I had someone else to bounce these things off of. Someone who remembers what it was like to be seventeen and confused."

"You've got good instincts, Elena. Trust them."

"Thanks. I hope so." She paused, and David could hear the sound of running water in the background—dishes being washed, the domestic soundtrack of a life filled with daily responsibilities. "What about you? Really, I mean. You sounded... I don't know, unsettled when you picked up."

David considered how much to share. Elena knew about his empathic episodes—had witnessed them firsthand during Michael's illness—but she lived three thousand miles away with problems of her own. Still, the need to voice what he'd been experiencing felt suddenly urgent.

"I had one of those moments," he said finally. "You know, the empathic thing. More intense than usual."

"When?"

"Last week. And again tonight." He found himself describing the encounters at the diner and the bus stop, the young man's obvious hardship, his own paralysis when faced with the opportunity to help.

Elena listened without interrupting, a skill she'd learned during the long months of Michael's decline when David had needed to talk through his fears and frustrations without being offered solutions he wasn't ready to hear.

"So you think this kid is homeless?" she asked when he finished.

"I think he's in trouble, yes. The empathic connection was... overwhelming. Fear, exhaustion, grief. But also strength, dignity. He's not giving up, but he's running out of options."

"And you want to help."

"I don't know what I want," David admitted. "I keep thinking about him, wondering where he is, whether he's safe. But I also recognize that might be my own loneliness talking, looking for purpose where none exists."

Elena was quiet for a moment. When she spoke, her voice was gentle but direct.

"David, I'm going to ask you a question, and I want you to really think about it before you answer."

"Okay."

"If you were that kid, and someone could potentially help you—someone with resources, someone who seemed decent—would you want them to try? Or would you rather they stayed silent out of fear?"

The question hung between them like a challenge. David sipped his scotch and watched the lights of Los Angeles spread out below him, eight million individual stories playing out in isolation.

"I think," he said slowly, "I'd want them to try."

"Then maybe the question isn't whether you should get involved. Maybe it's how."

After Elena hung up, David remained on the terrace for another hour, turning her words over in his mind. The young man was out there somewhere in the vast anonymity of the city, and David was here in his comfortable house, separated by more than just geography. But Elena was right—the choice wasn't whether to care, because that decision had apparently been made for him. The choice was whether to act on that caring or retreat back into the safety of professional distance.

For the first time in years, David found himself seriously considering taking a risk that had nothing to do with box office projections or career advancement. The thought was terrifying and exhilarating in equal measure.

Tomorrow, he decided, he would figure out how to find a stranger who might not want to be found.

four
elena's question

DAVID WOKE Friday morning with Elena's question echoing in his mind like a song he couldn't shake. *If you were that kid, and someone could potentially help you—someone with resources, someone who seemed decent—would you want them to try?*

He'd always been someone who processed emotions through analysis, breaking down complex feelings into manageable components the way he might dissect a marketing campaign or a distribution strategy. But this felt different—more personal than professional, more heart than head. As he went through his morning routine, David found himself remembering his own seventeen-year-old self, the boy who'd felt like a stranger in his own skin, carrying secrets that felt too dangerous to share.

The shower water was too hot, but he didn't adjust it. Sometimes physical discomfort helped sharpen mental focus, and this morning he needed clarity more than comfort. Elena's question assumed a level of courage he wasn't sure he possessed—the willingness to insert himself into someone else's crisis, to risk rejection or misunderstanding for the possibility of making a difference.

When had he become so careful? When had the distance between wanting to help and actually helping become so vast?

The answer, of course, was Michael.

David toweled off and dressed for work with the automatic precision of thirty years of professional routine, but his mind wandered back to just a few years ago, when everything had changed. Michael had been complaining of fatigue for weeks—nothing dramatic, just a persistent tiredness that sleep didn't seem to cure. As someone who'd lived through the worst years of the AIDS crisis, David's first instinct had been panic, but the HIV tests came back negative. Then came the other tests, the specialists, the diagnosis that arrived like a punch to the gut: prostate cancer, advanced and aggressive.

Five months. That's how long they'd had from diagnosis to the end. One hundred and forty-seven days of trying to compress a lifetime of love into whatever time remained. David had taken a leave of absence from work, something that would have been unthinkable under any other circumstances. He'd learned to navigate the healthcare system, to advocate for aggressive pain management, to coordinate hospice care. He'd held Michael's hand through chemo sessions that bought weeks rather than years, had slept in hospital chairs, had become fluent in the language of decline.

And through it all, Elena had been their anchor.

She'd flown in from Boston every weekend, sometimes more often when things got bad. She'd brought groceries and terrible movies and the kind of determined cheerfulness that masked profound grief. She'd held David when he cried, had argued with doctors when he couldn't find the words, had somehow maintained hope even when hope felt like a luxury they couldn't afford.

The morning Michael died, David had been holding his hand. They'd said their goodbyes the night before—Michael lucid enough for final words, for promises that felt both eternal and heartbreakingly temporary. When his breathing finally stopped, just after sunrise, David had called Elena before anyone else. She'd been on a plane within hours.

"I don't know how to be without him," David had told her that night, sitting in his kitchen while Elena made arrangements he couldn't face. "I don't remember who I was before we were us."

"You don't have to figure that out today," she'd said, setting a cup of tea in front of him. "Or this week, or this month. You just have to breathe."

But breathing had proved harder than expected. The grief was manageable during the day, when work provided structure and distraction. It was the evenings that nearly broke him—coming home to the house they'd shared, to the silence where Michael's laughter used to live. David had learned to stay late at the office, to accept dinner invitations from colleagues, to fill every available hour with activity that required no emotional investment.

The strategy had worked, perhaps too well. In the months after Michael's death, David realized he'd become someone who observed life rather than participating in it. A year later, that observation had hardened into habit. The distance felt less like protection and more like prison, but he'd forgotten how to close the gap.

Elena had noticed, of course. She'd been living in Boston since high school, where she'd met Robert, Michael's friend from their teenage years. Robert understood that Elena came with complications, chief among them a grieving friend who needed more care than he knew how to ask for. When Michael had gotten sick, Elena had flown in as often as she could, and David had watched her struggle to balance her own family responsibilities with supporting them through the crisis. Her boys had been younger then, but old enough to understand that something terrible was happening to Uncle Michael, old enough to worry about their mother's frequent trips to Los Angeles.

Now, sitting at his kitchen island with coffee and the morning trades, David wondered if Elena's question was really about the homeless young man at all, or if it was about something larger—about the choice between safety and connection, between protecting yourself and risking yourself for someone else.

His phone buzzed with a text from Tom Richter: *Director wants to meet about the campaign changes. 10 AM work for you?*

David typed back his confirmation, then gathered his things for another day of meetings and decisions that would affect box office numbers and quarterly reports but leave him essentially unchanged. The drive to the studio took twenty-five minutes, winding through morning traffic that moved with the predictable rhythm of a city devoted to the business of entertainment.

In his office, David tried to focus on the Jacobson project, on international tracking numbers, on the endless stream of emails that demanded his attention. But Elena's question kept surfacing like a song played on repeat. By lunch, he'd made a decision that surprised him with its clarity.

Instead of eating in the commissary or attending the networking lunch he'd been invited to, David got in his car and drove west on Pico Boulevard. He told himself he was simply exploring the neighborhood around Mel's Diner, getting a better sense of the area where he'd been spending his Thursday evenings. But as he drove slowly past bus stops and small restaurants, past a doggie daycare with a window full of puppies, past shops that served the working-class community that couldn't afford West Hollywood rents, he knew he was looking for someone.

The young man wasn't there, of course. David hadn't really expected him to be—Los Angeles was too vast, too anonymous for such coincidences. But the drive served another purpose: it made the theoretical practical, the abstract concrete. This was where the kid lived, somewhere in this grid of streets and storefronts and apartment buildings. This was where he navigated each day, where he tried to survive with whatever resources he could find.

David parked near a small community center and walked the block, observing details he'd never noticed from the driver's seat. A laundromat with hand-lettered signs in three languages. A corner market advertising phone cards and money transfers. A bus stop with a schedule posted in small print, routes that connected this neighborhood to others across the sprawling city.

It occurred to him that he'd lived in Los Angeles for over twenty years but had never really seen this part of it—not because it was hidden, but because his life moved in different circles, followed different patterns. The revelation felt both humbling and oddly hopeful. If he'd been blind to an entire community that existed fifteen minutes from his office, what else might he have missed? What other connections might be possible if he was willing to look beyond the boundaries of his carefully constructed life?

When David returned to the studio, he found three messages from Elena on his phone. He called her back during a brief break between meetings.

"I've been thinking about our conversation last night," she said without preamble. "About the question I asked you."

"So have I."

"I may have been projecting a little. Things with Aiden have me worried, and I think I was talking to myself as much as to you."

David leaned back in his chair, grateful for Elena's honesty. "What's going on with him?"

"I think he's gay, David. I think he's struggling with coming out, and I don't know how to help him without making it worse."

The words hung between them, weighted with the particular fear of a parent who wanted desperately to do right by her child. David thought about his own coming out process—the years of shame and secrecy, the terror of disappointing people he loved, the relief and regret that had accompanied finally telling the truth.

"What makes you think so?" he asked gently.

"A hundred little things. The way he flinches when his friends make jokes about girls. How he's never shown interest in dating, even when his friends are girl-crazy. The way he lights up when we watch movies with gay characters, then pretends he wasn't paying attention." Elena's voice was thick with emotion. "I want him to know it's okay, that I love him no matter what. But I'm afraid if I say something, I'll be forcing him into a conversation he's not ready for."

David understood the dilemma. Coming out was such a personal process, so tied to individual readiness and courage. Well-meaning parents could accidentally create pressure when they meant to create safety.

"Have you considered bringing him out here for a visit?" David heard himself say. "Not to force anything, just to give him a change of scenery. Sometimes it's easier to figure things out when you're not surrounded by all the usual expectations."

Elena was quiet for a moment. "That's not a terrible idea. He's been asking about you, actually. Wants to know more about your work, about living in Los Angeles."

"He's welcome anytime," David said, and meant it. "Both boys are."

"I might take you up on that. Maybe this summer, when school's out."

After they hung up, David sat in his office thinking about families— the ones you were born into and the ones you chose, the ways people could disappear from your life and the ways they could surprise you by showing up exactly when you needed them. Elena had been Michael's friend first, but grief had transformed their relationship into something deeper, more complex. She'd become the person who remembered the version of himself that had existed when he was part of something larger, and she'd refused to let him disappear entirely into professional success and emotional isolation.

Now she was asking him to remember that version of himself again— the man who'd been willing to take risks for love, who'd fought for Michael through illness and loss, who'd understood that some things were worth the possibility of heartbreak.

Elena's question wasn't really about the homeless young man, David realized. It was about whether he was ready to be that person again— someone who cared enough to act, who was willing to be vulnerable in service of connection.

The answer, he thought, was yes. He just had to figure out how.

Outside his office window, Los Angeles spread out in all directions, eight million stories unfolding simultaneously. Somewhere in that vastness, a young man was trying to survive another day. And somewhere else, David's godson-in-all-but-name was struggling with questions about identity and belonging that David remembered all too well.

For the first time in years, David felt the stirring of something he'd almost forgotten: the desire to be useful, to matter, to risk disappointment for the possibility of making a difference.

It was terrifying and exhilarating in equal measure. It was also, he suspected, exactly what Michael would have wanted him to feel.

five
reflections

DAVID HAD BEEN WORKING at the studio for three hours when he realized he hadn't absorbed a single word of the marketing reports spread across his desk. Friday afternoon sunlight streamed through his office windows, and somewhere in the building's depths, the familiar machinery of entertainment commerce hummed along without his attention. His mind kept returning to Elena's question, to the young man at the bus stop, to the growing certainty that he was standing at some kind of crossroads.

By two o'clock, he'd made a decision that would have surprised his colleagues. David Harmon, the executive who rarely left the office before seven, gathered his things and headed for the elevator.

"Taking the rest of the day?" his assistant asked, not quite hiding her surprise.

"I need some air," David said, which was true enough, though it didn't begin to explain the restlessness that had been building all week.

The drive west on Pico Boulevard felt different in daylight. The neighborhood around Mel's Diner revealed details that darkness had hidden—small markets with hand-lettered signs, a community center with basketball courts where teenagers gathered after school, apartment buildings that housed the working families who kept Los Angeles running. David had driven this route dozens of times but had never really seen it, never considered the lives being lived in the spaces between his familiar destinations.

He parked near the doggie daycare he'd noticed during yesterday's exploration, drawn by something he couldn't quite name. Through the large front window, a collection of small dogs tumbled and played with the kind of unself-conscious joy that seemed both foreign and familiar. David found himself standing on the sidewalk, watching a particularly energetic puppy—some kind of terrier mix—who seemed determined to engage every other dog in play.

There was something hypnotic about the scene, something that quieted the analytical voice in his head that was always calculating angles and outcomes. The puppy's enthusiasm was infectious, its tail wagging with such vigor that its entire body wiggled. Despite everything weighing on his mind, David found himself smiling.

He was so absorbed in watching the dogs that he didn't notice the young man approaching from the opposite direction until movement in his peripheral vision caught his attention. David's breath caught. It was him—the kid from the diner, from the bus stop. Walking slowly down Pico Boulevard, hands shoved deep in the pockets of jeans that had seen better days, shoulders hunched against more than just the afternoon breeze.

David's first instinct was to look away, to honor the unspoken rule his great-grandmother had taught him about not making eye contact with strangers on the street. But something held his gaze—perhaps the same quality that had made the young man so compelling in the diner, that particular combination of vulnerability and dignity that seemed to radiate from him even at a distance.

The young man stopped a few feet away from David, his attention caught by the same playful puppy. For a moment, they stood in parallel silence, two strangers united by the simple pleasure of watching something innocent and joyful. David could see the young man's face more clearly now—the sharp cheekbones that suggested he wasn't eating enough, the careful way he held himself, as if prepared to move quickly if necessary.

And then, without warning, David's empathic ability activated with an intensity that nearly brought him to his knees.

This time, the connection was complete and overwhelming. David felt himself pulled not just into the young man's emotional state, but into his entire world. The bone-deep exhaustion of weeks spent sleeping rough. The constant vigilance required to stay safe on the streets. The hollow ache of hunger that had become background noise. But more than the physical hardships, David felt the emotional weight—the grief of losing everything familiar, the shame of his circumstances, the growing despair that this might be his new reality.

Yet underneath it all, David sensed something that broke his heart and filled him with admiration simultaneously. This young man—this kid who couldn't be more than eighteen—was still fighting. Still choosing kindness when he encountered it. Still stopping to watch puppies play even when his world had collapsed around him. There was a core of goodness that remained unbroken despite everything that had tried to crush it.

The connection was so intense, so complete, that David felt tears streaming down his face before he realized he was crying. The young man's pain became his pain, the loneliness so profound it seemed to hollow out his chest. David gripped the window frame of the doggie daycare, using the physical anchor to try to pull himself back to his own consciousness, but the empathic link held firm.

That's when he heard the voice—soft, concerned, completely unexpected.

"Hey, are you okay?"

David blinked, tears still flowing, and found himself looking into a pair of brown eyes filled with genuine worry. The young man had turned toward him, his own problems temporarily forgotten in the face of David's obvious distress.

"I'm sorry," David managed, his voice rough with emotion. "I don't usually..."

"It's okay," the young man said gently, taking a half-step closer. "Whatever it is, it'll be okay. Trust me."

The kindness in his voice—this kid who had every reason to be suspicious of strangers, who was living circumstances that would break most people—offering comfort to someone who appeared to have everything together. David felt a fresh wave of tears, but these carried a different quality. Not just the overwhelming sadness he'd absorbed through the empathic connection, but his own grief at the unfairness of it all.

"I'm sorry," David said again, trying to pull himself together. "I'm embarrassing myself here."

"You're not embarrassing anybody," the young man replied, his voice carrying a maturity that seemed at odds with his youth. "We all have bad days. Whatever's going on, you don't have to go through it alone."

David almost laughed at the irony—here was someone who was literally going through his struggles alone, offering support to a stranger. He wiped his eyes with the back of his hand, trying to find his equilibrium.

"Thank you," he said. "That's... that's very kind of you."

The young man shrugged, but his eyes remained watchful, concerned. "Just paying it forward, I guess."

For a moment, they stood in awkward silence, both seeming to realize they'd shared something unexpectedly intimate. David's mind raced. This was his chance—the opportunity he'd been hoping for but hadn't known how to create. But how did he begin? How did he offer help without seeming predatory or patronizing?

"I know this is going to sound strange," David heard himself say, "but aren't you the person I saw at Mel's Diner a couple weeks ago? And at the bus stop?"

The young man's posture shifted slightly, becoming more guarded. "Maybe. Why?"

David felt heat rise in his cheeks. "This is going to sound even stranger, but I... I noticed you seemed like you might be going through a tough time. And I've been thinking about it since then."

"Thinking about what?"

"About whether I should... I mean, whether there was anything..." David stopped, shook his head, laughed at his own fumbling. "I'm making a complete mess of this. Let me start over."

The young man's expression had shifted from concern to curiosity, with an undertone of wariness that David completely understood.

"Look," David continued, "I know how this must sound. Random older guy approaches you on the street, says he's been watching you. I'm not... I don't want anything from you. I just had the feeling that maybe you could use a friend, and I wondered if you'd let me buy you lunch."

"Why?" The question was direct, not hostile, but clearly expecting an answer.

David considered several responses—the truth about his empathic episodes seemed too strange, too invasive. A lie about random charity felt insulting to both of them. Finally, he settled on something that was true, if incomplete.

"Because you just offered comfort to a complete stranger who was having a breakdown on the sidewalk. Because you seemed like a decent person who might be dealing with some difficult circumstances. And because..." He paused, remembering Elena's words. "Because if I were in a tough spot, I'd hope someone would take the chance."

The young man studied David's face for a long moment, as if trying to read something in his expression. Finally, he nodded toward the diner across the street.

"There's outdoor seating," he said. "Public, safe. If you're buying, I'm not going to say no to a meal."

David felt a rush of relief and nervousness in equal measure. "Perfect. I'm David, by the way."

"Marcus," the young man replied, then added with the ghost of a smile, "and for the record, you weren't embarrassing yourself. We all need to cry sometimes."

As they crossed Pico Boulevard together, David couldn't help but think that Elena would be proud of him for taking this chance. More importantly, he felt something he hadn't experienced in years—the possibility that he might actually be able to help someone, that his life might have purpose beyond professional success.

The thought was terrifying and exhilarating in equal measure. But as they approached the diner, Marcus walking slightly ahead with the careful awareness of someone accustomed to evaluating his surroundings, David knew he'd made the right choice.

Sometimes, he realized, the most important decisions were the ones that scared you most.

six
breaking bread

THE OUTDOOR SEATING at Mel's consisted of four small tables arranged along the sidewalk, each one positioned to catch the afternoon sun while remaining close enough to the restaurant's front door to feel safe and accessible. David chose the table farthest from foot traffic but closest to the window, hoping Marcus would appreciate both the privacy and the clear sightlines. As they settled into their chairs, David noticed how Marcus positioned himself facing the street, back to the restaurant wall—someone who'd learned to keep an eye on his surroundings.

"This okay?" David asked, gesturing to the table arrangement.

"Perfect," Marcus replied, and David caught a note of relief in his voice. The outdoor setting had been the right call.

A waitress appeared almost immediately—not Dolores, but a younger woman with kind eyes and a practiced smile. "Afternoon, gentlemen. Can I start you with something to drink?"

"Coffee, please," Marcus said quickly. "Black."

"Same," David added. "And could we see some menus?"

"Of course. Back in just a minute."

As the waitress disappeared inside, David found himself studying Marcus more closely than he'd been able to during their previous brief encounters. Up close, the young man's resilience was even more apparent. His clothes were worn but clean, his hair recently washed despite his obvious circumstances. There was a carefulness to his movements, an economy of gesture that suggested someone who'd learned to conserve energy and avoid drawing attention.

"So," Marcus said, his voice carrying a note of gentle challenge, "you want to tell me why you've really been watching me?"

David had been dreading this question, but Marcus's directness was somehow refreshing after a career built on strategic conversations and careful positioning. "The honest answer is going to sound strange."

"Try me."

David took a breath. "I have this... ability, I guess you'd call it. Sometimes when I'm around people, I can sense what they're feeling. Not read minds or anything that dramatic, but I pick up on emotions, experiences. It's not something I can control."

Marcus raised an eyebrow but didn't look skeptical, just curious. "And you sensed something about me?"

"The first time I saw you at the diner, it hit me like a wave. Your fear, your exhaustion, but also your strength. Your determination not to give up even when everything felt hopeless." David paused, studying Marcus's face for signs of discomfort or disbelief. "Today, when I saw you looking at the puppy, it happened again. More intensely than ever before."

"That's why you started crying."

"Yes. I felt what you were feeling, and it overwhelmed me."

Marcus was quiet for a moment, processing this information. When he spoke, his voice was thoughtful rather than dismissive. "That must be exhausting for you. Feeling everyone else's problems."

The response surprised David. He'd expected skepticism, maybe concern that he was mentally unstable. Instead, Marcus's first thought was about how the ability might affect David himself.

"It can be," David admitted. "I've learned to manage it, mostly. But sometimes it breaks through anyway."

The waitress returned with coffee and menus, giving both men a moment to collect their thoughts. David watched Marcus scan the menu with the focused attention of someone calculating cost against hunger. The lunch specials were reasonably priced, but David could see Marcus doing the math.

"Order whatever you want," David said quietly. "Please. I meant what I said about this being my treat."

Marcus looked up from the menu. "You sure? I mean, I could eat."

"I'm sure. When's the last time you had a real meal?"

"Define real." Marcus's smile was wry but not bitter. "I had a sandwich yesterday. Day before that, some leftover pizza someone gave me."

David felt his chest tighten. "Order whatever looks good. Seriously."

When the waitress returned, Marcus ordered the club sandwich with fries and a side of soup. David chose a salad, though his appetite had diminished as the reality of Marcus's situation became clearer.

"So," David said once they were alone again, "can I ask how long you've been... on your own?"

Marcus stirred sugar into his coffee with deliberate precision. "About eight months. Since last October."

"That's when you left home?"

"That's when home stopped being an option." Marcus's voice was matter-of-fact, but David caught the undertone of pain. "My dad found some text messages on my phone. Messages from a boy I liked. That was pretty much the end of that conversation."

David felt a familiar ache—the memory of his own coming out process, the fear and rejection that had shaped those early years. "I'm sorry. That must have been devastating."

"Yeah, well." Marcus shrugged, but David could see the careful control in the gesture. "Turns out some people's love comes with conditions. Who knew?"

The bitterness was brief, quickly replaced by the same quiet dignity David had sensed during their previous encounters. This kid had every right to be angry, to rage against the unfairness of his situation. Instead, he was sitting here having a civil conversation with a stranger, worried about David's well-being despite his own desperate circumstances.

"Where did you go? After you left home, I mean."

"Phoenix first—that's where I'm from. Then I figured if I was going to be homeless, I might as well be homeless somewhere with better weather." Marcus's attempt at humor was gentle, self-deprecating. "Los Angeles seemed like a good idea at the time."

"How did you get here?"

"Greyhound. Took most of my savings, but I thought maybe there would be more opportunities here. More resources for people like me."

David thought about the resources that did exist—LGBTQ+ youth centers, shelters, support services—and wondered what barriers had

prevented Marcus from accessing them. "Have you tried any of the orga-
nizations downtown? The LGBTQ+ youth services?"

Marcus's expression grew guarded. "I tried a few places when I first
got here. Didn't work out."

"What happened?"

"Nothing dramatic. Just... the system doesn't really work for people
like me. Too old for some programs, too young for others. Don't have the
right documentation for others. And honestly?" Marcus met David's eyes
directly. "I learned pretty quickly that accepting help often comes with
strings attached. People want something in return, even when they say
they don't."

David felt a chill as he understood the implication. "I'm sorry. That
must have made it hard to trust anyone."

"Trust is a luxury I can't afford right now."

The food arrived, and David watched Marcus take his first bite of the
sandwich with an expression of genuine gratitude. The young man ate
with careful appreciation, not wolfing down the food despite his obvious
hunger. Even in his desperation, he maintained his dignity.

"Can I ask you something?" Marcus said after a few bites.

"Of course."

"What do you do? For work, I mean. You seem..." Marcus gestured
vaguely at David's clothes, his general appearance. "Successful."

"I work at a movie studio. Marketing and distribution."

"Really? That's cool. What kind of movies?"

For the next few minutes, David found himself describing his work in
ways he hadn't thought about in years—not the budgets and demo-
graphics that usually dominated his conversations, but the stories themselves, the art of connecting audiences with narratives that might move or
inspire them. Marcus listened with genuine interest, asking thoughtful
questions that revealed both intelligence and curiosity.

"You really love it," Marcus observed. "The work, I mean."

"I do. Or I did. Sometimes I lose sight of why it matters."

"What made you get into it?"

David thought about his younger self, the Indiana kid who'd escaped
to Los Angeles with dreams of being part of something larger than
himself. "I wanted to tell stories that mattered. Stories about people who
didn't usually get to see themselves on screen."

"Like gay stories?"

"Among others, yes."

Marcus nodded thoughtfully. "That's important. When I was growing up, I never saw anyone like me in movies. Made me feel like maybe I didn't exist, you know?"

David knew exactly what he meant. The conversation felt natural, unforced—two people sharing stories over a meal, the fundamental human ritual of connection. For a moment, David forgot about the circumstances that had brought them together, forgot about the careful calculations of how to help without overstepping.

"David," Marcus said suddenly, his voice more serious. "Why are you doing this? Really. I mean, I appreciate the meal, don't get me wrong. But people don't usually go out of their way for strangers. What do you want?"

The question was direct, uncompromising. David set down his fork and considered how to answer honestly without overwhelming this fragile new connection.

"I want to help," he said finally. "I don't know exactly what that looks like yet, but I can't stop thinking about what I sensed when I saw you. Your situation, your strength, your refusal to give up. And I have resources—a house with empty rooms, connections in the city, financial stability. It seems wrong to have all that and not try to make a difference."

Marcus studied his face carefully. "And what would you want in return?"

"Nothing," David said immediately. "I'm gay, Marcus. I know what it's like to feel like you don't belong anywhere, to worry that the people who are supposed to love you might reject you instead. I know what it's like to be alone."

Something shifted in Marcus's expression—not complete trust, but a recognition of shared experience.

"I'm not trying to fix your life," David continued. "I can't undo what your family did to you, and I can't promise that everything will work out perfectly. But I can offer you a safe place to sleep, regular meals, and time to figure out what comes next. No strings attached."

Marcus was quiet for a long moment, finishing his sandwich while he processed David's offer. Finally, he looked up.

"This is a lot to think about," he said. "I've gotten pretty good at taking care of myself. It's hard to imagine trusting someone else with that responsibility."

"I understand. And I don't expect an answer today. But maybe we could start smaller? I could give you my phone number, you could think about it. Maybe we could meet for coffee again in a few days?"

Marcus nodded slowly. "That I could probably handle."

David pulled out his business card and wrote his personal cell phone number on the back. "Call or text me whenever you want. Even if it's just to talk. No pressure."

Marcus pocketed the card carefully. "David? Thank you. For the meal, for listening. For not making me feel like a charity case."

"Thank you for giving me a chance to help. And Marcus? You're not a charity case. You're a person going through a difficult time, and there's nothing shameful about accepting support."

As they stood to leave, David felt something he hadn't experienced in years: hope. Not just for Marcus, but for himself. For the possibility that his life might include something more meaningful than professional success.

It was a beginning, fragile and uncertain, but real nonetheless.

seven
get out

Arizona

MARCUS HAD BEEN TEXTING BACK and forth with Jake from his drama class, his heart racing with each exchange. They'd just crossed the line from friendship into something more—Jake had said Marcus had "beautiful eyes," and Marcus had responded that Jake's eyes "looked pretty good" too. The simple words "I like you" and "I like you, too!" had appeared on his screen like a miracle.

His mother's voice calling from the kitchen interrupted the moment. "Marcus, dinner!"

"Just a minute, Mom!" he called back, unable to tear his eyes away from Jake's last message.

"Marcus, your mother is calling you!" his father's voice boomed from his recliner, sharp with irritation.

Startled, Marcus dropped his phone on the sofa and ran to the kitchen, his face still glowing with happiness. He was barely through explaining to his mother that he'd be right there when his father's voice exploded from the living room.

"What... the fuck... is this?"

Marcus's blood turned to ice. He ran back to find his father holding up his phone, the screen displaying the text conversation that had just made him feel like he could fly.

"What the fuck! Are you some fuckin' queer? Is my son... a faggot!" His father's face was purple with rage as he hurled the phone at the wooden floor, the screen shattering on impact.

Marcus screamed—part shock, part devastation at losing not just his phone but the connection to Jake that had meant everything.

"You get your faggotty ass outta my house RIGHT NOW, you fucking queer! I didn't raise no son of mine to take it up the ass!" His father stepped forward, arm raised to strike.

His mother appeared from the kitchen, placing herself between them. "Don't you dare hit him!" she yelled, but her tiny frame barely seemed capable of stopping the rage radiating from her husband.

Marcus could hear his younger brothers' bedroom doors slamming down the hall, could hear eight-year-old Sofia crying from her room. His family was disintegrating in real time, and it was all his fault for being stupid enough to leave his phone unlocked.

He ran down the hall to the bedroom he shared with his brothers, who sat on their beds in shellshocked silence. Marcus grabbed his school backpack and dumped out the books, stuffing in whatever clothes he could grab from his drawers. His parents' voices echoed from the living room—his father's rage, his mother's desperate attempts to calm him down.

Marcus knew he had seconds. He grabbed the jar from his closet where he'd been saving money for college—bills and change that amounted to maybe three hundred dollars—and emptied it into the bag. Looking at his crying brothers, all he could do was nod once before running like a quarterback down the hall, past his arguing parents and through the screen door into the Phoenix night.

The Greyhound station in downtown Phoenix smelled of disinfectant and desperation. Marcus sat on a hard plastic chair, his backpack clutched to his chest like armor. He'd spent three weeks sleeping in parks and 24-hour diners, rationing his money and trying to figure out his next move. Los Angeles kept calling to him—a place where being different wasn't just tolerated but celebrated, or so he'd heard.

The ticket cost $89, leaving him with enough money for maybe two weeks if he was careful. A middle-aged woman sitting nearby noticed him counting and recounting his cash.

"First time traveling alone, honey?" she asked, her voice kind but weary.

Marcus nodded, not trusting himself to speak.

"L.A.'s a big city. You got people there?"

"Not exactly," Marcus admitted.

She reached into her purse and pulled out half a sandwich wrapped in plastic. "Turkey and Swiss. My daughter packed it, but I'm not hungry. You look like you could use it more than me."

He wanted to refuse—pride still intact despite everything—but hunger won. As he ate, she told him about youth services downtown, about shelters that didn't ask too many questions. "They help kids like you," she said gently, and Marcus wondered what she saw in his face that made his situation so obvious.

December

"Marcus, we can get you into emergency housing, but I need you to fill out these forms." The social worker looked exhausted, her desk piled high with similar folders containing similar stories. "And we'll need to contact your parents since you're still a minor."

Marcus stood up immediately, his chair scraping against the linoleum floor. "No. I told you what happened."

"I understand your situation is difficult, but legally—"

He was out the door before she could finish, his heart pounding with panic. Three hours of waiting in that sterile office for nothing. Outside, he counted his remaining money: $43.12. Not enough for a bus ticket home, even if home had still been an option.

That night, he slept in MacArthur Park, using his jacket as a pillow and his backpack as a shield against whatever dangers lurked in the darkness. When rain began to fall near dawn, he found shelter under a convenience store awning and made a promise to himself: never again would he trust anyone with power over his safety.

February

"You can crash with me if you want. I've got a tent setup near Venice."

Damon was twenty-two, with an easy smile and tattoos crawling up his neck like vines. He'd shared his In-N-Out burger with Marcus outside the convenience store where Marcus had been trying to figure out what food would stretch his last seven dollars the furthest.

"What's the catch?" Marcus asked, his street-learned suspicion kicking in automatically.

Damon laughed, but it sounded genuine. "Smart kid. No catch, just looking out. Been where you are. Got a little community going down by the beach. Safer than being alone out here."

Two days later, Marcus followed Damon to a collection of tents and makeshift shelters tucked between abandoned buildings near the Venice boardwalk. Six people lived there, all young, all with stories that echoed his own in different keys. There was Jamie, kicked out for being trans. Sarah, who'd aged out of foster care with nowhere to go. Miguel, whose parents had discovered his boyfriend and chosen their religion over their son.

For the first time in months, Marcus slept through the night without waking at every sound.

The community had rules: share what you could, watch out for each other, keep the space clean so the authorities wouldn't hassle them. Damon seemed to be the unofficial leader, the one who knew which restaurants threw out good food at closing time, which public restrooms had hot water, which social workers could be trusted and which ones couldn't.

"The key," Damon told Marcus one evening as they watched the sunset from the beach, "is staying invisible. Don't cause trouble, don't attract attention, and they'll mostly leave you alone."

Marcus learned to shower at the beach facilities early in the morning before the lifeguards arrived. He discovered the library branches where he could use computers and wifi without being hassled. He found the food pantries that didn't require extensive documentation, the churches that served meals without demanding conversion.

It wasn't much of a life, but it was survival. And survival, Marcus had learned, was its own kind of victory.

March

Marcus woke up to find Damon's tent gone. Not packed up—actually gone, along with the sleeping bag Marcus had saved weeks to buy and the twenty-dollar bill he'd hidden in his backpack. The others in the camp shrugged when he asked where Damon had gone.

"People move on," Jamie said with practiced indifference. "Don't take it personal."

But it felt personal. Damon had been the closest thing to a friend Marcus had found since leaving home, the person who'd taught him how to navigate this invisible world of the displaced and forgotten. Now he was alone again, with winter approaching and his resources dwindling.

The tent community began to disperse after that. Without Damon's leadership, the delicate ecosystem they'd built started to collapse. The city swept through one morning with cleanup crews and police, scattering what remained of their small society like leaves in the wind.

April

Marcus sat at the bus stop across from Mel's Diner, counting coins in his palm. Three dollars and seventy-six cents. Not enough for much of anything. His stomach had stopped growling hours ago, settling into the familiar hollow ache that had become his constant companion.

The older man from the diner was across the street again, standing by his expensive car. Marcus had noticed him before—the way he seemed to watch people, the sadness that clung to him like cologne. Most people looked through Marcus as if he didn't exist, but this man saw him. That should have been terrifying, but somehow it wasn't.

When the bus arrived, Marcus made a split-second decision to board it, not caring where it went as long as it carried him away from those searching eyes that seemed to see past his carefully constructed walls, into the pain he thought he'd buried deep enough that no one would ever find it.

But running away was getting harder. His body was wearing down, his spirit eroding like a cliff face under constant assault from the waves. He was eighteen years old, but he felt ancient, carved hollow by experiences that should have been unimaginable for someone his age.

As the bus pulled away from the curb, Marcus caught a glimpse of the man's face through the window—not predatory or dismissive, but genuinely concerned. For a moment, Marcus allowed himself to wonder what it would be like to trust someone again, to believe that help could come without hidden costs.

The thought was dangerous, he knew. Hope was a luxury he couldn't afford. But as the city blurred past the bus windows, Marcus found himself thinking about the kindness in the man's eyes, and wondering if maybe, just maybe, the world still contained people who helped simply because they could.

It was a fragile thought, barely more substantial than morning mist. But for the first time in months, Marcus found himself entertaining the possibility that his story might not have to end in invisibility and despair.

That had to count for something.

eight
small steps

THE BUS STOP bench on Pico Boulevard offered little comfort, but it was better than walking the streets all night. Marcus had found a spot partially hidden by an overgrown oleander bush, his backpack clutched against his chest like armor. The lunch with David felt like something from another lifetime, though only six hours had passed since they'd parted ways outside the diner.

He'd spent the afternoon walking, thinking about David's offer, about the business card tucked safely in his pocket. The conversation had felt real in a way that most interactions didn't anymore—no underlying agenda, no sense that he was being evaluated or judged. Just two people sharing a meal and honest conversation. But years of disappointment had taught Marcus to be cautious about hope, and he'd decided to sleep on it, literally, before making any decisions about calling.

The footsteps approached around ten-thirty, when the boulevard had quieted to the occasional passing car and the distant hum of late-night Los Angeles. Three men, moving with the kind of purposeful casualness that made Marcus's stomach clench with recognition.

"Hey, kid," the tallest one called out, his voice carrying false friendliness. "You got somewhere to be, or you just camping out here?"

Marcus kept his eyes down, his grip tightening on his backpack. "Just waiting for a bus."

"Bus don't run this late, sweetheart." Another voice, closer now. "Why don't you show us what's in that bag? Maybe we can help you out."

Marcus's heart hammered against his ribs. He'd managed to avoid this scenario for months, but his luck had finally run out. "I don't have anything worth taking."

"Let us be the judge of that."

The first man reached for his backpack, and Marcus bolted. He ran blindly down Pico Boulevard, his sneakers slapping against the pavement, the shouts behind him gradually fading as he put distance between himself and the bus stop. When he finally stopped, lungs burning and legs shaking, he found himself standing outside the familiar gates of Meridian Pictures.

The security booth glowed like a beacon in the darkness, and Marcus could see the guard inside reading something, probably a magazine or newspaper. David's business card felt heavy in his pocket as he approached the window.

"Excuse me," Marcus said quietly, trying to keep his voice steady. "I'm sorry to bother you, but could I possibly make a phone call?"

The guard looked up, his expression immediately shifting to suspicion as he took in Marcus's appearance—the worn clothes, the obvious exhaustion, the desperation that probably clung to him like cologne.

"Beat it, kid. This is private property."

"Please." Marcus pulled out David's business card, his hands trembling slightly. "I just need to call David Harmon. He works here. He gave me his card and wrote something on the back."

The guard's expression changed as he recognized the name, then shifted again as he read the handwritten note on the back of the card. He studied Marcus's face for a long moment, perhaps seeing something there that made him reconsider his initial dismissal.

"You sure about this? It's almost eleven-thirty."

"I'm sure," Marcus said, though he wasn't sure of anything except that he couldn't keep running much longer.

The guard picked up his phone and dialed. Marcus could hear it ringing through the speaker, once, twice, three times.

"David? It's Jerry at the front gate. Sorry to bother you so late, but I've got a young man here says you know him. Marcus?"

Marcus couldn't hear David's response, but he saw the guard's expression soften slightly.

"Yeah, he's got your card. Looks like he's had a rough night." The guard handed the phone through the window. "He wants to talk to you."

Marcus took the phone with unsteady hands. "David? I'm sorry to call so late, I just—"

"Marcus, are you okay? What happened?"

The genuine concern in David's voice was Marcus's undoing. The careful composure he'd maintained for months, the determination to handle everything on his own, the stubborn refusal to admit how close he was to breaking—all of it crumbled at once.

"I don't know why I'm calling," Marcus said, his voice cracking. "Some guys tried to rob me at the bus stop and I ran and I ended up here and I just... I can't keep doing this, David. I'm so tired."

The words came out in a rush, punctuated by tears he couldn't hold back anymore. Months of fear and anger and hurt and confusion poured out of him as he stood in the circle of light from the security booth, crying into a phone while a stranger looked on with uncomfortable sympathy.

"I'm coming to get you," David said immediately. 'Stay right there with Jerry. Don't move, okay? I'll be there in fifteen minutes."

"You don't have to—"

"I want to. Jerry, you still there?"

The guard took the phone back. "Yeah, David."

"Take care of him until I get there, will you?"

"Of course."

After hanging up, Jerry gestured toward a chair inside the booth. "Come on in, kid. You want some coffee? It's not great, but it's hot."

Marcus nodded gratefully, settling into the chair and wrapping his hands around the paper cup Jerry offered. The coffee was terrible, but the warmth felt like a luxury he'd almost forgotten existed.

"David's a good man," Jerry said after a few minutes. "Been working here longer than I have. Never heard a bad word about him from anybody."

Marcus managed a small smile. "He seems nice."

"Nice don't begin to cover it. You picked the right person to call."

Exactly fourteen minutes later, David's BMW pulled up to the gate.

Marcus watched through the window as David got out of the car, his hair slightly messed from sleep, wearing jeans and a sweater instead of his usual business attire. He looked younger somehow, more human.

"Thank you, Jerry," David said as Marcus emerged from the booth. "I owe you one."

"No problem. Take care of yourself, kid," Jerry added, looking at Marcus with something that might have been paternal concern.

They walked to David's car in silence, Marcus still clutching his backpack, David keeping a careful distance that somehow managed to feel protective rather than distant. It wasn't until they were both settled in the car that David spoke.

"Do you want to tell me what happened?"

Marcus gave him the basic facts—the attempted mugging, running until he found himself at the studio gates, not knowing where else to go. David listened without interrupting, his hands gripping the steering wheel as they drove through the quiet streets of West Hollywood.

"I'm glad you called," David said finally. "I'm glad you trusted me enough to reach out."

When they pulled into David's driveway, Marcus felt his breath catch. The house was beautiful in the way that houses in magazines were beautiful—clean lines and warm lighting, mature landscaping that looked effortless but probably cost more than his family's annual income. It was exactly the kind of place he'd imagined successful people lived in, but seeing it up close made him acutely aware of the gap between his world and David's.

"It's really beautiful," Marcus said as they walked toward the front door.

"Thank you. It's too big for one person, honestly, but I've gotten used to the space."

Inside, Marcus felt even more overwhelmed. The living room alone was larger than his family's entire front room back in Phoenix, filled with furniture that looked comfortable and expensive in equal measure. Art hung on the walls—real paintings, not prints—and everything was arranged with the kind of casual elegance that took money and taste to achieve.

"Marcus," David said, turning to face him as they stood in the entryway. "I want to say something, and I hope you'll hear me out."

Marcus nodded, still taking in his surroundings.

"I would very much like to give you a hug right now. You've had a terrible night, and you look like you could use some comfort. But I don't want you to think I have ulterior motives, or that there are strings attached to my offer to help. I simply want to provide some human kindness to someone who's been walking through this alone for too long."

The honesty in David's voice, the careful way he'd laid out his intentions, broke down another wall Marcus hadn't realized he'd built. Without thinking, he stepped forward and let David's arms close around him.

The hug was everything Marcus hadn't known he needed—warm and safe and unconditional. It smelled like expensive laundry detergent and aftershave, like stability and comfort. And as David held him, months of suppressed emotion finally found their release. Marcus cried against David's shoulder—for his lost family, for the boy he'd been before that terrible night in Phoenix, for the simple human contact he'd been denying himself out of necessity and fear.

David didn't say anything, just held him and let him cry, one hand rubbing gentle circles on his back. When Marcus finally pulled away, wiping his eyes with embarrassment, David handed him a tissue without comment.

"Thank you," Marcus said quietly. "I needed that more than I realized."

"We all need that sometimes."

Marcus took a shaky breath, then looked directly at David. "I want to be honest with you too. You seem like a really good person, and I'm grateful—more grateful than I can express. But I'm scared, David. What if you decide you don't want me here anymore and throw me out? What if you come into my room in the middle of the night wanting something I can't give? What if you're not who you seem to be?"

David nodded thoughtfully, as if he'd been expecting these questions. "Those are all reasonable concerns, Marcus. Let me try to address them."

They moved to the living room, where David gestured for Marcus to sit on the sofa while he took a chair across from him.

"First, I'm not going to throw you out. This isn't a whim or a temporary solution. I'm offering you a place to live while you figure out your next steps, however long that takes. Second, I will never, ever come to your room uninvited, and I will never ask you for anything sexual. I'm gay, Marcus, but I'm also a grown man who understands the difference between helping someone and taking advantage of them."

David paused, seeming to choose his words carefully.

"As for whether I'm who I seem to be—well, time will be the true test of your trust. I can say anything right now. You need to see it and feel it to believe it, and I understand and respect that completely. All I can do is be consistent, be honest, and give you the space you need to feel safe."

Marcus felt some of the tension leave his shoulders. "Thank you for not trying to convince me I'm being paranoid."

"You're not being paranoid. You're being smart. Anyone in your situation should ask these questions."

David stood up and gestured toward a hallway that led away from the main living areas. "Come on, let me show you where you'll be staying."

They walked down a short corridor to what David described as the guest wing—a bedroom with its own bathroom, a small kitchenette, and a sitting area with a television and bookshelf. There were locks on both the bedroom door and the door that connected the wing to the main house.

"This was designed to give guests complete privacy," David explained. "You can lock yourself in if it makes you feel safer. I won't be offended."

Marcus stood in the doorway, taking it all in. The room was larger than the bedroom he'd shared with his brothers, furnished with a comfortable-looking bed, a desk, and a dresser. The bathroom had a shower with glass doors and fluffy towels. The kitchenette included a small refrigerator and microwave.

"I've never stayed anywhere this nice," Marcus admitted.

"Well, it's yours for as long as you need it." David moved to the linen closet and pulled out fresh sheets and a blanket. "Tomorrow we'll go get you some clothes—and before you argue, this isn't charity. Think of it as an investment. I'd rather get you back to good health and stability. We can worry about repayment and jobs and all that later. For now, just focus on getting yourself grounded."

Marcus watched David move around the room, turning on lamps and adjusting the thermostat with the easy confidence of someone accustomed to taking care of details. "What do you want in return?"

"Nothing right now except for you to rest and recover. Next week, when you're feeling more settled, we can sit down and talk about goals, about what you want to do next. But tonight, just shower and sleep. Wake up whenever you want—I'm not going anywhere."

David paused in the doorway. "My room is upstairs on the opposite side of the house. If you need anything, anything at all, my number's programmed into the phone by the bed. Don't hesitate to call."

After David left, Marcus sat on the edge of the bed and looked around his temporary new home. The silence was different here—not the dangerous quiet of the streets, but the peaceful quiet of safety. For the first time in eight months, he was warm and clean and protected.

He was also exhausted. The emotional release of the evening, combined with months of inadequate sleep and constant stress, had left him feeling wrung out and hollow. He managed a quick shower, marveling at the hot water pressure and the collection of expensive-looking toiletries David had left for him, then fell into bed wearing the clean t-shirt and boxers he found laid out on the dresser.

As he drifted toward sleep, Marcus allowed himself to feel something he'd been denying for months: hope. It was fragile and tentative, but it was real. For the first time since that terrible night in Phoenix, he wasn't alone.

Tomorrow would bring new challenges, new questions about trust and independence and what came next. But tonight, he was safe. Tonight, he could rest.

That had to be enough.

nine
movement

MARCUS WOKE to silence so complete it felt foreign. No traffic rumble, no shouting voices, no rustling of other people moving in nearby tents or makeshift shelters. Just quiet—the kind of deep, peaceful quiet he'd almost forgotten existed. Sunlight filtered through curtains he didn't remember closing, casting soft patterns across a ceiling that wasn't a tent roof or a park bench or the inside of a bus shelter.

For a moment, confusion clouded his thoughts. Where was he? Then memory returned in gentle waves: the attempted mugging, the call from the studio gates, David's arms around him as months of held-back tears finally found their release. The guest wing. Safety.

Marcus turned his head toward the bedside clock and blinked in disbelief. 1:27 PM. He'd slept for nearly fourteen hours—the longest uninterrupted sleep he'd had in eight months. His body felt different, relaxed in ways he'd forgotten were possible. The duvet—was that what this fluffy, cloud-like covering was called?—seemed to cradle him like a gentle embrace.

But with the physical relief came an unexpected wave of guilt. While other kids his age were struggling on the streets, he was lying in luxury. While people who'd shown him kindness in the tent community were probably hungry and cold, he was warm and fed and safe. Had he somehow won a lottery he didn't deserve? Was this all too good to be true?

Marcus sat up slowly, his body protesting the movement after so much rest. The room looked even more beautiful in daylight—the furniture polished and inviting, the bathroom gleaming through the open door, everything clean and fresh and his. At least temporarily.

He remembered David's words about the locks, about privacy and safety. Tentatively, he tried the bedroom door handle and found it unlocked—he'd been too exhausted the night before to engage the mechanism. The knowledge that he could lock himself in anytime he needed to felt like another small gift.

Standing in just his boxers and the clean t-shirt David had provided, Marcus felt suddenly self-conscious. He should get dressed, but his own clothes lay in a crumpled pile where he'd dropped them after his shower —worn, dirty, carrying the smell of too many nights spent sleeping rough. The thought of putting them back on made his skin crawl.

After a moment's hesitation, Marcus unlocked the door connecting his wing to the main house and stepped into the hallway. He'd been too overwhelmed the night before to really explore, and now he found himself in unfamiliar territory. The hallway led to what appeared to be the main living area, but he could hear soft music coming from another direction—something classical and soothing.

Following the sound, Marcus discovered David in what was clearly a study or home office. Books lined the walls from floor to ceiling, and a comfortable reading chair sat near a window that looked out onto a small garden. David was settled in the chair with a hardcover book in his lap, his reading glasses perched on his nose, looking completely absorbed in whatever he was reading.

The music was coming from speakers Marcus couldn't see—something with strings and piano that seemed to float through the air like the morning light.

"David?" Marcus said softly, not wanting to startle him.

David looked up with a smile that seemed genuinely pleased rather than surprised. "Good afternoon, sleepyhead. How did you rest?"

"Better than I have in..." Marcus paused, realizing he was standing in David's study wearing only underwear and a t-shirt. Heat rose in his cheeks. "I'm sorry. I should have gotten dressed first, but my clothes are kind of..."

"Dirty?" David closed his book and set it aside. "Let's get that fixed then. You have to be hungry, and we can pick up a few things for you to wear while we're out."

David stood and gestured toward the door. "I have some sweatpants and a t-shirt or two that will fit. From... from Michael's things, if you don't mind wearing them."

Marcus caught the slight catch in David's voice, saw the way his expression shifted for just a moment—a shadow of grief crossing his features before he recovered his composure. Even now, years later, David still missed Michael. Marcus could feel it radiating from him like heat from a fire.

"I'd be honored to wear them," Marcus said quietly, and meant it.

Something in his tone seemed to reach David, who nodded gratefully before leading the way back toward the main part of the house.

Twenty minutes later, Marcus stood in David's kitchen wearing clothes that had belonged to a man he'd never met but somehow felt connected to. The sweatpants were soft with washing, the UCLA t-shirt comfortable and perfectly fitted. They smelled faintly of the same expensive laundry detergent that had scented David's embrace the night before.

"I don't want to overwhelm you," David said, pouring coffee into two mugs. "But I thought we could get you some basics today—clothes, toiletries, whatever you need to feel settled. We could grab lunch first, or shop first, or just stay here if you'd prefer. Whatever feels right to you."

Marcus appreciated the options, the way David was giving him control over decisions that affected him. It was such a contrast to the way most adults had treated him since leaving home—as a problem to be managed rather than a person with preferences and agency.

"Lunch sounds good," Marcus said. "And then shopping, I guess, though I have to warn you—I usually just grab whatever's cheapest and hope it fits. I don't really know about... nice stores."

David's smile was warm, tinged with something that might have been excitement. "Michael would have loved to take you shopping. He had excellent taste and a real eye for what looked good on people."

They drove to Nordstrom, and Marcus's first reaction was bewilderment. "There's a restaurant in the store?"

"Several, actually," David replied, leading him toward the café on the third floor. "Welcome to the world of upscale department stores."

Lunch was a revelation—not just the food, which was better than anything Marcus had eaten in months, but the entire experience. The way the servers treated him with the same courtesy they showed David, the quality of the coffee, the sense that this was just a normal part of some people's lives. Marcus found himself studying the other diners, trying to understand what it meant to move through the world with this kind of ease and comfort.

"This is really nice," Marcus said as they finished their meal. "I feel like I'm seeing how the other half lives."

"Well, you're part of it now," David replied simply. "For as long as you want to be."

The clothes shopping that followed was unlike anything Marcus had ever experienced. Instead of grabbing items off racks and hoping they'd work, David had him try on everything. A sales clerk named Patricia appeared as if summoned, taking measurements and bringing different sizes and styles for Marcus to consider.

At first, the constant trips to the dressing room were annoying. Marcus was used to making quick decisions and moving on. But as Patricia and David worked together to find clothes that actually fit him properly, that made him look older and more put-together, Marcus began to understand what he'd been missing.

"You have excellent proportions," Patricia told him as she adjusted the fit of a button-down shirt. "These colors really bring out your eyes."

Marcus caught his reflection in the three-way mirror and barely recognized himself. The young man looking back at him appeared confident, healthy, well-cared-for. It was startling to see what proper clothes and a good night's sleep could accomplish.

From Nordstrom, they went to what David called "Bloomingdale's"—another store Marcus had never heard of but which seemed to operate on the same principle of treating shopping like an art form. By the time they loaded the bags into David's BMW, Marcus was feeling overwhelmed in an entirely different way.

"Is this too much?" he asked, looking at the collection of shopping bags that filled the back seat. The guilt was returning, stronger now that he could see the physical evidence of David's generosity.

"Not at all," David replied, starting the car. "You've got nine outfits. That'll get you through a week and a half without doing laundry.

Though I think you could use more socks and underwear—no need to run out of those."

Marcus laughed despite himself. "Tell me about it. I could tell you stories..."

"I'm sure you could." David's voice was gentle, understanding. "But you don't have to worry about that anymore."

As they drove back toward David's house, Marcus found himself studying his companion. David seemed genuinely happy, more relaxed than he'd appeared during their previous encounters. There was something almost boyish about his enthusiasm for the shopping expedition.

"You seemed to really enjoy that," Marcus observed.

David glanced over with a slightly embarrassed smile. "I did. I don't get many chances to spoil anyone. I have nephews back in Indiana, but I rarely see them. This felt... nice. Familiar, somehow."

Marcus was quiet for a moment, processing the implications of that statement. Finally, he worked up the courage to ask the question that had been forming in his mind.

"Can I ask you something personal?"

"You can ask me anything you'd like."

"Did you and Michael ever think about having kids?"

David's hands tightened almost imperceptibly on the steering wheel, but his voice remained steady. "Yes, we talked about it. Michael would have loved to have children. He was so good with kids—natural in a way I never felt I was."

"But you decided not to?"

"We never really decided anything definitively. My career was always so demanding, and..." David paused, seeming to choose his words carefully. "Truth is, I was afraid I wouldn't be a good father."

Marcus turned in his seat to study David's profile. "How so?"

"Because I wasn't sure about myself. I wasn't sure if I knew what I was doing. I mean, I think I'm a good person—I try to be. And I know how to love unconditionally. But..."

"But what? Sounds like you would have been the perfect dad to me."

David shook his head. "I was afraid I'd say something wrong, or inadvertently do something that would hurt them. Kids seemed so fragile. I know I was."

"How were you fragile?"

"Well, like... what if I was busy at work and wasn't paying enough attention? Or missed a piano recital or couldn't go to a basketball game? Or maybe I'd say they looked 'lovely' when I should have said they looked 'sick' or whatever kids say these days..."

Marcus burst out laughing—the first genuine, unguarded laugh he'd had in eight months. It felt so good he couldn't stop, even when David looked at him with puzzled concern.

"What?" David asked. "Why are you laughing?"

"Because you worry about stupid shit!" Marcus managed between giggles.

"I do not!" David protested, but he was laughing too now, his indignation completely undermined by his amusement.

"Okay, maybe Michael used to accuse me of the same thing," David admitted. "But in my defense, I just want to be a good person. To be a good..."

"Dad," Marcus finished for him. "Yeah, I know. And you would have been."

They drove in comfortable silence for a few minutes, both lost in their own thoughts. Finally, Marcus spoke again, his voice softer now.

"David?"

"Yeah?"

"Just keep being honest, and you'll be perfect."

David glanced over at him, and Marcus saw something in his expression that looked like gratitude mixed with wonder, as if he couldn't quite believe this conversation was happening.

"Thank you," David said quietly. "That means more than you know."

As they pulled into David's driveway, Marcus felt something shift inside him—a loosening of the tight control he'd maintained for so long. For the first time since leaving Phoenix, he allowed himself to imagine what it might be like to belong somewhere again, to be part of something larger than mere survival.

It was a dangerous thought, he knew. Hope had proven unreliable in the past. But sitting in David's car, wearing Michael's clothes, surrounded by bags full of new possibilities, Marcus found himself willing to take the risk.

Maybe, just maybe, he'd found his way home.

ten
opening doors

TEN DAYS HAD PASSED since Marcus first slept in David's guest wing, and a comfortable rhythm had begun to emerge between them. David would leave for work around seven-thirty, always checking quietly to see if Marcus was awake—which he rarely was—and leaving a note about what was in the refrigerator for lunch. Marcus typically surfaced around eleven or noon, his body still adjusting to the luxury of uninterrupted sleep.

This morning, David found Marcus in the kitchen at ten-forty-five, looking more rested than he had since arriving. The dark circles under his eyes had faded, and he'd gained a few pounds that filled out his face and made him look his age again.

"Morning," Marcus said, pouring himself coffee from the pot David had left warming. "You're still here."

"Conference call got pushed back an hour," David replied, setting down his laptop. "How did you sleep?"

"Good. Really good, actually." Marcus settled at the kitchen island, wrapping his hands around the mug. "I've been thinking, though—I feel like I'm turning into a teenager again, sleeping until noon every day. Is that normal?"

David smiled, remembering conversations with Elena about teenage sleep patterns. "Your body's been in survival mode for eight months. It's going to take time to reset your natural rhythms. But if you're concerned about it, we could try establishing more of a routine."

"What do you mean?"

"Well, you're going to bed around ten, which is great. But maybe we could add some structure to your days? Some light exercise might help regulate your sleep cycle. I have a small gym downstairs, or..." David paused, suddenly feeling self-conscious about his next suggestion.

"Or what?"

"There's a pool. I never use it, but it's there if you're interested."

Marcus's face lit up with the first genuine excitement David had seen from him. "You have a pool? Like, a real swimming pool?"

"Want to see it?"

David led him through the sliding doors off the living room onto a terrace that overlooked the backyard. The pool was modest by Hollywood standards but beautifully maintained, surrounded by mature landscaping that provided privacy from neighboring houses.

"This is incredible," Marcus breathed, walking to the edge and looking down into the clear blue water. "I used to swim in high school. Not competitively or anything, just for fun. I'd forgotten how much I missed it."

"Feel free to use it whenever you want. There are towels in the pool house, and I can pick up some swim shorts for you today.'

Marcus turned back to David with something approaching wonder. "You'd really let me swim in your pool?"

"Marcus, this is your home now. You don't need permission to use anything here."

They stood in comfortable silence for a moment, both looking out over the water. Finally, Marcus spoke again, his voice quieter.

"I keep waiting for the catch, you know? For you to tell me what you really want in return for all this."

David understood the wariness—it was probably what had kept Marcus safe on the streets. "The only thing I want is for you to feel secure enough to figure out what comes next for you. That's it."

Marcus nodded slowly, then surprised David by asking, "Could we maybe make a list? Of things that need to be done around here? I feel like I should be contributing somehow."

An hour later, they sat at David's dining room table with a legal pad between them, brainstorming what David diplomatically called "household tasks" and Marcus insisted on calling "chores."

"Okay," David said, writing at the top of the page. "Pool maintenance —I have a service for that, so that's covered. Groceries..."

"I could do groceries," Marcus offered immediately. "And cleaning. I'm good at cleaning. And laundry. Cooking, maybe, though I should probably learn more than ramen and sandwiches."

David looked up from the list. "Marcus, you don't have to take on everything."

"I want to. I need to feel useful." Marcus's voice carried an edge of urgency. "I've been taking care of myself for months. I'm not helpless."

"I know you're not. But this isn't about earning your keep. You're not my tenant."

"Then what am I?"

The question hung in the air between them. David set down his pen and considered how to answer honestly.

"You're someone I care about. Someone I want to help get back on his feet. Someone who's become..." David paused, searching for the right word. "Important to me."

Marcus was quiet for a moment, processing this. Finally, he said, "Okay. But I still want to do my share. It'll make me feel better about being here."

They compromised. Marcus would handle grocery shopping, most of the cleaning, and his own laundry. David would continue managing the yard service, pool maintenance, and major household repairs. They'd split cooking duties, with David teaching Marcus some basic techniques.

"What about school?" David asked as they finished the list. "Have you thought about that?"

Marcus's pen stopped moving. "Some. I was supposed to graduate this spring, but obviously that didn't happen. I guess I need to figure out how to get my GED."

"We can look into that. There might be other options too—programs for students in situations like yours."

"You mean homeless kids?"

"I mean young people who've had their education interrupted. You're not the first person this has happened to, Marcus. There are resources."

Marcus nodded, but David could see him retreating slightly into himself. The mention of school seemed to bring back memories of the life he'd lost.

"We don't have to decide anything today," David said gently. "Just something to think about."

That evening, after they'd shared a dinner of pasta and salad—Marcus's first attempt at cooking something more complex than sandwiches—they found themselves lingering at the table, neither quite ready to end the day.

"Can I ask you something?" Marcus said, swirling the last of his iced tea in his glass.

"Always."

"What was it like growing up in Indiana? I mean, being gay in a small town?"

David leaned back in his chair, surprised by the question. "Lonely, mostly. And scary. I knew I was different from a very young age, but I didn't have words for it. This was the eighties—there wasn't much representation, no internet, no gay-straight alliances at school."

"Did you come out to your family?"

"No." David's voice was quiet. "I never found the courage. My parents were... traditional. Conservative. I convinced myself it would destroy them to know the truth about me."

"Do you regret that?"

David considered the question. "Sometimes. My father died when I was thirty-five, and my mother a few years later. I think about whether things might have been different if I'd trusted them with the truth. But I was so afraid of losing them that I never gave them the chance to surprise me."

Marcus nodded thoughtfully. "When did you have your first boyfriend?"

"Michael was my first everything. First kiss, first relationship, first time I held hands with someone in public. I was twenty-four when we met."

"Twenty-four?" Marcus's eyes widened. "That seems so old for a first kiss."

David laughed. "It felt old at the time too. I was convinced I was going to die alone and inexperienced." He paused, then turned the question back. "What about you? First kiss? First boyfriend?"

Marcus felt heat rise in his cheeks. "I never... I mean, there was Jake back home, but we never got past texting. And the kissing thing..." He trailed off, embarrassed.

"Never?"

"Never. I'm still a virgin, actually." Marcus said it quickly, as if rushing the words might make them less mortifying to admit.

To his surprise, David's face lit up with something that looked like pride. "Congratulations."

"Congratulations?" Marcus stared at him. "For being an eighteen-year-old virgin? That's not exactly an accomplishment."

"Yes, it is." David's voice was firm, serious. "Marcus, you've been through hell these past eight months. You've been vulnerable, alone, probably approached by people who wanted to take advantage of that vulnerability. The fact that you held onto something so personal, that you saved it for someone who matters to you—that shows incredible character."

Marcus blinked, processing this unexpected response. "Really?"

"Really. I wouldn't think less of you if you'd made different choices—everyone's path is different. But the fact that you protected that part of yourself through everything you've endured? That's remarkable."

Marcus felt something warm unfurl in his chest—a feeling he couldn't quite name but that felt like being truly seen and valued. He ducked his head, suddenly shy.

"Thank you," he said quietly. "I never thought about it that way."

They sat in comfortable silence for a few minutes before David's phone rang. Elena's name appeared on the screen.

"Mind if I take this?" David asked. "It's my friend Elena."

Marcus nodded, and David answered the call.

"Hey, Elena... Yes, he's doing wonderfully... Actually, he's right here if you'd like to say hello."

David held out the phone to Marcus, who took it with nervous curiosity.

"Hi, Elena."

"Marcus! I've heard so much about you. David sounds like a proud father when he talks about you."

Marcus glanced at David, who was pretending to clean up dinner dishes but was clearly listening. "He's been really good to me."

"I'm so glad. David needs someone to take care of. He's been rattling around in that big house alone for too long."

They chatted for a few minutes before Elena asked to speak to David again. Marcus handed back the phone and moved to the kitchen to give David some privacy, but he could still hear fragments of the conversation.

"...Aiden's been asking about visiting... this summer maybe... I think you're right about him struggling with his identity... would Marcus be okay with having another teenager around?"

David walked into the kitchen, still talking. "Actually, having Marcus here makes me look forward to spending time with Aiden. And if you're right about what he's going through, maybe I can help. Maybe they can help each other."

After David hung up, Marcus asked, "Is Aiden Elena's son?"

"Her seventeen-year-old. She thinks he might be gay and struggling with coming out. She's been worried about him."

Marcus felt a flutter of recognition and sympathy. "That's hard. Being seventeen and not knowing how to tell people who you really are."

"Would you be okay with him visiting this summer? Elena's thinking about sending both boys out for a few weeks."

"Both boys?"

"Aiden and his younger brother Noah. Fourteen."

Marcus considered this. The idea of sharing this space, this new sense of safety, with strangers felt intimidating. But the thought of helping another kid who might be going through what he'd experienced—that felt important.

"Yeah," he said finally. "I think I'd like that. Especially if Aiden needs someone to talk to who gets it."

David smiled. "I think you'd be good for each other."

As they finished cleaning up the kitchen, Marcus reflected on how much had changed in just ten days. He had a routine now, responsibilities, a sense of belonging he'd almost forgotten was possible. And maybe, soon, he'd have the chance to be what David had been for him—someone who showed up when it mattered most.

The thought was both exciting and terrifying. But for the first time in months, Marcus felt ready for whatever came next.

eleven
the call

SATURDAY AFTERNOON SUN streamed through the windows of David's study as he settled into his favorite reading chair with a cup of coffee and the latest issue of *Variety*. The house was peaceful—Marcus had been in the pool for the past hour, and David could occasionally hear the splash of water as he swam laps. It was exactly the kind of quiet weekend moment David had grown to cherish since Marcus had moved in.

His phone rang just as he was getting absorbed in an article about international distribution trends. Elena's name appeared on the screen, and David smiled as he answered.

"Perfect timing," he said. "I was just thinking I should call you."

"Great minds," Elena replied, but David caught something in her voice—a tension that hadn't been there during their conversation the week before. "Are you free to talk? Really talk? I mean, no work calls or Marcus needing anything?"

"Marcus is swimming, and my weekend is completely clear. What's going on?"

Elena sighed, and David could picture her settling into her kitchen chair, the one by the window where she always sat for serious conversations. "It's Aiden. Things have gotten worse since we talked last week."

David set aside his magazine and gave Elena his full attention. "Worse how?"

"He's spending almost all his time in his room now. When he does come out, he barely speaks to any of us. The other day I suggested he invite some friends over, and he just gave me this look—like I'd suggested something ridiculous. Today's actually unusual—he went out with Noah and some of Noah's friends, but only because I practically forced him."

"What about school? How are his grades?"

"Still good, thankfully. But his teachers have mentioned he seems withdrawn in class. And David..." Elena paused, seeming to gather her thoughts. "That spark in his eyes? It's just gone. He used to be so animated when he talked about things he was passionate about—theater, books, music. Now he just shrugs when I ask about anything."

David felt a familiar ache in his chest, remembering his own teenage years of hiding and self-doubt. "Has he said anything specific? Given you any clues about what's bothering him?"

"Not directly. But he's become really protective of his phone. Like, panic-level protective. Last week I jokingly threatened to check his browser history if he didn't clean his room, and I swear he went white as a sheet."

"Do you think he's sending inappropriate photos? Or talking to strangers online?"

"No, I don't think it's anything predatory. I've tried to give him subtle openings—you know, mentioning how proud I am of people who live authentically, gay or straight. I've brought you up a few times as an example of someone I admire who happens to be gay."

"How does he react to that?"

"That's the thing—he perks up when I mention your name. His whole demeanor changes, like he's suddenly paying attention. But then he catches himself and shuts down again."

David stood and moved to the window, watching Marcus execute a perfect flip turn at the far end of the pool. "It sounds like he's definitely struggling with something identity-related. What finally convinced you?"

Elena laughed, but it carried a note of maternal exasperation. "Last night I was in the living room grading papers, and Aiden was on the couch with his phone. He thought I wasn't paying attention, but I glanced over and caught a glimpse of what he was watching."

"Which was?"

"Some YouTube video of shirtless guys working out. Very attractive, very muscular shirtless guys."

David couldn't help but smile. "And what's wrong with that?"

"Nothing! They were hot!" Elena said with a laugh. "But straight seventeen-year-old boys don't typically spend their Friday nights watching videos of hot shirtless guys, David."

They both laughed, and David felt some of the tension ease from the conversation. "Sounds like he's at least curious. That's a healthy start."

"I think so too. But I'm worried about pushing too hard, you know? If I confront him directly about being gay, I'm afraid he'll shut down completely. He needs to come to this realization on his own timeline."

David was about to respond when he caught sight of Marcus approaching the study, dripping wet with a towel around his shoulders. Marcus had clearly heard David's laughter and stopped in the doorway, looking curious but uncertain about interrupting.

"Elena, hold on a second," David said, gesturing for Marcus to come in. "Marcus just came in from swimming, and I think he might have over-heard us talking about hot shirtless guys."

Marcus's eyebrows shot up in surprise, and David couldn't help but grin at his expression.

"Marcus, do you mind if I put Elena on speaker? She'd probably like to say hello."

Marcus nodded, settling into the chair across from David's desk as David switched to speakerphone.

"Hi, Marcus!" Elena's voice filled the study. "Sorry if you walked in on us discussing attractive men. We weren't talking about you, I promise."

Marcus's face broke into the kind of mischievous grin David had rarely seen from him. "So I'm not hot?" he asked with mock offense.

Elena's laughter echoed through the room. "Boy, we can't win, can we, David? Teenagers and their egos!"

David found himself laughing harder than he had in weeks, and he noticed Marcus looked genuinely delighted to be included in the family banter.

"Were you talking about Aiden?" Marcus asked, his tone shifting to something more serious. "Is it okay if I ask about that? I don't want to get into your personal business."

"It's fine, Marcus," Elena said warmly. "Why do you ask?"

Marcus glanced at David, as if seeking permission to continue. David nodded encouragingly.

"Well, maybe I could... I don't know, maybe talk with him or something? I mean, I've got time, and David's going to be working while he's out here, right?"

David started to object. "Well, I'm planning to take some time off, but I do have several meetings I'll need to attend—"

"And I don't know," Marcus continued, his words coming faster now, "maybe he'd like to hang out with me? We're about the same age and all, and... I don't know if I can help, but..." He paused, seeming to lose confidence. "I'm probably not making any sense, but I know what it's like to not know who to talk to, especially if you think you're..."

Marcus trailed off, suddenly looking uncertain.

"Gay?" Elena finished gently.

"Yeah," Marcus said quietly. "I remember feeling so alone with all those questions. Maybe having someone close to his age who's been through it might help?"

David felt something warm and proud unfurl in his chest. Here was Marcus, still healing from his own trauma, offering to help another young person navigate similar struggles. It was exactly the kind of generosity of spirit that had drawn David to him in the first place.

"Marcus, that's incredibly thoughtful," Elena said, her voice thick with emotion. "I think that might be exactly what Aiden needs."

"Really?" Marcus brightened. "I mean, I can't promise I'll know what to say, but I remember wishing I had someone who understood. Someone who wouldn't judge me for the questions I was too scared to ask out loud."

"When were you thinking about having them visit?" David asked.

"I was hoping for a couple weeks this summer," Elena replied. "School gets out in early June, and I thought maybe July? That would give me time to prepare them, and give you time to prepare Marcus for the invasion."

Marcus laughed. "I like the idea of an invasion. This house is too quiet sometimes."

"Speaking of which," Elena continued, "what about Noah? I don't want him to feel like a fourth wheel while Aiden and Marcus are bonding. He's only fourteen, but he's perceptive. He'll notice if his brother suddenly has this special connection with someone."

David hadn't considered that dynamic, and he felt a flutter of anxiety at the complexity of managing multiple teenagers with different needs. "That's a really good point. Maybe I could spend some uncle time with Noah while Marcus and Aiden hang out together? Though I suppose a lot depends on how well they all get along."

"Boy, raising children is complicated," David muttered, more to himself than to anyone else.

"You think?" Elena teased. "David, you're sounding like a true parent! Welcome to the club."

Marcus grinned at David's slightly panicked expression. "Don't worry, David. I think you're going to be great at this. You've had plenty of practice with me."

"That's different," David protested. "You were... well, you are easier than most teenagers."

"Give me time," Marcus said with mock seriousness. "I might start being difficult just to prepare you for Aiden and Noah."

Elena's laughter filled the room again. "Oh, Marcus, I like you already. You're going to fit right into this family."

As they wrapped up the call with tentative plans for a July visit, David found himself marveling at how naturally Marcus had inserted himself into the conversation, how easily he'd offered to help, how comfortable he seemed with the idea of being part of something larger than just the two of them.

After Elena hung up, Marcus remained in his chair, still wrapped in his towel, looking thoughtful.

"You sure you're okay with this?" David asked. "Having two other teenagers around for a few weeks? It'll change the dynamic here significantly."

Marcus considered this. "I think I want that. I like what we have, David—I love it, actually. But I think I'm ready to try being the person who helps instead of the person who needs help. Does that make sense?"

David nodded, understanding completely. "It makes perfect sense. And Marcus? I'm proud of you for offering. That took courage."

"I learned from the best," Marcus replied with a smile. "Besides, someone once told me that when you've been through something difficult, sometimes the best thing you can do is help the next person who's going through the same thing."

"When did I say that?"

"You didn't. But you've been showing me that every day since we met."

David felt his throat tighten with emotion. In just a few weeks, Marcus had gone from a desperate young man with nowhere to turn to someone ready to be a mentor and friend to others in need. It was exactly the kind of transformation David had hoped for but hadn't dared to expect.

"Well," David said, standing and stretching, "I guess we'd better start planning for houseguests. Think the pool can handle three teenagers?"

Marcus grinned and headed for the door. "Only one way to find out. Want to join me for a swim and we can discuss logistics?"

David looked at his pile of weekend reading, then at Marcus's hopeful expression. "You know what? That sounds perfect.'

As they headed toward the pool together, David realized that some-where along the way, without quite noticing when it had happened, he'd stopped thinking of Marcus as someone he was helping and started thinking of him as family. And now that family was about to grow.

twelve
meeting

AIDEN SAT on the edge of his bed, watching Noah pack his oversized suitcase with the methodical precision of someone who'd clearly been planning this trip for weeks. His younger brother had laid out every shirt, every pair of shorts, arranging them like he was preparing for a military inspection rather than a summer vacation.

"You know we're only going for two weeks, right?" Aiden said, trying to keep his voice light. "Not moving there permanently."

Noah looked up from his careful folding. "I want to be prepared. What if we go somewhere fancy? What if we meet celebrities? What if—"

"What if you calm down?" Aiden interrupted, but he was smiling. Noah's excitement was infectious, even if it made Aiden's own nervousness feel sharper by comparison.

Noah threw a rolled-up sock at him. "Easy for you to say. You've been all weird and quiet for weeks. At least I'm excited about something."

The comment hit closer to home than Noah probably intended. Aiden had been weird and quiet, carrying around questions and feelings he didn't know how to voice. And now, sitting here in their shared space, with Noah being so openly trusting and enthusiastic, Aiden felt the familiar urge to tell him everything.

"Noah," Aiden started, then stopped. His brother was still organizing his suitcase, not really paying attention. "Can I... can I tell you something?"

"Sure." Noah didn't look up from debating between two nearly identical t-shirts.

Aiden took a breath, feeling his heart rate accelerate. "I've been thinking about... about things. About myself. About..."

Now Noah did look up, sensing something different in his brother's tone. "About what?"

The words were right there, balanced on the tip of Aiden's tongue. *About being gay. About liking boys instead of girls. About feeling like a fraud every time someone assumes I'm straight.* But looking at Noah's expectant face, so trusting and uncomplicated, Aiden lost his nerve.

"About college," he finished lamely. "About what I want to study."

Noah's expression shifted to mild disappointment. "That's what you've been all weird about? College? Dude, you're only going to be a senior. You have time to figure that out."

"Boys!" Elena's voice carried up the stairs, sharp with the particular urgency of a mother running behind schedule. "We need to leave for the airport in ten minutes! Aiden, are you packed?"

Aiden gestured to his own suitcase, considerably less organized than Noah's but packed nonetheless. "Yeah, Mom!"

"Then get down here! Both of you!"

Noah grabbed his suitcase handle and headed for the door, then paused to look back at his brother. "You know you can tell me stuff, right? Real stuff, not just college worries."

Aiden felt his throat tighten. "I know."

"Good. Because you've been acting like you're carrying around some huge secret, and it's kind of annoying."

If only you knew, Aiden thought, but he just nodded and followed Noah downstairs.

Elena was waiting in the kitchen, her own coffee mug in hand and that particular expression she got when she was trying to manage multiple emotions at once—pride, worry, excitement, and maternal protectiveness all competing for space on her face.

"Okay," she said, setting down her mug and turning to face both boys. "Last chance for me to give you the lecture about being responsible, looking out for each other, and not doing anything that would make me regret letting you travel alone."

Noah grinned. "We've heard the lecture, Mom. Like, five times."

"Then hear it a sixth time," Elena replied, but she was smiling too. "Aiden, you're the older brother. I'm trusting you to make good decisions, not just for yourself but for Noah too. That's a big responsibility."

Aiden felt the weight of her trust settle on his shoulders—not uncomfortable, exactly, but significant. He was the older brother, the one she was counting on to be mature and responsible. The one she trusted to take care of Noah in a city three thousand miles from home.

"I know, Mom. I won't let you down."

Elena stepped forward and cupped his face in her hands, the way she'd done since he was small. "You are special, Aiden. You are loved, exactly as you are. And if you need to talk about anything—anything at all—you can call me. Or you can talk to David. He's... he understands things about growing up that might be hard to discuss with your mother."

Aiden felt heat rise in his cheeks. Did she know? Had she figured out what he'd been struggling with? "Mom—"

"I'm just saying," Elena continued gently, "that sometimes it helps to have adults in your life who've been where you are. David is someone I trust completely, and he cares about you boys."

Noah, who'd been listening with the impatience of someone eager to get to the airport, finally spoke up. "Who's Marcus again? You explained before, but I still don't really get it."

Elena released Aiden's face and turned to Noah, her expression becoming more careful. "Marcus is a young man who's been staying with David. He's about Aiden's age—maybe a year older. He's had some difficult circumstances in his life, and David has been helping him get back on his feet."

"What kind of difficult circumstances?" Noah pressed.

Elena glanced at Aiden, then back to Noah. "That's Marcus's story to tell if he wants to share it. What I can tell you is that he's a good person who's been through some challenges, and David thinks you boys might enjoy spending time with someone closer to your age."

"Is he gay too?" Noah asked with the blunt curiosity of a fourteen-year-old.

"Noah!" Aiden said, mortified.

Elena held up a hand. "It's okay, Aiden. Yes, Noah, Marcus is gay. But that's not why David is helping him—David helps him because he's a good person who needed support. Just like David isn't special because he's gay, he's special because he's kind and generous and has become like family to us."

Noah nodded thoughtfully. "Cool. I've never really hung out with other gay people before. I mean, besides David, but that was only for a few days last time."

Aiden felt something twist in his stomach. Would Noah be equally accepting if he knew about his brother? Or would it be different when it was someone in his own family rather than a friend of the family?

Elena checked her watch and clapped her hands together. "Okay, enough questions for now. You'll meet Marcus in a few hours and can ask him whatever you want—within reason. But right now, we need to get to Logan before you miss your flight."

The drive to the airport passed in a blur of final reminders and reassurances. Elena quizzed them on their flight information, made sure they had David's address and phone number written down in addition to having it in their phones, and reminded them at least three times to call her as soon as they landed.

At the departure gate, she hugged them both fiercely, holding on perhaps a moment longer than necessary.

"I love you both," she said, looking between them. "Take care of each other, have fun, and remember—this is a big deal. I'm trusting you to be mature and responsible. Don't make me regret it."

"We won't," Aiden promised, and meant it.

As they walked toward the jetway, Noah turned back to wave at their mother one more time. "I can't believe she's actually letting us do this alone."

"Yeah," Aiden agreed, but his mind was already racing ahead to Los Angeles, to David's house, to meeting Marcus. To the possibility of finally having someone to talk to who might understand the questions he'd been carrying around for months.

The flight to LAX felt both eternal and impossibly short. Noah spent most of it reading a book about special effects in movies, occasionally sharing particularly interesting facts with Aiden whether he wanted to hear them or not. Aiden tried to read, tried to listen to music, tried to focus on anything other than the growing nervousness in his chest.

What if he and Marcus didn't get along? What if David had changed since their last visit and wasn't as welcoming as Elena seemed to think? What if he said something that revealed too much about what he was struggling with?

But underneath the nervousness was something else—a flutter of anticipation that felt almost like hope. For the first time in months, he was going somewhere new, meeting someone new, escaping the familiar patterns of home where he felt so trapped by his own uncertainty.

When the plane began its descent into Los Angeles, Noah pressed his face to the window like a kid half his age.

"Look at all those palm trees!" he said, as if he hadn't seen them during their previous visit. "And the mountains! God, I love this place already."

Aiden leaned over to look past his brother at the sprawling city below. Los Angeles stretched out in all directions, vast and sun-soaked and full of possibilities. Somewhere down there, David was probably driving to the airport to pick them up. Somewhere down there, Marcus was waiting to meet them.

"Yeah," Aiden said quietly. "I love it too."

The baggage claim at LAX was chaos, as always—crowds of travelers speaking dozens of languages, families reuniting, business travelers hurrying toward ground transportation. Aiden kept a protective eye on Noah while scanning the crowd for David's familiar face.

"There!" Noah said suddenly, pointing toward the arrivals area. "I see him!"

David was walking toward them with a smile that seemed to light up his entire face, looking more relaxed and happy than Aiden remembered from their previous visit. Beside him walked someone who had to be Marcus—tall and lean with dark hair, wearing jeans and a t-shirt that looked expensive but not flashy. Even from a distance, there was something about his posture that suggested confidence mixed with careful awareness of his surroundings.

"Boys!" David called out as they approached, opening his arms for hugs. "Look at you! You've both grown at least six inches since I saw you last."

Noah launched himself into David's embrace with the enthusiasm of someone who'd been looking forward to this moment for weeks. "David! This is so cool! I can't believe Mom actually let us come by ourselves!"

"Well, you're practically adults now," David replied, ruffling Noah's hair. "I'm proud of her for trusting you, and proud of you for being trustworthy."

When David turned to Aiden, his hug was just as warm but somehow more thoughtful, as if he was really seeing him. "And how are you doing, Aiden? Really?"

The question caught Aiden off guard—not the words themselves, but the way David asked it, as if he genuinely wanted to know and had time to listen to whatever the answer might be.

"I'm good," Aiden said, then found himself adding, "Better now that we're here."

David smiled at that, then turned to Marcus, who'd been hanging back slightly, giving them space for their reunion.

"Boys, I'd like you to meet Marcus. Marcus, this is Aiden and Noah."

Marcus stepped forward with an easy smile that reached his eyes. "Hey, guys. David's told me a lot about you. I'm really glad you're here."

There was something in Marcus's voice—a warmth that felt genuine rather than polite, and an undercurrent of understanding that Aiden couldn't quite identify but that made him feel immediately more comfortable.

"Hi," Aiden said, suddenly feeling shy. "Thanks for... I mean, David said you might hang out with us some while we're here."

"If you want to," Marcus replied. "No pressure. But I thought it might be fun to have someone closer to your age to show you around. David's great, but his idea of a good time might be different from ours."

Noah laughed. "What do you mean?"

"Well," Marcus said with a grin, "David's probably thinking museums and educational tours. I'm thinking maybe we hit the Beverly Center, check out some actual movie locations, maybe get some In-N-Out burgers."

"Yes!" Noah said immediately. "That sounds way better than museums."

David held up his hands in mock offense. "Hey, I like In-N-Out! And I never said anything about museums."

"But you were thinking it," Marcus teased, and Aiden was struck by the easy familiarity between them. Whatever Marcus's story was, he and David clearly had a comfortable relationship built on genuine affection.

As they walked toward the parking garage, Noah peppered Marcus with questions about Los Angeles, about movie stars he might have seen, about whether the beaches were really as awesome as they looked in movies. Marcus answered patiently, occasionally throwing in details that made Noah's eyes widen with excitement.

Aiden found himself hanging back slightly, watching the interaction with a mixture of curiosity and something that might have been envy. Marcus seemed so comfortable in his own skin, so at ease with meeting new people and answering questions. He had the kind of natural confidence Aiden wished he possessed.

But there was something else, too—moments when Marcus's expression would shift slightly, becoming more thoughtful, as if he was remembering something or considering his words more carefully. It was subtle, but Aiden noticed it, and it made him wonder what experiences had shaped the young man walking beside them.

David's BMW was exactly as Aiden remembered it—sleek and comfortable and unmistakably expensive. As they loaded their luggage into the trunk, David turned to both boys with a slightly nervous expression.

"So, I should mention—I've set up separate rooms for you this time. I figured you might appreciate some privacy now that you're older. But they're right next to each other, so if you want to stay close..."

"Separate rooms?" Noah's face lit up. "Really? Like, my own room?"

"Your own room," David confirmed. "With your own bathroom and everything."

Noah turned to Aiden with excitement. "Did you hear that? We get our own rooms! This is the best vacation ever."

Aiden smiled at his brother's enthusiasm, but found himself feeling a flutter of uncertainty. He was used to sharing space with Noah, used to having his brother's familiar presence nearby when he felt anxious or unsettled. Having his own room sounded great in theory, but it also felt like another step toward the independence he wasn't sure he was ready for.

Marcus seemed to sense his hesitation. "The rooms are literally right next door to each other," he said quietly. "And David's house is really comfortable. You'll love having your own space, but you won't feel isolated."

"Where do you stay?" Aiden asked.

"I have a guest wing on the other side of the house. My own little apartment, basically. David set it up so I could have complete privacy when I need it."

There was something in the way Marcus said it that suggested the privacy had been important for reasons beyond just comfort. Aiden filed that observation away, along with his growing curiosity about Marcus's story.

The drive from LAX to West Hollywood took nearly an hour in traffic, but it passed quickly. David pointed out landmarks and changes since their last visit, while Marcus added commentary about his favorite spots and hidden gems that tourists usually missed. Noah kept up a steady stream of questions and observations, his excitement infectious.

But it was the quieter moments that caught Aiden's attention—when Marcus would catch his eye in the rearview mirror and smile, or when David would glance back to check on them both, his expression soft with something that looked like contentment. There was a warmth in the car that felt like family, but also like something new and undefined.

When they pulled into David's driveway, Aiden felt a rush of recognition mixed with surprise. The house looked exactly as he remembered, but somehow more welcoming. Maybe it was the mature landscaping, or maybe it was David's obvious happiness, but the place felt more like a home than the impressive but sterile house they'd visited two years ago.

"Okay," David said as they gathered their luggage, "house tour first, then we'll figure out lunch. Marcus, you want to show them around while I check messages?"

"Sure," Marcus replied, then turned to the boys with a grin. "Come on, let me show you guys your new temporary headquarters."

The house was even more beautiful than Aiden remembered. Marcus led them through the main living areas, pointing out the kitchen, the study where David liked to read, the terrace that overlooked the pool. Everything was tasteful and comfortable, clearly expensive but not ostentatious.

"This place is insane," Noah said, running his hand along the granite countertop in the kitchen. "David must make serious money."

"The movie business has been good to him," Marcus agreed. "But honestly, he's not really into showing off. He just likes beautiful things and comfortable spaces."

When they reached the guest bedrooms, Aiden understood why David had been slightly nervous about the arrangements. The rooms were gorgeous—each with its own bathroom, comfortable furniture, and large windows that looked out over the landscaped backyard. But they were clearly meant for adults, sophisticated and elegant in a way that might have intimidated younger kids.

"These are incredible," Aiden said, setting his suitcase down in what David had designated as his room. "Are you sure it's okay for us to stay here?"

Marcus leaned against the doorframe, his expression gentle. "David wants you to be comfortable. He wants you to feel like this is your space while you're here, not like you're visitors who have to be careful about everything."

Noah poked his head out of his room next door. "Marcus, can I ask you something?"

"Shoot."

"My mom said you've had some difficult circumstances. I don't want to be nosy, but... are you okay now? I mean, are you happy here?"

Aiden held his breath, curious about how Marcus would handle Noah's characteristic directness.

Marcus was quiet for a moment, seeming to consider his answer carefully. "Yeah, I'm okay now. Better than okay, actually. David helped me when I really needed it, and now I'm figuring out what comes next for me. Sometimes life throws you curveballs, you know? The important thing is having people who care about you when things get tough."

"Did your family not care about you?" Noah pressed.

"Noah," Aiden said quietly, sensing they were moving into territory that might be too personal.

But Marcus held up a hand. "It's okay. The short answer is that my family and I had some disagreements about who I am and what my life should look like. They couldn't accept certain things about me, so I had to leave home and figure things out on my own."

"Because you're gay?" Noah asked.

"That was part of it, yeah."

Noah was quiet for a moment, processing this. Finally, he said, "That sucks. I'm sorry that happened to you."

"Thanks. It did suck for a while. But I'm in a much better place now, and I've learned that family isn't always the people you're born with. Sometimes it's the people who choose to love and support you."

Aiden felt something twist in his chest at Marcus's words. The idea of family rejecting someone for being gay was his worst fear, the nightmare scenario that kept him awake some nights. But hearing Marcus talk about it so openly, with sadness but without bitterness, made it seem somehow more manageable.

"Are you and David...?" Noah started, then seemed to realize he wasn't sure how to finish the question.

Marcus laughed. "No, we're not dating. David's more like... well, he's been like a father to me, I guess. Or a really great uncle. Someone who stepped in when I needed guidance and support."

David's voice came from downstairs. "Boys! Are you ready for some lunch? I was thinking we could walk to this great little café, unless you'd rather drive somewhere."

"Walking sounds good!" Noah called back, already heading for the stairs with his characteristic enthusiasm.

Marcus turned to follow, then paused when he noticed Aiden hadn't moved from his position by the window.

"You okay?" Marcus asked quietly.

Aiden looked at him—really looked at him—and saw something in Marcus's expression that he recognized. A kind of understanding that went beyond their brief acquaintance, a sense that Marcus might genuinely comprehend the questions and fears that Aiden had been carrying around for months.

"Yeah," Aiden said finally. "I think I'm going to be okay."

Marcus smiled, and for the first time since leaving Boston, Aiden felt like that might actually be true.

"Come on," Marcus said, gesturing toward the stairs. "Let's go explore the neighborhood. And fair warning—Noah's about to discover that Los Angeles has the best Mexican food on the planet. We might not get him to eat anything else for the rest of the trip."

As they headed downstairs to rejoin David, Aiden found himself thinking about Marcus's words about chosen family, about people who choose to love and support you. Looking around David's beautiful house, seeing the easy affection between David and Marcus, watching Noah's excitement about every new discovery, Aiden began to understand what that might feel like.

Maybe, for the next two weeks, he could let himself imagine what it would be like to be part of something like this—a family built on acceptance rather than expectations, on love rather than obligation. Maybe, if he was brave enough, he could even start to be honest about who he really was.

The thought was terrifying and exhilarating in equal measure. But as he followed Marcus and Noah downstairs, hearing David's laughter echoing from the kitchen, Aiden felt something he hadn't experienced in months: hope.

thirteen
the brother problem

THE RIDE back from dinner had been filled with Noah's animated recap of everything they'd seen at the studio that day. David smiled as he listened to the fourteen-year-old's enthusiasm, remembering his own first glimpse behind the Hollywood curtain decades ago. Marcus and Aiden had been quieter, but David had attributed that to the full day they'd all shared.

It wasn't until they pulled into his driveway that David noticed it—the way Aiden's eyes followed Marcus as the older boy climbed out of the BMW and headed toward the front door. There was something in that glance, something David recognized from his own youth, and before he could prepare himself, his empathic ability activated with stunning intensity.

Suddenly David was drowning in Aiden's emotions. The careful attraction the seventeen-year-old had been nurturing all day, the way his heart had skipped when Marcus had laughed at his jokes during lunch. The fear that came with these feelings—not fear of Marcus, but fear of what wanting Marcus meant about himself. The relief of being around someone who understood, mixed with terror at how naturally this felt. And underneath it all, a deep longing for connection that felt both thrilling and terrifying.

David gripped the steering wheel as the wave of emotion crashed over him, trying to pull himself back to his own consciousness. When he finally managed to break the connection, he found Aiden looking at him with concern.

"David? Are you okay?"

"I'm fine," David managed, his voice slightly unsteady. "Just... tired from the long day, I think."

But as they walked into the house together, David's mind was racing. Aiden was exactly where David had suspected he might be—wrestling with his identity, drawn to Marcus but not yet ready to name what that meant. Elena had been right to worry, and right to send him here.

The evening settled into a comfortable rhythm. Noah claimed the living room TV for a video game he'd been wanting to try, while David retreated to his study to catch up on emails. Marcus and Aiden gravitated toward the kitchen, ostensibly to make popcorn but really, David suspected, to continue the conversations that had been building between them all day.

From his study, David could hear their voices—not the words, but the tone. The careful politeness of their first meeting had evolved into something warmer, more natural. Marcus's laugh came easier now, and Aiden sounded more like the confident young man Elena had described rather than the withdrawn teenager she'd been worried about.

"So," Aiden said, settling onto one of the kitchen stools while Marcus rummaged through David's impressively stocked pantry, "can I ask you something?"

Marcus paused, his hand hovering over a bag of kettle corn. "Sure."

"Yesterday, when we were talking about your family..." Aiden's voice grew more careful. "How did you know? I mean, how did you know for sure that leaving was the right choice?"

Marcus turned to face him, and Aiden was surprised to see something dark flicker across his expression.

"I didn't leave," Marcus said quietly. "I was forced out. There's a difference."

Aiden felt his stomach drop. "What do you mean?"

Marcus set down the popcorn bag and leaned against the counter, his arms crossed as if protecting himself from the memory. "I mean my father found some text messages on my phone, called me a faggot, and told me to get out of his house. When I tried to explain, he raised his hand to hit me. My mother had to physically hold him back."

"Oh my God," Aiden breathed. "I thought... I mean, when you said 'kicked out,' I thought maybe it was like an argument that got out of hand, or..."

"Or that I chose to leave dramatically?" Marcus's smile was bitter. "I packed whatever I could fit in my school backpack, took my college savings, and left at dawn before he could decide to finish what he'd started the night before."

Aiden stared at him, the full weight of Marcus's experience finally hitting him. "You were afraid he would hurt you?"

"My father looked at me like something disgusting that had stuck to the bottom of his shoe. His eyes... it's like they turned black and he was no longer my dad. Yeah, I was scared shitless. If it hadn't been for Mom..." Marcus trailed off, his voice catching slightly.

"What did she do?"

"She threw herself between us. This tiny woman, barely five feet tall, standing up to a man who was twice her size and furious beyond reason. She probably saved my life that night."

"But she didn't stop him from making you leave?"

Marcus's expression grew complicated. "She couldn't. She had three other kids to protect, and challenging him further would have put all of us at risk. I understood that, even then."

"Most people don't," Marcus continued, his expression softening slightly. "When you tell people you're homeless because you're gay, they assume it was some kind of mutual decision, or that families just need time to 'come around.' They don't realize that for some of us, coming out isn't a choice—it's something that gets discovered, and then everything changes in a single night."

Aiden felt tears prick his eyes as the reality of Marcus's situation truly sank in. "Were you scared? Out there on your own?"

"Terrified," Marcus admitted. "But I was more scared of going back and pretending to be someone I wasn't just to avoid another beating."

They were quiet for a moment, the weight of Marcus's words settling between them. Finally, Aiden spoke again, his voice barely above a whisper.

"Marcus? I think I'm gay."

The confession came out in a rush, as if Aiden had been holding it back and could no longer contain it. Marcus felt his heart clench with recognition and sympathy and something else he wasn't ready to name.

"Thank you for telling me," Marcus said simply. "That took courage."

"Did it? I feel like a coward most of the time. Especially after hearing what you went through."

"You're not a coward, Aiden. And what happened to me—that's not your fault, and it doesn't make your experience any less valid." Marcus moved to sit on the stool next to Aiden's. "Being scared is normal. Being careful is smart. You get to come out on your own timeline, in your own way."

"But what if my family can't accept it?" Aiden's voice was small, vulnerable.

Marcus was quiet for a moment, choosing his words carefully. "Well, your mom is best friends with David... and he's gay... so she's probably pretty cool about these things. Besides, she might already know."

Aiden's eyes widened. "She knows?!"

"I don't know... I'm just saying that moms often know things... you know?"

Aiden considered this, then shook his head. "I just... I can't imagine my mom looking at me the way your father looked at you."

"Then you're probably already safer than I was," Marcus said gently. "The fact that you can't imagine it probably means it won't happen."

"Can I tell you something?" Marcus asked, settling more comfortably on his stool.

"Anything."

"When I was living on the streets, there were nights when I thought about going back home. Even after everything my father said, even knowing he didn't want me there, I would think about calling and apologizing for being who I am, just so I could sleep in my own bed again."

Aiden's eyes widened. "Really?"

"Really. And you know what stopped me? The realization that apologizing for being gay would be like apologizing for having brown eyes or being tall. It's not something I chose—it's just part of who I am."

"But what if my family can't accept it?"

Marcus reached over and gently squeezed Aiden's shoulder. "But even if the worst happened—which I really don't think it will—you wouldn't be alone. You'd have people who care about you, who see you for who you really are."

"Like you?"

The question was asked so quietly Marcus almost missed it. When he looked at Aiden, he saw vulnerability and hope and something that made his breath catch.

"Like me," Marcus confirmed, though his voice was rougher than he'd intended.

They talked for another hour, their conversation ranging from the practical aspects of coming out to the deeper questions about identity and belonging. Marcus found himself sharing details about his journey that he'd never told anyone—not just the trauma of his father's rejection, but the smaller moments of discovery and acceptance that had shaped his understanding of himself.

By the time they made their way upstairs, it was nearly midnight. Noah had long since disappeared to his room, and David's study was dark. The house felt peaceful, settled in that particular way that homes do late at night.

"Marcus?" Aiden said as they reached the landing where their rooms diverged.

"Yeah?"

"Thank you. For listening. For understanding. For..." Aiden trailed off, seeming to search for words.

"For being you," Marcus finished gently.

Aiden smiled, the first completely unguarded smile Marcus had seen from him. "Good night."

"Good night, Aiden."

But as Marcus headed toward his room, he couldn't shake the feeling that something had shifted between them tonight. Not just the trust that came with shared secrets, but something deeper, more complex. Something that both thrilled and terrified him.

Three doors down, Noah lay in his unfamiliar bed, staring at the ceiling of his temporary room. The shadows here were different from the ones at home—sharper, more angular, cast by the streetlights outside rather than the familiar patterns of tree branches he was used to.

He'd been lying there for over an hour, waiting for the sound he'd grown accustomed to over the years he'd shared a room with his brother. Waiting for Aiden to appear in his doorway, or for the soft knock that meant it was time for their nightly conversation.

It was a tradition that had started when they were small, born out of necessity when Noah had gone through a phase of nightmares around age five. Aiden, barely seven himself, had started climbing into Noah's bed to tell him stories until he fell asleep. As they grew older, the stories evolved into conversations—about school, about friends, about the confusing world of growing up.

Some of Noah's most important memories were tied to those late-night talks. When he was nine and worried about whether their parents loved him as much as they loved Aiden, it was in the darkness of their shared room that Aiden had reassured him. When Aiden was thirteen and awkward and convinced no one would ever want to be his friend, Noah had listed every reason why he was wrong, speaking to the ceiling so his brother wouldn't see him blush at being so sincere.

The conversations had gotten more complex as they grew older. It was during one of those talks, when Noah was twelve and his body was starting to change in ways that embarrassed and confused him, that Aiden had patiently answered every awkward question without once making him feel stupid.

And it was during another late-night conversation, just a few months ago, that Aiden had asked the strangest question Noah had ever heard from his brother.

"Noah?" Aiden had said into the darkness, his voice unusually hesitant.

"Yeah?"

"What would you think if someone in our family was... different? Like, really different in a way that might disappoint Mom?"

Noah had turned toward his brother's bed, trying to make out his expression in the dim light. "What kind of different?"

"I don't know. Just... what if someone couldn't be what everyone expected them to be?"

"Then I'd tell them that being yourself is more important than meeting other people's expectations," Noah had said without hesitation.

"And I'd tell them that family means loving people exactly as they are, not as you wish they were."

Aiden had been quiet for so long Noah thought he'd fallen asleep. Finally, his brother's voice came through the darkness, thick with emotion.

"I love you, Noah."

"I love you too, Aiden."

Now, lying alone in David's guest room, Noah realized that conversation had probably been about more than hypothetical family members. Aiden had been trying to tell him something, and Noah had been too young or too dense to understand what.

But he was starting to understand now. The way Aiden looked at Marcus, the way his whole demeanor had changed since they'd arrived in Los Angeles, the way he'd seemed lighter today than he had in months back home.

What hurt wasn't the realization that his brother might be gay— Noah had suspected that for a while, even if he hadn't known how to address it. What hurt was that Aiden was sharing his thoughts and fears with someone else now. That the person he'd always turned to for those important conversations was Marcus instead of him.

Noah understood why, logically. Marcus was closer to Aiden's age, had experience with things Noah couldn't imagine, could offer perspective that a fourteen-year-old brother simply couldn't provide. But understanding didn't make the abandonment hurt less.

For the first time in his life, Noah fell asleep without hearing his brother's voice telling him good night, without the familiar comfort of knowing that whatever else happened, they were in this together.

And for the first time since arriving in Los Angeles, Noah wondered if this trip had been a mistake.

fourteen
almost

DAVID STOOD at the kitchen island, coffee mug in hand, watching the three boys navigate their breakfast with the careful choreography of people still figuring out how to be around each other. Noah attacked his cereal with more vigor than necessary, while Marcus and Aiden sat close enough that their elbows occasionally brushed—small contacts that seemed both accidental and entirely deliberate.

"So," David said, setting down his mug, "what would you like to do today? We could go shopping, catch a movie, do some sightseeing around the city..."

"Disneyland!" Noah shouted, his face lighting up with the first genuine enthusiasm David had seen from him since yesterday evening.

David laughed, charmed by Noah's immediate excitement. "Well, we've actually got tickets for Disneyland next week. I thought we'd make a whole day of it."

Noah's face fell slightly, but he recovered quickly. "Oh. Cool. Next week's good too."

Marcus looked up from his toast. "What about the beach? It's supposed to be beautiful today, and I bet Noah's never seen the Pacific Ocean."

"You mean like Malibu?" Aiden asked, his face lighting up with interest. "Isn't that the beach out here?"

Noah nodded eagerly. "Yeah, I want to see where all the movie stars go!"

David laughed, recognizing the influence of his own industry—TV and movies had given everyone the idea that beach equals Malibu, and his profession bore some of the blame for that misconception. "I know a place I've been going to since I moved out here, just south of Malibu, that's a bit more open and less of a scene. The view is gorgeous, and it's not too crowded on weekdays."

"I've never really been to a California beach," Noah admitted, some of his earlier enthusiasm returning.

"Then it's settled," David replied, already mentally planning the logistics. "Beach day it is."

Will Rogers State Beach stretched out before them like something from a postcard—golden sand meeting endless blue water under a sky so clear it seemed artificial. Noah stood at the edge of the parking lot, his mouth slightly open as he took in the vastness of the Pacific Ocean.

"It's huge," he breathed, then seemed embarrassed by his obvious statement.

"Wait until you see the sunset," Marcus said, shouldering the beach bag David had packed. "It's incredible from here."

They found a spot near the lifeguard station, close enough to feel safe but far enough from other beachgoers to have some privacy. David spread out the blankets while the boys kicked off their shoes, Noah immediately running toward the water's edge with the uncomplicated joy of a fourteen-year-old experiencing something new.

"First time seeing the ocean?" Marcus asked Aiden as they watched Noah dance around the incoming waves.

"Technically it's the second, but we were like five so I don't remember it." Aiden's voice was soft, thoughtful. "It's weird how different things feel now, you know?"

Marcus nodded, understanding the subtext. Everything felt different for Aiden now—not just because he was older, but because he was finally beginning to understand himself. Marcus remembered that feeling, the way the world had seemed to shift and reshape itself once he'd acknowledged who he really was. Though he realized he wasn't that much older than Aiden and had plenty to learn about himself as well.

David noticed the moment when Noah's solo exploration of the tide pools began to feel lonely. The fourteen-year-old kept glancing back at where Marcus and Aiden sat talking quietly on the blanket, their heads bent close together as they shared some private joke. The distance between Noah and his brother seemed to grow with each passing minute.

"Noah," David called out, getting to his feet. "Want to show me those tide pools? I haven't explored this part of the beach in years."

Noah's face brightened with relief and gratitude. "Really? There are some really cool hermit crabs over here."

As David walked away with Noah, he caught Marcus's eye and nodded slightly—a subtle permission that seemed to say *take your time, I've got this covered*. Marcus felt a rush of appreciation for David's intuitive understanding of the situation.

For the next hour, David let Noah guide him through a thorough exploration of the rocky tide pools, listening with genuine interest as the boy pointed out sea anemones and tiny fish darting between the rocks. Noah's enthusiasm was infectious, and David found himself remembering the simple pleasure of discovery, of having someone's full attention while sharing something that excited you.

Meanwhile, Marcus and Aiden had gravitated toward the water's edge, walking slowly along the shoreline where the sand was firm and cool beneath their feet. The beach was expansive enough that they could talk without being overheard, and for the first time since meeting, they felt completely free to be themselves with each other.

Marcus had pulled off his shirt when they'd first arrived, and Aiden found his eyes drawn to the lean muscles of Marcus's chest and shoulders, evidence of the physical work he'd done to survive on his own. He forced himself to look away, heat rising in his cheeks that had nothing to do with the California sun.

Marcus, for his part, was fighting his own battle. Aiden's developing physique was becoming harder to ignore—the way his shoulders had broadened, the definition starting to show in his chest. Marcus made a conscious effort to keep his eyes on Aiden's face, but they kept wandering despite his best intentions.

"Can I ask you something?" Aiden said, stopping to pick up a piece of sea glass that had caught the light.

"Sure."

"Do you ever think about... like, what would've happened if things were different? With your dad, I mean."

Marcus considered the question as a wave rolled up toward their feet, both boys stepping back instinctively. "Sometimes. But I don't know... I think I'm figuring out who I'm supposed to be, you know? Even the shitty parts... they're part of what happened to me."

"I keep thinking about what you said last night. About not saying sorry for who you are." Aiden turned the sea glass over in his palm, watching how the light caught the smooth edges. "I spend so much time apologizing for stuff I haven't even done yet."

"Like what?"

"Like... disappointing people. Like not being the son my mom thought I'd be, or the brother Noah wants me to be." Aiden's voice grew quieter. "Like wanting things I'm probably not supposed to want."

Marcus felt his heart skip at the last part, but he forced himself to stay focused on Aiden's needs rather than his own growing feelings. "What kind of things?"

Aiden looked at him then, really looked at him, and Marcus saw something in his expression that made his breath catch. But before either of them could say anything more, Noah's voice carried across the beach.

"Marcus! Aiden! Come see this! David found an octopus!"

The moment broke, but something had shifted between them—like they'd almost said something important but ran out of time.

The drive home was subdued, all four of them tired from the sun and salt air. Noah dozed in the back seat, his face slightly sunburned despite David's diligent application of sunscreen. Marcus and Aiden sat on opposite sides of the car, but David could see them stealing glances at each other in the rearview mirror.

David's mind wandered as he navigated the late afternoon traffic. Watching the boys today had stirred up memories he hadn't accessed in years—the confusion and longing of his own teenage years, the boys he'd found attractive but could never approach, the crushing isolation of growing up gay in a small Indiana town during the height of the AIDS crisis.

He remembered being Aiden's age and feeling like he was carrying a secret so dangerous it might destroy everything he touched. There had been no Marcus in his life then, no one who understood what he was going through. He'd had to figure it out alone, through stolen glances at magazines and careful observation of the few openly gay men he encountered.

The thought of Aiden going through even a fraction of that internal struggle made David's chest tighten with protective instinct. Elena had sent her son here because she'd sensed he needed support, and David was beginning to understand just how crucial this timing might be.

But there was also Marcus to consider. David could see the way the young man looked at Aiden—with affection and desire and something deeper that was just beginning to take shape. Marcus deserved happiness, deserved the chance to experience young love without the trauma that had defined so much of his recent past. But he was also still healing, still building his sense of security and self-worth.

And then there was Noah, who was clearly struggling with the shifting dynamics in his family. David remembered being fourteen, that particular vulnerability that came with being too old to be coddled but too young to be included in adult conversations. Noah needed attention and reassurance, needed to know that his relationship with his brother wasn't being threatened by new connections.

It was a delicate balance, and David wasn't entirely sure how to navigate it. But watching Noah's face light up when they'd discovered the octopus, seeing the way Marcus and Aiden had looked at each other by the water's edge, David felt something he hadn't experienced in years: the deep satisfaction of being needed, of having a family to worry about and protect.

Dinner was a casual affair—takeout from a Thai restaurant that David had discovered years ago, eaten on the terrace as the sun began to set behind the Hollywood Hills. The boys were tired but content, their skin warm from the day's sun, their conversation flowing easily around stories from the beach.

It was after they'd cleaned up, when David had retreated to his study to answer some work emails, that the evening's first real conflict arose.

"Want to play Mario Kart?" Noah asked Aiden, already heading toward the living room where David's gaming console waited. "We can do our usual tournament."

Aiden hesitated, glancing toward Marcus, who was loading the dishwasher. "Actually, I thought maybe I'd just hang out upstairs for a while. I'm pretty tired."

"Come on," Noah pressed, his voice carrying a note of pleading that made Marcus look up from the dishes. "We always play Mario Kart. What's wrong? You didn't even do anything today except walk around."

"I know, but—"

"I could play with you," Marcus offered gently, recognizing the tension building between the brothers. "I'm terrible at Mario Kart, but I could give it a try."

Noah's face darkened. "I don't want to play with you. I want to play with my brother."

"Noah," Aiden said, his voice carrying a warning edge. "Marcus was just trying to be nice."

"I don't care if he's being nice. What's wrong with you? You've been acting weird ever since we got here."

"We spent the whole day together."

"No, we didn't. You spent the whole day with Marcus, and I spent it with David."

Marcus stepped back from the dishwasher, recognizing that he'd become part of a family dynamic he didn't fully understand. "Maybe I should—"

"Maybe you should mind your own business," Noah snapped, then immediately looked stricken by his own rudeness.

"Noah!" Aiden's voice was sharp now, protective. "Apologize. Right now."

"No." Noah's chin jutted out stubbornly. "I'm tired of pretending everything's fine when it's not. I'm tired of you acting like I don't exist."

"I'm not acting like you don't exist. I'm just—"

"You're just too busy with your new boyfriend to care about anyone else."

The words hung in the air like a challenge. Aiden's face flushed red, and Marcus felt his stomach drop. From his study, David could hear the rising voices and the pointed silence that followed Noah's accusation.

"Fine," Aiden said finally, his voice tight with hurt and anger. "If that's what you think, then fine. Go play your stupid video games by yourself."

"Fine!" Noah shot back, louder than necessary. "Maybe I will!"

The sound of Noah's footsteps pounding up the stairs echoed through the house, followed by the decisive slam of his bedroom door.

Marcus stood frozen by the dishwasher, uncertain whether he should apologize, explain, or simply disappear. Aiden remained by the kitchen island, his hands clenched into fists at his sides.

"He'll be fine," Aiden said, but his voice lacked conviction. "He's just being dramatic. He always gets like this when he doesn't get his way."

Marcus nodded, but he couldn't shake the image of Noah's hurt expression, or the way the fourteen-year-old had looked at him like he was an intruder in his family. "Maybe I should just... I don't know, give you guys some space for a while? Until things cool down?"

"No," Aiden said quickly, then seemed embarrassed by how fast he'd responded. "I mean... you don't have to do that."

Marcus studied Aiden's face, recognizing the conflict there. "I just don't want to make things worse between you and Noah. I know what it feels like to be left out."

"You're not making anything worse," Aiden said, though he didn't sound entirely convinced. "It's just... Noah's been weird since we got here, and I don't know what to do about it."

They stood in awkward silence for a moment, the tension from Noah's outburst still hanging between them. Finally, Aiden fumbled for words.

"We could... maybe go upstairs? Just while he cools off? If that's okay with you?"

Marcus hesitated. "You sure? I don't want to cause more problems."

"You're not," Aiden said, his voice gaining strength. "Come on."

From his study, David heard the argument wind down and debated whether to intervene immediately or give everyone time to cool off. After a few minutes of silence, he decided that Noah probably needed some space to process his emotions before anyone tried to talk to him.

But the guilt was already settling in David's chest. He'd been so focused on facilitating the connection between Marcus and Aiden that he'd perhaps underestimated how difficult this transition would be for Noah.

Twenty minutes later, he climbed the stairs to check on his youngest houseguest.

They climbed the stairs together, and Aiden led Marcus to his temporary room—a space that had already begun to feel familiar after just a few days. Aiden pulled out his phone and connected it to a small Bluetooth speaker David had provided.

"What kind of music do you like?" Aiden asked, scrolling through his Spotify playlists.

"Pretty much everything. What about you?"

"This is going to sound weird, but I'm kind of obsessed with eighties music. Like... uhm... Depeche Mode, that kinda stuff." Aiden paused, looking slightly embarrassed.

Marcus's eyes widened, and Aiden quickly misread his expression. "I know it's like old and stuff, but there's something fun about it..." he trailed off, worried he was blowing it.

"I love that stuff!" Marcus said with genuine excitement. "Especially Tears for Fears."

"Really?" Aiden's face lit up as he realized Marcus wasn't weirded out at all. "Everyone at school thinks I'm weird for liking this old stuff..."

"Their loss. Put on 'The Hurting'—that whole record is perfect."

As the opening notes filled the room, both boys settled onto Aiden's bed, sitting close enough that their shoulders touched. The music seemed to create a bubble of intimacy around them, a shared space where they could be completely themselves.

"Do you think David ever saw them in concert?" Marcus asked as "Mad World" began to play. "I mean, he's ancient so he probably saw them, right?"

They both laughed, and Aiden grinned. "He's not that old. But yeah, maybe. We should totally ask him."

They talked easily as the record played, sharing stories about songs that had gotten them through difficult times, laughing about the dramatic lyrics that somehow perfectly captured the intensity of teenage emotion. Marcus found himself watching the way Aiden's face animated when he talked about music, the way his hands moved as he tried to explain why certain songs affected him so deeply.

But underneath the easy conversation, both boys were thinking about Noah's accusation. The word "boyfriend" hung between them, unspoken but present, making every casual touch and shared glance feel more charged.

"You know what's funny?" Aiden said as they debated the best song. "This music is all about pain and like, not belonging and stuff, but listening to it makes me feel less alone."

"That's not funny," Marcus said softly. "That's exactly what good music should do."

Their eyes met and held, and Marcus felt the same electric tension that had been building between them all day. Aiden was sitting cross-legged on the bed, close enough that Marcus could see the flecks of gold in his brown eyes, could smell the lingering salt air in his hair from their day at the beach.

"Marcus," Aiden said quietly, his voice barely audible over the music. "What Noah said earlier... about us being..."

"Yeah," Marcus said, his heart racing. "I heard."

But instead of continuing that conversation, Aiden grabbed one of the pillows from behind him and lobbed it at Marcus's head with a grin. "For making me listen to 'Everybody Wants to Rule the World' like seventeen times in a row."

"Hey!" Marcus protested, catching the pillow and immediately launching it back. "That song is awesome!"

"It's so overplayed!"

"Take that back!"

They wrestled for control of the pillow, both of them laughing and trying to keep their voices down. Marcus was stronger, but Aiden was quicker, and their mock battle quickly devolved into them rolling around on the bed, each trying to pin the other while maintaining possession of the pillow.

"Shh!" Aiden gasped between giggles as Marcus got an arm around his waist. "We shouldn't be... Noah's probably still upset and we're up here just..."

"Then surrender!" Marcus whispered back, but he was laughing too hard to sound threatening, even as guilt flickered across his face.

"Never!"

They were both breathing hard when the wrestling match finally ended, Marcus pinning Aiden to the bed with the pillow trapped between them. The laughter faded as they realized how close they were— Marcus's face inches from Aiden's, their bodies pressed together, both of them suddenly very aware of the warmth and weight of the other.

"Aiden," Marcus breathed, his voice rough with something that had nothing to do with their playful fight.

Aiden's eyes fluttered closed as Marcus began to lean down, the space between them disappearing by degrees. Marcus could feel Aiden's heartbeat against his chest, could see the slight parting of his lips in anticipation.

They were a breath away from their first kiss when the bedroom door opened.

"Aiden?" Noah's voice was small, uncertain. "I'm sorry about... oh."

Both boys sprang apart as if they'd been electrocuted, Marcus rolling off the bed entirely in his haste to put distance between them. Aiden sat up quickly, his face burning with embarrassment and something that might have been guilt.

"Noah... uh... you what... uh..." Aiden stammered, clearly unsure what words he was trying to say.

Noah stood frozen in the doorway, his face flushed red as he took in the scene—the rumpled bedsheets, Marcus scrambling to his feet, the way both older boys looked anywhere but at him. He'd been lying in bed feeling terrible about yelling at them, wanting to apologize and ask Aiden how he should make things right with Marcus too. But now... this was like last year when he'd barged into the bathroom without knocking. Private stuff he wasn't supposed to see.

"I was just... I felt bad about earlier and wanted to say sorry, but..." Noah's voice trailed off as his cheeks burned with embarrassment. "I didn't mean to..." He couldn't finish the sentence.

"Noah, it's not..." Aiden started, but he couldn't figure out how to finish the sentence.

Marcus, still standing awkwardly by the side of the bed, looked mortified. "We weren't... I mean, we were just..."

"It's okay," Noah said quickly, backing toward the door. "I'll... I'll talk to you tomorrow or something. I'm really sorry for barging in."

"Wait, Noah—" Aiden began, but his brother was already disappearing down the hall, his footsteps quick and embarrassed.

The door closed with a quiet click, leaving Marcus and Aiden alone with the weight of what had almost happened and the complicated reality of what Noah had witnessed.

They sat in silence for a long moment, the music still playing softly in the background, both of them processing the magnitude of the moment that had just been interrupted and the new complications it would bring to their already fragile family dynamic.

"I should go," Marcus said finally, his voice barely above a whisper.

Aiden nodded, but his eyes were bright with unshed tears—whether from frustration, embarrassment, or worry about his brother, Marcus couldn't tell.

"Good night, Aiden."

"Good night."

But as Marcus made his way back to his own room, and as Aiden lay staring at the ceiling long into the night, both boys knew that everything had changed. The almost-kiss hung between them like a promise and a complication, and tomorrow would bring questions neither of them was sure how to answer.

Down the hall, Noah lay in his own bed, staring at the same shadows on the ceiling, finally understanding that his brother was growing up in ways that would take him places Noah couldn't follow. For the first time in his life, Noah felt truly alone.

fifteen
firsts

THE KITCHEN FELT like a minefield the next morning. David stood at the coffee maker, glancing between the three boys who sat at the island picking at their cereal with all the enthusiasm of students taking a pop quiz. Noah kept his eyes glued to his phone, Aiden stared into his bowl like it might contain the secrets of the universe, and Marcus seemed fascinated by the nutrition information on the cereal box.

"So," David said, settling into his chair with his coffee, "what should we do today? The weather's supposed to be perfect again."

"Don't care," Noah mumbled without looking up.

Aiden shrugged. "Whatever."

Marcus nodded vaguely in agreement.

David tried again. "We could check out the Hollywood Walk of Fame, or maybe drive up to Griffith Observatory..."

Three more noncommittal grunts.

This was definitely about last night's argument. David had climbed the stairs intending to talk to Noah after he'd heard the shouting, but by the time he'd reached the boy's room, the door was closed and everything had gone quiet. He'd figured Noah needed time to cool off, that they could address it in the morning.

Clearly, he'd been wrong.

"Are you guys still upset about what happened last night?" David asked gently. "Because we can talk about it."

The question produced an immediate reaction, though not the one David expected. Noah's head shot up, his face flushing red, while Aiden nearly choked on his cereal. Marcus went very still, like a deer sensing a predator.

"It's fine," Aiden said quickly, his voice cracking slightly. "Everything's fine."

"Yeah, totally fine," Noah echoed, but his voice had that artificially bright quality that screamed the opposite.

David studied their faces, confused by the intensity of their reactions. It had just been a typical sibling argument, hadn't it? But the way they were all avoiding eye contact, the tension crackling between them...

Then Noah glanced up, and for just a moment, their eyes met. David felt his empathic ability activate like a switch being flipped, and suddenly he was drowning in the fourteen-year-old's emotions.

Noah wasn't angry. He was worried, uncertain, embarrassed about something. There was guilt there too, and confusion, and underneath it all, a desperate desire to make things right but not knowing how. The feelings were so intense, so complicated for someone his age, that David had to grip his coffee mug to anchor himself back to his own consciousness.

What had happened last night that would make Noah feel this way?

"Okay," David said slowly, still trying to process what he'd just experienced. "Well, if anyone wants to talk about anything—anything at all—you know I'm here, right?"

Three vigorous nods, followed by a return to the fascinating world of cereal and phones.

David sipped his coffee and wondered what he was missing.

The day passed in a strange sort of suspended animation. The boys stayed close to the house, not quite avoiding each other but not exactly seeking each other out either. David caught glimpses of them throughout the afternoon—Marcus reading by the pool while Aiden swam laps, Noah playing video games in the living room with the volume turned up just loud enough to be heard from anywhere in the house.

It wasn't until after dinner, when they were all sitting around the terrace picking at the remnants of Chinese takeout, that Marcus cleared his throat and made a suggestion that surprised everyone.

"Hey," he said, looking directly at Noah, "want to play some Mario Kart? We could do teams—me and David against you and Aiden."

Noah's face immediately brightened with interest, but then he caught himself and the enthusiasm dimmed. "David doesn't play video games."

"I could learn," David offered, though the idea of mastering hand-eye coordination with a controller felt about as likely as him suddenly developing the ability to fly.

Marcus caught his eye across the table, and David felt that empathic pull again—not overwhelming this time, but clear enough to understand what Marcus was really asking. This wasn't about the game. This was about giving Noah a reason to belong, a way to connect with his brother again, a chance for all of them to be in the same space without the weird tension that had defined the entire day.

David found himself nodding before he'd consciously decided to agree. "Actually, that sounds like fun. Fair warning though—I'm probably going to be terrible."

"That's kind of the point," Marcus said with a grin. "Noah and Aiden are going to destroy us."

And just like that, Noah was fully engaged again. "Really? You want to play?" He looked between Marcus and David as if they'd just offered him tickets to Disney World.

"Absolutely," David said, getting to his feet. "But I'm going to need some serious coaching if we're going to put up any kind of fight."

Twenty minutes later, David found himself holding a controller that felt like it had been designed by aliens, listening to Marcus explain the basic mechanics of a game that seemed to involve cartoon characters driving impossibly fast cars around tracks that defied all known laws of physics.

"The key is the power slides," Marcus was saying, demonstrating a move that sent his character drifting around a corner while somehow gaining speed. "And watch out for the banana peels."

"Banana peels," David repeated solemnly. "Got it."

Noah giggled from the other couch. "Uncle David, you sound like you're taking notes for a business meeting."

"Hey, I take my gaming very seriously," David shot back, which made Noah laugh harder.

The first race was a disaster. David's character spent most of the time driving into walls or going backwards, while Marcus valiantly tried to carry their team despite David's best efforts to sabotage them. But something magical happened as they played—the awkwardness that had been hanging over them all day began to dissolve.

"David, you're supposed to steer INTO the turn, not away from it!" Marcus called out, laughing as David's character sailed off the track for the third time.

"I'm trying!" David protested. "This thing has a mind of its own!"

"Maybe the controller's broken," Aiden suggested innocently, which earned him a pillow thrown by his uncle.

By the third race, David was starting to get the hang of it, and Marcus was proving to be a surprisingly good teacher. They were still losing spectacularly, but they were making it entertaining.

"You know what?" Noah said as they finished another race, his earlier mood completely transformed. "We should switch teams. Marcus and me against David and Aiden."

Everyone looked surprised by the suggestion, but Noah was already scooting over to make room for Marcus on the couch.

"You sure?" Marcus asked.

"Totally. I can teach you some tricks Aiden doesn't know about." Noah leaned over and whispered something in Marcus's ear that made the older boy's face light up with understanding.

David felt a warm glow in his chest as he watched the interaction. This was Noah's way of accepting Marcus, of bringing him into the family circle. The gesture was so natural, so generous, that David had to blink back unexpected tears.

"Alright then," Aiden said, moving to sit next to David. "Prepare to get schooled, little brother."

"Bring it on," Noah shot back, but he was grinning.

The second round of races was much more competitive. Noah proved to be an excellent coach, whispering strategies and pointing out shortcuts that Marcus picked up with impressive speed. Meanwhile, Aiden patiently guided David through more advanced techniques, their roles completely reversed from what anyone would have expected.

"No, like this," Aiden said, reaching over to adjust David's grip on the controller. "And don't brake so much in the turns."

"I'm starting to think you're just trying to make me look bad," David said, which made Aiden snort with laughter.

"You don't need my help for that."

The final race came down to the wire, with Marcus and Noah barely edging out a victory. Before he could even stop himself, Noah gave Marcus a celebratory hug and yelled out "In your face!" to his opponents —nothing mean, just pure fun.

Marcus was taken aback at how well he had been "let in" to Noah's circle, squeezing back when Noah hugged him. The gesture didn't escape notice from both David and Aiden, the latter being gobsmacked. Aiden had always known Noah was the more rambunctious and emotional between the two of them, but he'd never seen his brother take to someone so quickly. Marcus was the first guy who had ever started to capture Aiden's attention so much, and the fact that Noah had practically caught them kissing just a short while after he'd yelled at them, calling Marcus his boyfriend... this was such a turnaround.

David got up and stretched, indicating he was heading to bed. Tomorrow would be another busy day. Truth told, he planned to give the boys their space. He wasn't sure what that meant, really, but he could tell that Aiden and Marcus wanted to spend time together.

"Noah, I forgot to give you something the other night for your room," he said, more to get Noah out of their hair than anything else. The game had gone well and whatever had happened between the three of them the night before seemed to have dissolved. But David also remembered his own youth and figured a fourteen-year-old wasn't conducive to hanging out with a future boyfriend. At least that was the vibe David got.

Noah predictably looked curious about whatever it was that David had forgotten about. So did the other two. But David quickly settled the mystery: He had a small television and Apple TV box for the guest room Noah was staying in. He'd picked them up some time back but had forgotten about them, both sitting in their unopened boxes in his home office closet that he'd come across the other day.

Noah was predictably happy and both jumped up to set up the new toys for his room, leaving Aiden and Marcus alone in the living room.

It was already well into the evening, just before 9 PM, and Marcus looked over at Aiden and asked if he'd like to go another round of Mario Kart, now that he had the hang of it better. Aiden smiled. Sure.

They sat next to each other, both getting competitive and into the game, before they realized they had scooted so close they were elbowing each other as they twisted and turned the cars in the game, laughing and trash talking as two teens would. Aiden narrowly won, but gave street cred to Marcus. One day, he said, you just might beat me.

They both fell back into the cushy sofa laughing and talking about the game, where Marcus almost had him had it not been for him fumbling the controller. Aiden's hands reached over to demonstrate, and for a moment, they both were holding each other's hands on Marcus's controller, continuing to trash talk and laugh.

Aiden dropped his hand, which landed on Marcus's leg as they both laughed, and then it became quiet. Marcus saw—and felt—Aiden's hand resting innocently on his leg before Aiden noticed it and quickly pulled away, muttering an apology and turning red.

Marcus decided he liked it and reached over and pulled Aiden's hand back before placing his on top of it. "No need to be sorry. I liked it."

"Really?"

Marcus nodded before they both heard distant Noah and David voices from upstairs as they got the TV hooked up. Aiden instinctively pulled his hand back, but Marcus grabbed it, their palms slipping together as Marcus intertwined his fingers around Aiden's, properly closing their hands. Aiden looked down at his hand clasped in Marcus's. He was actually... holding hands... with a boy! Looking up into Marcus's eyes, he noticed that Marcus had a sweet smile.

Softly, he whispered, "Uh... Marcus..." while darting his eyes up towards the stairs and the hallway back to the voices of his little brother and uncle.

"Yeah?" Marcus whispered sweetly in return.

"Uh..." Aiden bit his lip.

"What?" Marcus smiled, knowing where this was going... or hoping it would go there.

"Uh... remember last night?"

Of course he did. Marcus nodded.

"Uh... what... never mind... it's stupid." Aiden went to pull his hand away, feeling embarrassed. Marcus held tighter and caused Aiden to stop and turn, his smile betraying him through the red face.

"What?"

"No... it's dumb..."

Marcus leaned forward on the sofa and turned to look at him, keeping his hand clasped to Aiden's. He glanced up towards the top of the stairs and then back to Aiden, whose eyes had followed his. This felt a little secretive, like any moment, David or Noah might bustle down the stairs and "catch them"... doing what? They weren't doing anything bad, he told himself and continued.

"Nothing is dumb, Aiden. What were you going to say?"

"Well... do you..." Aiden clearly had difficulty trying to ask something.

"Do I what?"

"Do you think that if Noah hadn't barged in last night..." he stopped again, clearly embarrassed.

"Do this?" Marcus found his courage. Things were flowing inside him, practically eliminating any fear of being caught or disturbed. He felt this was the time... now or never. Marcus leaned forward on the sofa, took his free hand and lightly caressed Aiden's cheek, pulling closer before noticing Aiden's face—a mixture of fear, expectation, heart and... wanting. Aiden's eyes closed just as his lips that he'd been biting opened slightly. Pressing his lips to Aiden's, Marcus felt the soft, wet pleasure of a first kiss... warm and unsure, feeling Aiden's breath pause, his body slowly freezing as if adapting to this new sensation before relaxing and pressing back in return.

Marcus felt his hand that had been clasped in Aiden's break free as Aiden's arms reached around and pulled Marcus into him, drawing them close, their heads angling to become more comfortable, never breaking the kiss. After a moment, he felt Aiden's chest rise again and then his breath break free as if he was breathing for both of them together. Marcus hadn't realized he had his own breath held—the excitement taking over his entire system—but the moment was so tender, so inno-cent, so... wonderful.

Slowly pulling away, both gasped as if they'd been underwater, faces just inches from each other and looking into newly opened eyes. Sharing the moment that always goes unspoken, yet is clear as anything they'd ever hear in their lives... the intimacy of giving away yourself for the first time... the first kiss that signaled a new milestone... a budding affection and a desire to share it with the other.

Upstairs, Noah had yelled out in happiness about some game he could play on the Apple TV and his uncle's shared joy in his nephew's fun. Downstairs, Marcus and Aiden looked up at the stairs and then back at each other like they'd gotten away with something and smiled. Both didn't say a word but giggled—a shared understanding.

"Hey Marcus!" Noah had yelled from his bedroom down the hall. "You wanna play this game with me?"

Marcus smiled and looked right into Aiden's eyes, which looked equal parts scared that they might be caught and affectionate that his little brother had asked his boyfriend to play a game before him. Perhaps Noah would be okay with Marcus being his boyfriend after all?

Wait! Were they boyfriends?

"Sounds fun, Noah! I'll be up in a sec," Marcus yelled back, his arms still intertwined with Aiden, before pulling Aiden into a quick kiss, almost as if he said "I'm gonna go play with your brother, but I love you." At least that's how Aiden took it before releasing his clasp and following Marcus up the stairs, lovestruck.

Walking down the hall, Marcus yelled out, "So, what's the game I'm gonna beat you at?" and laughed, followed closely by Aiden.

Noah began trash talking him back, but laughing. David sat on the edge of the bed, clearly enjoying watching his nephew's excitement at this new toy, but noticed Aiden walking in behind Marcus and suddenly caught his eye.

He's in love.

sixteen
full disclosure

IT HAD BEEN three days since the first kiss, and Aiden was pretty sure he and Marcus were being incredibly subtle about their new relationship. They kept their distance during the day, only stealing glances when they thought no one was looking. They sat on opposite ends of the couch during movies. They made sure to include Noah in everything they did.

What Aiden didn't realize was that love has a way of making itself known, despite the best efforts to hide it. The way his face lit up whenever Marcus walked into a room. The unconscious way he leaned toward Marcus during conversations. The soft smile that played at his lips when Marcus made him laugh. The careful way they said goodnight to each other, lingering just a moment too long in the hallway.

David noticed, of course. He'd been young and in love once, and he recognized the signs. But he also understood the need for privacy, for the boys to figure things out at their own pace. So he smiled to himself and gave them space, letting them think they were being discreet.

Noah noticed too, but his observations came with a fourteen-year-old's bluntness and a brother's protective instincts. He watched Aiden watching Marcus. He saw the way they found excuses to brush hands when passing snacks during movie night. He heard the muffled laughter coming from Aiden's room in the evenings before Marcus would emerge to play video games with him.

By Monday night, Noah had made up his mind. It was time for a talk.

Aiden was lying in bed reading when Noah just walked in without knocking.

"Dude," Noah said, then stopped and looked around awkwardly.

"What?" Aiden looked up from his book, feeling a flutter of anxiety. Noah had been acting strange all day—not hostile like before, but watchful in a way that made Aiden uncomfortable.

Noah closed the door behind him and padded over to sit on the edge of Aiden's bed, the way he used to when they were younger and he'd had a nightmare.

"Okay so like... you and Marcus are totally dating, right?" Noah said, fidgeting with the hem of his t-shirt.

Aiden's face went scarlet. "What? No! We're just... why would you even—"

"Oh my God, Aiden, come on. You guys are like, super obvious about it."

"We are not obvious!" Aiden protested, his voice cracking slightly. "We're just friends who—"

"Who hold hands and stuff when you think nobody's looking?" Noah interrupted, but he was kind of smiling. "And you're always whispering and being all... I don't know, couple-y. You look at each other like... I don't know, like how Mom used to look at Dad before everything got weird."

Aiden opened his mouth to deny it again, but the words wouldn't come. His little brother was looking at him with such gentle understanding that all his carefully constructed defenses crumbled.

"Are we really that obvious?" Aiden whispered, covering his face with his hands.

"Only cause I know you really well," Noah said softly. "David probably knows too but he's being cool about it."

"You're not... you're not like, mad or anything?"

"Why would I be mad?" Noah looked genuinely confused.

"Because I didn't tell you! And because everything's different now and—"

"Dude, chill. Yeah, it kinda sucked that you didn't tell me, but like... this is scary stuff, right? The whole gay thing?"

Aiden nodded, not trusting his voice.

"And I'm not mad about Marcus," Noah continued. "I like him. He's cool, and he's nice to me, and he makes you happy. Like, really happy. I haven't seen you smile this much in... I don't know, maybe ever."

"Really?"

"Really. Plus, he's actually getting better at Mario Kart, so that's something."

Despite everything, Aiden laughed. "He's been practicing on his phone."

"I figured." Noah grinned, then his expression grew more serious. "But Aiden? I need to tell you something, and don't get weird about it, okay?"

Aiden braced himself. "Okay."

"But I don't want everything to be weird now, okay?" Noah said quietly, fidgeting with his shirt. "Like, I still want to hang out with you guys. I don't want to be the annoying little brother who's always in the way."

Aiden felt his heart clench. "Noah, you're never in the way. You're my brother. That's never going to change, no matter what."

"But it's different now!" Noah said. "You guys want to do... boyfriend stuff." He made a face. "Without me watching, which is totally fine! I'm not trying to be gross about it. I just mean like, you want to hold hands and kiss and... whatever... without your little brother there."

"Noah—"

"It's okay!" Noah said quickly. "I just don't want to pretend I don't know what's going on, you know?"

Aiden stared at his brother, amazed by his maturity. "When did you get so smart?"

"I've always been smart," Noah said, then shrugged. "I mean... I don't know. You just never really... like, you're always doing the big brother thing, so..."

They sat in comfortable silence for a moment, the weight of years of shared secrets and sibling solidarity settling between them.

"So like... do you actually want to tell me? Instead of me just guessing and you freaking out about it?"

Aiden took a deep breath, feeling like he was standing at the edge of a cliff. "I'm gay, Noah. And Marcus is my boyfriend."

Noah's face broke into a huge grin. "Cool. How long?"

"How long what?"

"How long have you known? How long have you guys been together?"

"I've known for like... maybe a year? But Marcus and I just... we had our first kiss Friday."

"Your first kiss ever?"

"Yeah."

"Dude, that's awesome," Noah said with genuine excitement. "Was it good? Did you know what to do?"

"NOAH!" Aiden laughed, throwing a pillow at his brother. "That's kind of personal."

"Sorry, sorry. I'm just curious! I've never kissed anyone either."

"You just... do, I guess. It's instinct or something."

Noah nodded thoughtfully. "Can I ask you something else?"

"Sure."

"Are you happy? Like, really happy?"

Aiden considered the question. Three days ago, he'd been terrified of Noah finding out, convinced it would ruin everything between them. Now, sitting here with his brother's acceptance and support, he felt lighter than he had in months.

"Yeah," he said softly. "I'm really happy."

"Good," Noah said, standing up and heading toward the door. "That's all I wanted to know."

"Noah?"

His brother turned back. "Yeah?"

"Thank you. For being... for being okay with all this. For being my brother."

Noah's expression grew serious. "Aiden, you're gay. So what? Like... you're still you, right? You still helped me learn to ride my bike and stuff. And you listen to me complain about everything. Being gay doesn't... I mean, it doesn't change who you are or whatever."

"But what if people at school find out? What if they say stuff about you having a gay brother?"

Noah shrugged. "Then I'll tell them my brother is awesome and they can shut up about it. Besides, half the kids at my school probably don't even know what gay means."

Aiden laughed. "You're probably right."

"I usually am," Noah said with a grin. "Oh, and one more thing?"

"What?"

"I promise not to barge into your room anymore without knocking. I learned my lesson the other night." Noah paused, then grinned mischievously. "I mean, I could tell you guys were really... excited... about something." He glanced down meaningfully and wiggled his eyebrows.

Aiden's face flamed red again. "Oh God, you saw—"

"I didn't see anything!" Noah said quickly, but he was still grinning at how mortified his brother looked. "But I could tell I interrupted something. So from now on, I'll knock and wait for you to say it's okay to come in. Deal?"

"Deal," Aiden said, relief flooding through him.

"And maybe you guys could put a sock on the door handle or something when you want privacy? That's what they do in movies."

"NOAH!"

"What? I'm just trying to be helpful!" Noah was laughing now, clearly enjoying his brother's embarrassment. "I'm going to bed. Good night, Aiden."

"Good night, Noah."

As his brother reached for the door handle, Aiden called out one more time. "Hey, Noah?"

"Yeah?"

"I love you."

Noah's smile was soft and genuine. "I love you too. Feel better?"

Aiden thought about it—the weight of secrets lifted, the fear of rejection replaced by acceptance, the joy of being known and loved exactly as he was.

"Yeah," he said, his voice thick with emotion. "Yeah, I do."

After Noah left, Aiden lay back against his pillows, staring at the ceiling with a smile he couldn't seem to wipe off his face. His phone buzzed with a text from Marcus.

Everything okay? Heard voices in the hallway.

Aiden typed back quickly: *Everything's perfect. Noah knows about us. He's happy for us.*

A few minutes later, there was a soft knock on his door.

"Come in," Aiden called out, expecting it to be Marcus.

Marcus slipped through the door, closing it quietly behind him. His face was bright with relief and excitement.

"Really?" Marcus whispered, moving to sit on the edge of Aiden's bed. "Noah's really okay with us?"

"Really. He said we're obvious, but he likes you and wants me to be happy."

"We're obvious?"

"Apparently very obvious."

Marcus was quiet for a moment, studying Aiden's face. "Are you okay with that? With him knowing?"

Aiden thought about Noah's acceptance, his maturity, his promise to respect their privacy while still wanting to be part of their lives. "More than okay. It feels... it feels really good to not have to hide from him anymore."

"So no more sneaking around?"

"Well, we probably shouldn't make out in front of him or anything," Aiden said, laughing. "But yeah, no more sneaking around. At least not from Noah."

"What about David?"

"I think David already knows. Noah thinks he does too."

"Huh." Marcus looked thoughtful. "Maybe we're worse at hiding this than we thought."

"Maybe we don't need to hide it anymore."

"Maybe not," Marcus agreed softly, reaching over to take Aiden's hand. "I'm really glad Noah's okay with us."

"Me too," Aiden said, squeezing Marcus's hand. "It feels like everything's finally falling into place."

Marcus stood up to leave, but Aiden pulled him into a quick kiss, still glancing nervously at the door. As they broke apart, Aiden looked at the door handle and started laughing.

"What?" Marcus asked, confused by the sudden laughter.

"Noah said we should put a sock or something on the door when we... you know... so he knows not to barge in."

"What?" Marcus's eyes widened.

"Really."

"Seriously?" Marcus started laughing too.

Aiden scooted off the bed and opened his dresser drawer to pull out a sock, which caused Marcus to laugh even harder before he covered his mouth to silence himself. Aiden opened the door quickly and put the sock on the handle before closing it.

They both laughed quietly so hard they practically fell on the floor and into each other's arms.

Outside in the hallway, Noah heard something and opened his door slightly, seeing the sock on Aiden's door handle. He nearly burst with laughter himself. *He doesn't waste any time, Romeo,* he thought and went back to bed with a grin.

After Marcus finally left to go back to his room, both boys still grinning from their shared laughter, Aiden settled back into bed, feeling like the world had shifted in some fundamental way. For the first time in his life, he was completely honest with someone about who he was, and instead of rejection, he'd found acceptance. Instead of losing his brother, he'd somehow grown closer to him.

Sometimes, if you were lucky, it meant finding out they loved you even more.

seventeen
check-ins

DAVID STOOD on his terrace with his morning coffee, watching the three boys splash around in the pool below. It was barely nine AM, but they'd been up for an hour already, their laughter echoing off the water as Noah attempted some elaborate diving technique that Marcus was trying to teach him. Aiden floated nearby, supposedly reading a book but obviously more interested in watching Marcus demonstrate proper form.

The domestic scene filled David with a contentment he hadn't experienced in years. Two weeks into what had become a month-long visit, his house had transformed from a quiet sanctuary into something that actually felt like a home. Wet towels appeared in unexpected places. The refrigerator emptied at an alarming rate. Video game controllers migrated from room to room like nomadic tribes.

And David loved every chaotic minute of it.

His phone rang, Elena's name appearing on the screen with perfect timing.

"Good morning," he answered, settling into one of the terrace chairs. "How's Boston treating you?"

"Like a cold, wet bitch," Elena replied without missing a beat. "Sixty-eight degrees and drizzling. Meanwhile you're posting Instagram stories of eternal sunshine like some asshole influencer. How are my boys?"

"Your boys are fucking perfect. They're in the pool right now, and

I'm pretty sure Noah's trying to convince Marcus to teach him how to do a backflip off the diving board."

"Jesus Christ, please tell me you're going to stop him."

"Are you kidding? I'm taking video for evidence." David grinned, watching Noah's increasingly theatrical attempts to impress his audience. "Seriously though, El, they're thriving here. Aiden especially—kid's like a completely different person than the one who got off the plane."

"Different how?"

David considered how to phrase it. "Confident. Happy as hell. He laughs all the time now, and not just polite chuckles—real, unguarded belly laughs. He's been helping Marcus with some cooking projects, and yesterday I caught them having this intense debate about whether Blade Runner or The Matrix is the better sci-fi movie. Just... engaged with life in a way he wasn't before."

"And Noah?"

"Noah's in heaven. Kid's got two older brothers now instead of just one, and Marcus treats him like he's genuinely cool rather than just the annoying little brother. They've got this whole Mario Kart tournament thing going, and I think Noah actually lets Marcus win sometimes without making it obvious."

Elena was quiet for a moment. "And Marcus? How's he adjusting to having my chaos demons invade his space?"

"That's the thing—I don't think he sees it as an invasion at all. He's been like the perfect big brother to Noah, patient and funny and protective. And with Aiden..." David paused, choosing his words carefully.

"What about with Aiden?"

Elena's tone had shifted into full mama bear mode. David had forgotten how she could go from zero to protective in half a second when something concerned her boys.

"They've become very close," David said, testing the waters.

"Close how? And don't you dare give me some bullshit diplomatic answer, Harmon."

So much for subtlety. This was Elena, after all—the woman who'd grilled him about his intentions before she'd let him take Michael on their first real date. She didn't do subtle when it came to people she loved.

"Close like they understand each other," David said honestly. "Close like Aiden has found someone who gets what he's going through. Close like maybe Marcus is the first person Aiden's been able to be completely himself around."

"David." Elena's voice carried that particular warning tone he remembered from their early days. "Quit dancing around it. Are you trying to tell me something specific here?"

David looked down at the pool, where Aiden had abandoned all pretense of reading and was now openly watching Marcus explain diving technique to Noah. Even from this distance, David could see the soft expression on Aiden's face, the way his attention never wavered from Marcus's movements.

"I think your son might have found his first boyfriend," David said bluntly.

Elena was silent for so long that David began to wonder if the call had dropped.

"Elena? You still breathing over there?"

"I'm here." Her voice was thick with emotion. "Fuck, David, are you sure?"

"As sure as I can be without asking directly. They're careful around me, but they're teenagers—they're not exactly masters of subtlety. The way they look at each other, the way they find excuses to be in the same space, the way Aiden's whole face lights up when Marcus walks into a room..." David smiled. "It's actually pretty damn sweet."

"And you're okay with this? With them being... close... under your roof?"

David considered the question seriously. "More than okay, El. Marcus has been through absolute hell. His family threw him out for being gay, and he's spent months just trying to survive. If he can find some happiness, some connection with someone as good as Aiden... how could I not be okay with that?"

"What about Aiden? Is he okay? I mean, this would all be new for him, right? Coming to terms with his feelings, having his first... close friendship like this..."

"He's more than okay. He's fucking flourishing."

"Your boys are remarkable, Elena. Both of them. You should be proud."

"I am proud. I'm also terrified and excited and..." Elena paused.

"Should I say something when I call them later? Let Aiden know it's okay to tell me?"

"Remember, El, we don't officially know anything," David said carefully. "Give Aiden some time. He'll do it when and if he's ready. Just be yourself."

"If I were myself, I'd be calling him right now asking if he and Marcus are fucking."

David nearly did a spit take, coffee going down the wrong way as he started laughing. "Jesus, El, quit beating around the bush and tell me how you really feel."

Elena was laughing too. "But seriously, David... are they fucking?"

"I... I don't know."

"You don't know?"

"I don't have blacklights looking for cum stains on their sheets, El!" David laughed again. They could always speak this boldly around each other—it was one of the things he'd missed most about having someone who really knew him.

"Well, why not?!" Elena shot back, making him laugh even harder.

"Seriously though," she continued after their laughter died down, "maybe... maybe it's time you had the talk with Aiden."

"I'm pretty sure he knows about sex, El."

"Not *that* talk, David. The 'don't get HIV' talk."

David's laughter stopped. He was well aware of that responsibility. Elena had told him years ago, when Aiden wasn't even born yet, that at some point it would fall to him and Michael to give her boys the safe sex talk. *Why can't you?* he had responded, but Michael had understood immediately. Now Michael wasn't here, and it fell to David alone.

"I suppose," David said quietly. "But what am I supposed to do, El? Pass the potatoes and 'are you two fucking?' over dinner tonight?"

Elena laughed despite the serious turn. "You'll figure it out. You always do."

They talked for another few minutes about logistics—the planned trip to Disneyland, a possible weekend in San Diego, David's gradual return to work now that the boys were settled. Elena mentioned that her own mother was coming to visit next week, which meant the boys could potentially extend their stay even longer if they wanted to.

"Speaking of extending stays," Elena said, her tone shifting slightly, "I was looking at the calendar this morning, and I realized... next Tuesday is the anniversary."

David's coffee mug stopped halfway to his lips. "Shit."

"Michael's anniversary. July 18th. It'll be six years."

The terrace seemed to tilt slightly. David set down his mug with exaggerated care, as if sudden movements might shatter something fragile. Six years. How had he not been counting down to it the way he usually did?

"David? You still breathing?"

"Yeah, I'm... fuck. I didn't realize it was so close."

"You forgot." Elena's voice carried gentle surprise rather than judgment. "You actually forgot the date."

"I guess I did." David felt a strange mixture of guilt and relief. "I've been so focused on the boys, on making sure they're happy and settled..."

"That's not a bad thing, David. It means you're living in the present instead of camping out in the past."

"But I should remember. I should always remember."

"You will remember. But maybe this year it doesn't have to be the thing that fucks up your entire week. Maybe this year you can remember Michael without it destroying you."

David watched Marcus boost Noah up to the pool's edge, both of them laughing as Noah executed a reasonably successful cannonball. Aiden applauded from his float, genuinely delighted by his brother's progress.

"I keep thinking about how much he would have loved this," David said quietly. "All of it. The boys, the chaos, the family dinners on the terrace. Michael always wanted kids, you know? He would have been such a good father."

"He would have been an amazing father," Elena agreed. "But David? You're being an amazing father right now. To Marcus, to my boys... you're giving them exactly what they need."

"But I'm not Michael."

"No, you're not. You're David. And that's exactly who they need you to be."

David felt tears prick his eyes as he watched the boys below. "I miss him, El. I miss having someone to share this with. Someone who would understand how incredible this feels, having them here."

"I know you do. And he'd be so fucking proud of you for opening your heart again, for letting these boys become your family. Michael never wanted you to be alone forever, you stubborn ass."

"I know. I just... the anniversary always hits me like a truck. And this year, with the boys here..."

"This year might be different. This year you don't have to grieve alone. You have people who care about you, who've become part of your life. Maybe it's time to let them in on that part of your story too."

David considered this. The boys had never asked about the framed photos around the house, the ones where a younger, happier David stood next to a slight, laughing man with kind eyes. They'd accepted them as part of the landscape, the way teenagers accepted most adult mysteries.

But maybe Elena was right. Maybe this year could be different.

"The boys don't really know about him," David said. "Not the whole story, anyway. They know I had a partner who died, but they don't know... they don't know what he meant to me."

"Maybe it's time they did. Maybe sharing that with them would help you process the anniversary differently this year. Stop treating it like some sacred secret and start treating it like what it is—part of your story that made you who you are."

Below, Marcus was teaching both brothers some kind of synchronized swimming routine that was going terribly wrong and making all three of them laugh until they could barely stay afloat. The joy on their faces was infectious, and David found himself smiling despite the weight of the conversation.

"You know what the hardest part is?" David said. "Not that he's gone —I've made my peace with that, mostly. It's that he's missing this. He's missing watching me figure out how to be a father, missing seeing these boys grow up, missing all the good stuff that's finally happening again."

"But David, what if he's not missing it? What if this is exactly what he wanted for you? What if finding Marcus, having Aiden and Noah in your life... what if this is Michael's gift to you?"

David felt something shift in his chest, a loosening of tension he hadn't realized he'd been carrying. "That's a nice thought."

"It's not just a nice thought, asshole. It's Michael. You know how much he loved bringing people together, how he was always trying to fix everyone's problems and make sure no one felt left out. Does this really seem like a coincidence to you?"

David laughed, surprising himself. "You think Michael's playing matchmaker from beyond the grave?"

"I think Michael's love is still working in the world, and you're finally ready to receive it again. Through Marcus, through my boys, through all the ways your life is expanding instead of contracting. Stop being such a dumbass about it."

They sat in comfortable silence for a moment, David processing Elena's words while watching the ongoing aquatic comedy below. Finally, Elena spoke again.

"David? Will you do something for me?"

"Depends what it is."

"This year, on the anniversary, don't spend it alone. Whatever you usually do—the visiting his grave, the looking through photo albums, the general wallowing—do it with your family instead. Let them be part of remembering him."

"I don't know if I'm ready for that shit."

"You don't have to be ready. You just have to be willing to try something different. Besides, those boys are going to love hearing about Michael. He was such a huge part of who you are—sharing that with them will help them understand you better."

David thought about it. Six years of private grief, of careful commemoration, of treating the anniversary like a sacred ritual that belonged only to him. The idea of sharing it felt both terrifying and oddly appealing.

"I'll think about it," he said finally.

"That's all I ask, you stubborn bastard. And David?"

"Yeah?"

"Stop overthinking this. The boys are going to be fine. You're going to be fine. And Michael would be laughing his ass off at how scared you are to let people love you."

"You're one to talk, Missus 'are they fucking?'" David shot back, lightening the mood.

"Moi? I'm just being a careful and loving mother," Elena attempted to sound innocent, but could barely get out the phrase without laughing.

"You're so full of shit!" David laughed back, and they had collectively enjoyed the conversation. "I miss this, El..."

"I know you do... but you've got two mini-me's there to help you along," she replied.

"Correction, I think they're more like Michael and me."

"You think? How?"

"Noah doesn't give a shit and just says it like he sees it..."

"Yeah, and that's me, right?"

"Well... maybe... but remember, Michael could put you in your place..."

"True."

"And Aiden I suppose is you?" she added.

"In some ways, I connect with him... he reminds me of my shyness and worry over making everyone else happy..."

"I can see that... but David?"

"Yeah?"

"He has the best opportunity to learn how to be happy with himself now that he has you."

After they hung up, David remained on the terrace, watching his makeshift family and thinking about anniversaries, about the difference between remembering and living, about the possibility that love didn't end with death but transformed into something else entirely.

Maybe this year would be different. Maybe this year, instead of mourning what Michael had missed, David could celebrate what he'd helped make possible.

The thought felt like the beginning of something new.

eighteen
the happiest place on earth

THE LINE for the Matterhorn Bobsleds stretched ahead of them, winding through the Swiss-themed queue like a snake, but Noah's excitement was infectious enough to make even the wait feel like part of the adventure. He bounced on his toes, craning his neck to catch glimpses of the mountain through the trees, his enthusiasm ramped up to levels that made David grin despite himself.

"I can't believe we're actually here," Noah said for the fifth time in ten minutes. "I mean, I've seen it in movies and stuff, but this is actually real!"

David had been to Disneyland countless times before. He and Michael had held annual passes for years, coming down from West Hollywood just to have dinner sometimes, to walk around and people-watch, to escape into a world where magic felt possible even for cynical adults. But he'd never been here with kids before, and it was like looking through some magical lens he never knew existed—one that only being there with children, even big kids like these boys, could illuminate.

Everything felt new again. The familiar sights and sounds took on a different quality when filtered through Noah's wonder, Marcus's quiet amazement, and Aiden's barely contained joy. David found himself seeing the park through their eyes, remembering what it felt like to believe in magic.

"Next!" called the cast member, and their group shuffled forward to claim their bobsled. Noah immediately dove for the front seat, leaving

David to slide in behind him. In the bobsled directly behind them, Aiden claimed the front position with Marcus settling in behind him, close enough that David could see Marcus's hands resting lightly on either side of Aiden's waist.

The ride launched them into darkness, winding through the mountain's interior with a series of hairpin turns and sudden drops. It was on one of the sharpest curves, where they whipped around to zoom past the Abominable Snowman, that Noah let out a loud "Fuuucckk!" before catching himself and clapping a hand over his mouth.

David couldn't help but laugh. Elena would be proud, he thought, imagining her reaction to her son's enthusiastic profanity.

Behind them, Aiden and Marcus were having their own experience with the ride's physics, each sharp turn and sudden drop pushing Aiden back into Marcus's arms. David caught glimpses of them in the brief moments when their bobsleds aligned—the way Marcus instinctively tightened his grip to keep Aiden steady, the way Aiden relaxed into the contact like it was the most natural thing in the world.

"Where next?" David asked as they stumbled off the ride, all four of them grinning and slightly dizzy. It was only eleven AM, and they were obviously having the time of their lives.

"Small World?" Marcus suggested, to everyone's surprise.

"What?" he said, defensive when he caught their expressions. "I like the song."

"Fine!" Noah declared, already heading toward the attraction. "But I'm warning you, that song gets stuck in your head for like three days."

"Most annoying song ever," Aiden added, but he was smiling as he said it.

The four of them squeezed into the same row in the middle of the boat, David on the end next to Noah, then Marcus and Aiden on the other side. As they drifted through the colorful displays of singing children from around the world, David could swear he caught Marcus's hand brushing against Aiden's under the cover of the boat's edge. He smiled to himself, remembering the simple pleasure of secret touches in public places.

"Well, now I know how to sing that song in ten languages!" Aiden announced as they exited over the bridge and through the inevitable gift shop.

"Let's take the train!" Noah interrupted, spotting the Disneyland Railroad as it pulled into the station behind them.

The train swung around the side of the park, past the Autopia cars and into a long tunnel filled with elaborate dinosaur dioramas. The darkness gave Aiden the perfect opportunity to reach over and instinctively grab Marcus's hand. Noah was pressed up against the rail, taking in every detail of the moving displays, while David felt distinctly like a father wondering if his kids were ever going to officially tell him they were together.

He smiled, thinking about Michael putting his arm around his shoulder whenever they'd taken this same train ride. He missed that connection, the easy intimacy of shared experiences. But watching Aiden and Marcus discover the simple pleasure of holding hands in the dark, seeing the love they conveyed with such small gestures while still enjoying the ride—it filled something in David's chest that had been empty for too long.

"Next stop: New Orleans Square and Pirates of the Caribbean," David announced as they disembarked.

Having been to the park so many times, David knew a shortcut through some of the back-alley stores, past the Blue Bayou restaurant and directly to the attraction's entrance. Noah took one look at the queue snaking around the building and complained, "The line looks huge!"

"It'll go pretty quick," David assured him, though Noah remained skeptical. Aiden and Marcus were too absorbed in stealing glances at each other to really care about wait times.

The ride was everything everyone wanted—a dark, atmospheric journey through pirate-infested waters that provided plenty of opportunities for the lovebirds to hold hands and squeeze closer together during the exciting moments, enough animatronic pirates and cannon fire to keep Noah thoroughly entertained, and a flood of memories for David. This had been Michael's favorite ride, for all the right reasons.

"C'mon," David said as they exited, leading them left into a narrow alleyway instead of following the crowd back into the main square. Making another sharp left, the boys found themselves in a hidden courtyard with a magnificent staircase leading up to an ornate balcony. The space was beautifully decorated with wrought iron and climbing vines—the perfect setting for photos.

"Okay, boys, picture time! Put on your pretty faces!" David said, allowing himself to camp it up a little for his nephews' benefit. They found his uncharacteristic flamboyance both hilarious and endearing— they weren't used to seeing this side of their usually composed uncle.

Even Noah got in on the act, snapping his fingers and attempting his own camp version of "You go, girl!" which made everyone dissolve into laughter.

David took several pictures of the three boys on the elegant staircase before Noah suddenly said, "Hold on!" and ran out of the courtyard, leaving the other three confused.

He returned moments later with a park employee in tow. "All four of us," Noah declared, handing David's phone to the cast member.

They arranged themselves on the steps—David in the middle with his arms around Noah's shoulders on his left and Marcus's on his right, Aiden standing between Marcus and Noah. The photo captured a moment of pure happiness, four people who'd become a family grinning in the California sunshine. It would become cherished for decades to come.

"Marcus, Aiden, why don't I get a picture of just you two?" David suggested after thanking the cast member.

Both boys looked suddenly surprised, as if David knowing their secret had caught them off guard.

"C'mon, scoot together," David gestured when they seemed awkward and uncertain.

Noah, apparently done with subtlety, took charge. "For God's sake, Aiden, at least pretend to like your boyfriend!" he yelled before catching his slip and slapping his hand over his mouth. Aiden's eyes bulged in horror while Marcus looked like he wanted to melt into the staircase.

David had to stifle a laugh. Little brothers were never good with state secrets, and Aiden was finding that out now. Elena would've laughed her ass off, he thought.

"Guys," David said, figuring that sounded better than 'boys'—it felt like acknowledgment that they were maturing and he was going to treat them like adults going forward. "Guys, it's okay. I'm happy for you. Really."

Both Marcus and Aiden still looked mortified, with a distinct "I'm going to kill you" look coming from Aiden toward his little brother. Noah had instinctively backed up next to David for protection.

David decided to diffuse the situation with humor. "Guys... I'm gay, remember?" He intentionally camped it up, doing a stereotypical limp wrist gesture and snapping in a circle, trying to get them to laugh and loosen up. It worked—they couldn't help but crack up seeing their usually proper and refined uncle acting like a drag queen.

"Seriously, guys, it's cool. I really am happy for you."

"Really?" Marcus asked, his voice small.

"Yes, really."

They talked about it for a few more minutes, with Noah interjecting apologies and David reassuring them that he'd suspected for a while and was genuinely thrilled for them both.

"Should we move on to the Haunted Mansion?" David suggested, pointing down the path. "It's just down the way."

This time, David made a point of suggesting that Noah ride with him in one doom buggy while Aiden could sit with his boyfriend. He intentionally used the term 'boyfriend,' which made both boys turn red, but David knew that after a while they'd get used to it, the same way he had with Michael all those years ago. So he kept using it.

In fact, after four or five references to them as boyfriends, they began using the term themselves, as if they'd been given permission. Even Noah started calling them that without thinking about it. David thought that's how it should be—sometimes people just needed someone they saw as an authority or respected figure to help normalize what should be obvious and loving.

"Dinner, guys?" David asked as they emerged from the mansion, blinking in the late afternoon sunlight.

"Yes! I'm starving," Noah declared. The boyfriends nodded their agreement, and David noticed they were now holding hands openly. He smiled but didn't call attention to it, letting his focus return to Noah.

"Well, let's head to Michael's favorite spot."

"Michael?" Noah looked confused as they walked toward the Carnation Café near the castle.

David stopped and turned. "My partner."

Noah still looked puzzled—he'd been very little when Michael died.

"You may not remember him, but he really loved you when you were little and we'd visit. He was your mom's best friend a long time ago."

"What happened to him?" Noah asked with the directness that only children possessed.

Kids always knew how to zero in on the most painful bits without realizing it.

David took a breath. "I'll tell you, but let's get food first, okay?"

Marcus managed to stake out an umbrella table in the crowd of dinner-goers while they collected trays of fried chicken and mashed potatoes. Once they were settled and eating, David began to share Michael's story—who he was, what he'd meant to David, how he'd died. The boys asked questions between bites and seemed genuinely interested, treating the conversation with the seriousness it deserved.

Before too long, David noticed other families hovering nearby, waiting for tables. "We should probably let someone else have this table," he said. "It's getting busy."

"Are we a family?" Noah asked innocently, apparently struck by David's phrasing since only he and Aiden were actually related.

"Yes, Noah," David said without hesitation. "All of us are a family."

The words felt true in a way that surprised him with its completeness.

"Let's go to Space Mountain!" Aiden suddenly yelled out, and everyone agreed, the mood lifting as they headed toward their next adventure together.

Family, indeed.

nineteen
ghosts

THE DRIVE HOME from Disneyland stretched ahead of them through the orange glow of Los Angeles traffic, the 5 Freeway packed with families making their way back from a day of magic. In the back seat, Aiden sat openly holding Marcus's hand for the first time in the car, their fingers intertwined as they watched the city lights blur past the windows. Noah had claimed the front passenger seat and was staring out at the passing landscape with the satisfied exhaustion that only came from a perfect day.

It was Aiden who broke the comfortable silence, his voice thoughtful as he leaned forward slightly. "David? At dinner when you talked about Michael... how'd you guys meet?"

Noah perked up immediately, turning away from the window with renewed interest. "Yeah, I wanna know too."

David glanced in the rearview mirror and caught Marcus's eyes. There was something gentle in the young man's expression—compassion mixed with understanding. He didn't know the details, but he seemed to recognize that this was difficult territory.

David took a breath, easing into the story as traffic crawled forward around them. "We met at work, actually. This was 1990, and I was a marketing assistant at Sony Pictures. Michael was a UCLA student doing an internship in the publicity department."

"Wait, Mom never told us you guys worked together," Noah said.

"There's a lot your mom never told you," David said with a smile. "Anyway, Michael was... God, he was this tiny, skinny kid with the biggest personality you've ever seen. All energy and laughter and zero filter. I was the serious, buttoned-up guy who kept his head down and did his work, and Michael was this whirlwind who made friends with everyone."

"But how'd you actually meet though?" Aiden pressed.

"The Xerox machine," David laughed, remembering. "I was making copies of some marketing materials, and I dropped the whole stack. Papers everywhere. Michael appeared out of nowhere and helped me pick them up, and while we're crawling around on the floor, he just starts talking. Asking about the project, about what department I worked in, making jokes about office coffee. Twenty minutes later, we're still standing by that damn copy machine and I'm laughing harder than I had in months."

"That sounds like Uncle Mike," Noah said quietly. "I mean, from what I remember."

"He was infectious that way. Michael could make anyone feel like the most interesting person in the room." David's voice grew warmer with the memory. "He asked me out that same day. Right there by the copy machine. I was terrified—I'd never been on a date with another guy, never even held hands with anyone. But Michael just had this way of making everything feel possible."

Marcus squeezed Aiden's hand, understanding something about first relationships and taking chances.

"So what happened? On the first date?" Aiden asked.

"Michael took me to this terrible Chinese restaurant in Hollywood because it was the only place he could afford on his intern salary. The food was awful, but we talked for three hours. About movies, about our families, about what we wanted to do with our lives. I told him things I'd never told anyone." David smiled, lost in the memory. "When he walked me to my car afterward, he kissed me. Right there in the parking lot under the streetlights. My first kiss with another man."

"Dude, that's actually really sweet," Noah said with genuine emotion.

"It was. And I was hooked. Michael just... he brought out parts of me I didn't know existed. Made me funnier, braver, more willing to take risks. Before I met him, I was this careful, controlled person who never colored outside the lines. Michael taught me how to be spontaneous."

"How'd you meet Mom?" Aiden asked.

David's expression shifted slightly, becoming both fond and amused. "Elena was Michael's best friend from high school. And she was not having any of me at first."

"Really? Mom was like that?"

"Oh, and worse," David laughed. "She grilled me like I was applying for security clearance. What were my intentions? Was I going to hurt her best friend? Did I understand how special Michael was? She basically told me that if I broke his heart, she'd make my life a living hell."

The boys grinned, trying to imagine their mother as a fierce protector in "the olden days."

"Don't make me pull this car over," David jested at the old age jokes, which caused everyone to laugh. It felt good remembering Michael with them, sharing the joy rather than just the sadness. Michael would want it that way.

"So..." Aiden started, then hesitated, clearly wanting to ask something but unsure how.

David recognized the tone and decided to spare them the discomfort of asking directly. "Michael got sick about six years ago. Cancer. It happened really fast—from diagnosis to... to the end was only about five months."

"That's fucked up!" Aiden said, a tear hitting his cheek. He immediately looked embarrassed. "Sorry, I didn't mean to—"

"You're right, Aiden. It was fucked up," David said, ensuring he knew that there were some places where that language was not only appropriate, but true to what he was describing. The other boys looked at each other and made note. It wasn't often they heard David speak this way, but they'd heard their mom free with her casual use of the f-bomb, so perhaps it was okay sometimes—at least with adults. With each other, they'd use it all the time anyway.

The car grew quiet except for the hum of traffic around them.

"Your mom was my lifeline through all of it," David continued, his voice steady but soft. "She drove down from San Francisco every weekend, sometimes more when things got bad. She helped me navigate the doctors, the treatments, the decisions. When Michael died, she was the one who held me together."

"I remember Mom being really sad," Noah said quietly. "I didn't get why at the time, but I remember asking where Uncle Mike went."

"I remember more," Aiden said. "It was like, the first time anyone I knew died, except for my hamster Mr. Tickles."

"Dude, you had a pet hamster named Mr. Tickles?" Marcus interjected, momentarily breaking the serious mood.

"Yeah, and I was like, devastated when he died."

"Mr. Tickles?" Marcus repeated, trying not to smile.

"Yes!"

Noah didn't remember Mr. Tickles but found the name funny. David listened with some amusement—it wasn't funny that Aiden's pet had died, but it had helped him learn about the lifecycle of living, about loss and grief on a scale he could understand.

Marcus squeezed Aiden's hand in support, recognizing that this memory was important to his boyfriend, even if the name was endearing.

"I wish Uncle Mike was here to go to Disneyland with us," Noah said aloud what everyone had been thinking.

"Me too, buddy. Me too," David said, wiping away a tear that had started to form and focusing back on the traffic ahead.

Aiden and Marcus exchanged a look, both suddenly struck by the same sobering thought. Would they end up like David someday? One of them dying young while the other was left alone? Would they have nephews to take to Disneyland when they were older? How could anyone manage living alone after sharing so much time and love with someone?

It seemed too overwhelming to contemplate.

"But you know what, guys?" David said, his voice shifting to a more upbeat tone—partly to cheer them up from this heavy conversation, but mostly for himself.

"What?" Marcus replied for all of them.

"Uncle Mike is here. We're talking about him, so in my book, that means he's still alive in our memories. And... I like that."

They all smiled, unsure of how to respond but feeling the truth in his words.

"And Uncle Mike would go home tonight and have a great big bowl of ice cream while flipping through all the pictures I took of you goof-balls on the teacups!"

"You mean where Noah almost hurled after spinning too fast?" Aiden laughed.

"I didn't hurl!" Noah protested.

"You almost threw up on my lap!" Marcus added with a grin.

"And he would've laughed his ass off about it," David said, joining in their laughter. "Michael loved chaos. He would've gotten such a kick out of today."

As their laughter filled the car, David felt something he hadn't experienced in years—the sense that Michael's memory could be a source of joy rather than just grief. That sharing these stories didn't diminish the love they'd shared, but multiplied it, spreading it to new people who could carry it forward.

Somewhere, David thought, Michael was laughing along with them.

twenty
the talk

TWO DAYS after their Disneyland adventure, David found himself staring at his home office ceiling, wondering how the hell he was supposed to bring up safe sex with two teenagers who'd already been accidentally outed by a fourteen-year-old. He'd promised Elena he'd have this conversation, and he knew it was important—crucial, even—but that didn't make it any less awkward to contemplate.

He'd considered talking to them separately, but good luck finding an excuse for one-on-one time with each boy without the other getting suspicious. Besides, if he spoke with one first, the other would inevitably hear about it before David could have the second conversation. Better to rip the band-aid off all at once.

The truth was, they'd be mortified no matter how he brought it up, so he might as well address it head-on. Acknowledge that it was awkward, get over the "embarrassment and shame bullshit," and speak like adults. If he came right out and stated he expected to treat them as adults, maybe they could learn to discuss sensitive subjects in an adult manner.

After dinner that night—pizza, because David had made sure everyone got their favorite—he took a deep breath and made his move.

"Aiden, Marcus, could you join me in my office for a few minutes?"

Both boys froze, forks halfway to their mouths. David recognized the look immediately—it was the universal expression of teenagers wondering what they'd done wrong.

"Yes, you're both in serious trouble," David said with a grin, which earned him nervous laughter and helped ease the tension slightly. "Come on."

Noah looked wide-eyed as the older boys followed David down the hall. "Wait, what happened? Who's in trouble?"

"Nobody's in trouble," David called back. "Finish your pizza."

In his office, David settled into his desk chair while Aiden and Marcus perched awkwardly on the leather couch, looking like they were waiting for a prison sentence.

"Relax, guys. This isn't a detention." David leaned back, choosing his words carefully. "Look, I'm going to be straight with you. This is going to be uncomfortable for all of us at first, but we're going to get through it like adults, okay?"

The boys exchanged glances, their nervousness ratcheting up another notch.

"When I was in seventh grade," David began, "I had to change into PE clothes for the first time. In front of other guys. In a locker room." He paused, letting that sink in. "I was absolutely mortified. Red-faced, wanted to hide in a bathroom stall, the whole thing."

Aiden and Marcus giggled slightly, some of the tension breaking.

"You didn't have a brother?" Aiden asked. "I've seen Noah naked like a thousand times. No big deal."

"Me too," Marcus added. "It's just bodies."

"Exactly," David said. "But for me, it was new. Foreign. No one had seen me without at least shorts on since I was a little kid, so I was ashamed of my body, worried someone would make fun of me, that sort of thing. But I did it the first day, then the second. By the third time, I wasn't really thinking about it. By the end of the week, it was second nature. No big deal."

The boys nodded, not sure where this was going but listening.

"It's similar to how I felt the first time Michael and I... well, had sex. I had no clue what I was doing. Who was the top, who was the bottom—I didn't even know what those terms meant. Did I 'stick it in' or did he?"

Aiden and Marcus blushed but couldn't help laughing a little. They'd wondered the same things themselves.

"See?" David smiled. "Getting this stuff out there might seem weird or uncomfortable at first, but after a while, it doesn't have to be. More importantly, knowing the answers to these questions can literally save your lives—HIV and other diseases—but it also helps with your emotional and mental health, how you treat each other, how you see your bodies and your relationship. Lots of reasons to be honest and open about sex."

Marcus seemed to be listening without visible embarrassment, which gave Aiden permission to relax slightly. This wasn't as mortifying as he'd expected.

"So," David continued, "let's talk about some basics. Have you guys... I mean, how far have you gone?"

"We've kissed," Aiden said quietly. "And like... made out. But that's it."

"Good. No rush on anything else. But when you're ready—and only when you're both ready—there are things you need to know." David shifted into his straightforward mode. "Let's start with the big one: anal sex. It's probably what you're thinking about most, right?"

Both boys turned red but nodded.

"Does it hurt?" Aiden asked suddenly, then looked surprised at his own boldness.

David answered without judgment or discomfort. "It can, if you don't do it right. But if you take your time, use plenty of lube, and communicate with each other, it doesn't have to. The key is patience and preparation."

Seeing that David was treating their questions seriously made both boys more comfortable asking more.

"But like, how do you know who's the top and who's the bottom?" Marcus asked.

"You talk about it. You try things. Maybe you switch off. There's no rule that says you have to be one or the other forever." David leaned forward. "The important thing is that you both want to do whatever you're doing. If one of you doesn't want to try anal but the other does, then you find something else you both enjoy."

"What if Marcus wanted to... you know... fuck me, but I wasn't in the mood, so he went out and found some random guy at a club?" Aiden asked, then immediately looked jealous just at the thought.

"NO!" Marcus said emphatically. "I'd never do that to you!"

"See?" David said. "That's an example of both the physical and emotional ramifications of your sexual choices. Random hookups increase your risk of STDs because you don't know the other person's status. But it also takes an emotional toll on your relationship."

The conversation continued for over an hour, with the boys gradually becoming more comfortable using frank language—words like fuck and dick and ass that might sound profane out of context but helped them speak openly about the topic at hand.

They asked about oral sex ("Do you really need a condom for just sucking dick?"), about practical concerns ("What if you cum first?"), about hygiene issues they were too embarrassed to voice until David saved them the humiliation by bringing them up himself.

"What happens if there's... you know... shit?" Marcus finally managed to ask.

"It happens," David said matter-of-factly. "Don't worry about it. There are things you can do beforehand to minimize it, but bodies are bodies. You deal with it and move on."

"Can you use hand lotion instead of real lube?" Aiden asked.

"God, no. You'll give yourself chemical burns. Invest in the real stuff."

By the end of the conversation, they'd covered HIV prevention, PrEP, the importance of regular testing, and the difference between sex motivated by love versus just "getting off."

"Look," David said as they wrapped up, "I'm not saying you have to rush into anything. You're both young, you're figuring things out, and that's normal. But I want you to be safe—physically and emotionally. And I want you to know you can come to me with questions without feeling embarrassed or judged."

"Really?" Aiden asked.

"Really. Michael was patient with me when I was learning all this stuff. If he hadn't been so open about his own experiences, if he hadn't taught me how to do things right... I wouldn't be able to be this comfortable talking about it now."

The boys left David's office with more answers than they'd had before, but also with more questions—many of them about each other. More importantly, they left with a new sense of trust in David and in themselves, as if something had fundamentally changed and they'd been admitted to some kind of adult club.

As they headed back toward the living room, David heard Marcus whisper to Aiden, "That wasn't as bad as I thought it'd be."

"Yeah," Aiden whispered back. "And now we actually know stuff."

David smiled to himself. Elena would be proud. And somewhere, he thought, Michael would be too.

twenty-one
conversations

NOAH WAS WAITING in the living room when Marcus and Aiden emerged from David's office, his curiosity written all over his face.

"So?" he demanded. "What happened? Are you guys in trouble?"

Aiden and Marcus exchanged a look, and some silent communication passed between them.

"We had the safe sex talk," Aiden said matter-of-factly.

Noah's eyes went wide. "The what now?"

"You know," Marcus added with a completely serious expression, "about butt fucking and blow jobs and—"

"LALALALALA!" Noah clapped his hands over his ears and bolted toward the stairs. "I CAN'T HEAR YOU! I'M GOING TO PLAY GAMES!"

The older boys burst into laughter as Noah's voice continued to drift down from upstairs: "I DON'T WANT TO KNOW ABOUT YOUR GROSS STUFF!"

"That worked better than I expected," Marcus grinned.

"Come on," Aiden said, heading toward the kitchen. "Let's grab some Cokes and go outside."

———

David closed his office door and settled behind his desk, pulling out his phone. Given the time difference, Elena would still be awake, probably reading in bed or catching up on work emails. He'd promised to call her after having the conversation, and besides, she needed to be on the same page about what her sons were learning.

Elena picked up on the second ring. "Please tell me you survived."

"Barely," David said with a laugh. "But it went better than I expected."

"Start talking. I want details."

———

By the pool, Marcus and Aiden dangled their feet in the water, the underwater lights casting a soft blue glow across their faces. The evening air was warm, and the house behind them felt safely distant.

"So," Aiden said, then stopped, clearly struggling with something.

"So what?" Marcus prompted gently.

"I... uh..." Aiden took a long sip of his Coke, buying time.

Marcus remembered David's advice about being open and honest. "Just say it, whatever it is. I'm not going to judge you."

"Do you..." Aiden started, then stopped again. "This is embarrassing."

"More embarrassing than David asking us about shit on dicks?"

That got a laugh. "Fair point." Aiden took a breath. "Do you ever... you know... jerk off thinking about us? Doing stuff?"

Marcus felt his cheeks warm, but he pushed through it. "What kind of stuff?"

"Do I really have to say it?"

"You started this conversation," Marcus pointed out, reaching over to take Aiden's hand. "I won't judge, remember?"

———

"They asked good questions," David was telling Elena. "Smart questions. Some I expected, some I didn't."

"Like what?"

"Practical stuff mostly. How to know who tops, what it actually feels like, hygiene concerns. But also emotional stuff—how to know if they're ready, how to talk to each other about what they want."

"Jesus," Elena said. "My baby is really growing up, isn't he?"

"He's handling it well, El. They both are. Better than I did at their age, that's for sure."

———

"I jerk off thinking about you... topping me," Aiden said in a rush, his face burning red.

"Really?" Marcus's voice was soft, surprised.

"Yeah. Do you... do you want to do that? Someday, I mean. Not now! This is still weird and—"

"Yeah," Marcus interrupted. "I would. Only if you want to, though. I don't want to just... you know... fuck. I want it to mean something."

They both fell quiet for a moment, processing the weight of that admission.

"What about you?" Aiden asked, turning the tables. "What do you think about?"

Now it was Marcus's turn to look embarrassed. "I, uh..."

"I said it," Aiden pointed out. "You can too."

"Fine. I want you to... you know... suck me."

"Suck you? Like your dick?"

"No," Marcus said sarcastically, "my thumb!" He pretended to suck his thumb like a toddler.

Aiden smacked his shoulder and they both burst into laughter, the awkwardness dissolving into something more comfortable.

Marcus took a drink of his Coke, and after their laughter died down, Aiden said quietly, "I will if you want."

"What?" Marcus had almost forgotten what they were talking about after all the laughing.

"Suck your dick."

Marcus choked on his soda, the liquid going down the wrong pipe. Aiden immediately started slapping his back to help him cough it out.

"Really?" Marcus finally managed to ask, his eyes still watering.

———

"The thing is," David continued, "they're already thinking about this stuff. At least now they have actual information instead of whatever they might pick up from porn or locker room talk."

"Did you cover everything? PrEP, testing, emotional readiness?"

"Most of it. This was just the first conversation, El. There'll be more."

Elena was quiet for a moment. "It's weird hearing about my son's... desires. But I'm glad he's talking to someone about it. Glad it's you."

"I told them they could come to me with questions. No judgment, no telling parents unless it's a safety issue."

"Good. That's exactly what they need."

———

The boys continued talking by the pool, their conversation meandering through dreams and desires, the difference between lust and love, practical concerns about their inexperience.

"How do we even get condoms and lube?" Aiden wondered. "I'm not walking into CVS and buying that stuff."

"We could ask David," Marcus suggested. "He said we could come to him with questions."

"Would he tell my mom?"

"I don't think so. He said no judgment, right?"

"But is this too soon? We're both virgins. What should we do next? Just stick to kissing?"

"We could do other things," Marcus said carefully. "Things that aren't... you know. Full sex."

"Like what?"

Marcus gestured vaguely. "Hands? Just... touching each other?"

———

"The important thing," David said, "is that they felt comfortable asking questions. Even the embarrassing ones. I think if we keep the communication open, they'll make good choices."

"I hope so," Elena said. "I just want them to be safe. And happy. And not rush into anything they're not ready for."

"They're smart kids, El. And they clearly care about each other. That's more than a lot of people have."

"True. And they have you looking out for them."

"They have both of us."

———

"So what do we do now?" Aiden asked as they sat by the pool, their Cokes forgotten beside them.

"I don't know," Marcus admitted. "Take it slow? See how things feel?"

"I'm really glad we can talk about this stuff," Aiden said quietly. "With each other, I mean. And with David."

"Yeah, me too."

They sat in comfortable silence for a moment, feet creating small ripples in the pool water.

"This is pretty crazy," Aiden said finally.

"What is?"

"A month ago, I'd never even kissed anyone. Now I'm sitting here talking about... all this stuff. With my boyfriend."

Marcus smiled. "Your boyfriend?"

"Yeah. You are, right? My boyfriend?"

"Yeah," Marcus said, squeezing his hand. "I am."

———

"I should let you get some sleep," David said, noting the time.

"Thanks for doing this," Elena said. "For having that conversation. I know it wasn't easy."

"It was important. And honestly? It wasn't as bad as I thought it would be. They're good kids, El."

"The best. Give them my love."

"Will do. Talk soon."

After hanging up, David sat in his office for a moment, thinking about how much had changed in just a few weeks. Three boys who'd become a family, conversations that would have been unimaginable a month ago, and the gradual understanding that maybe he was better at this whole surrogate father thing than he'd given himself credit for.

———

Outside by the pool, Marcus and Aiden were coming to their own realizations about how much their world had expanded. They had each other, they had David's support, and they had the beginnings of understanding about what it meant to love someone completely.

"We should probably go inside," Marcus said as the evening air began to cool.

"Yeah," Aiden agreed, but neither of them moved.

They sat there a little longer, hands linked, feet dangling in the water, both of them thinking about the future and all the conversations—awkward and beautiful and necessary—that lay ahead.

twenty-two
the studio

THE MORNING LIGHT streaming through the kitchen windows caught the rim of Michael's reading glasses where they sat on the side table next to the sofa, just as they had for the past six years. David had never moved them, had never quite been able to put them away, and until this week, the boys had never thought to ask about them.

"Does David wear glasses?" Marcus asked Aiden and Noah, turning the wire frames over in his hands. "I don't think I've ever seen him with any."

"No, I don't think so," Aiden said, looking uncertain.

"Definitely not," Noah confirmed. "So whose are these?"

Aiden looked up from where he sat cross-legged on the floor, studying a small abstract painting that hung near the bookshelf. "Yo, check this out," he said, pointing to the lower right corner. "M. Santos, 1998. So Michael was like an artist or whatever?"

"Among other things," David said, appearing in the doorway with a cup of coffee. He'd been listening to their exploration for the past few minutes, unsure whether to interrupt or let them discover these pieces of Michael on their own. "He dabbled in a lot of creative things. That one was from a series he did the year we bought this house."

Noah emerged from David's study holding a simple gold band. "David, there's this ring just sitting on your desk? Seems like a weird place to keep jewelry and stuff."

David's breath caught slightly. Michael's wedding ring—they'd never legally married, of course, but they'd exchanged rings on their tenth anniversary. David still wore his own, but Michael's had sat on that desk since the day he'd taken it off when his fingers became too thin.

"Yes," David said simply. "That was Michael's."

The boys exchanged glances, suddenly realizing they'd stumbled into something more significant than casual curiosity.

"Shit, sorry," Aiden said quickly. "We weren't trying to be nosy or anything."

"You weren't being nosy," David assured them, settling into his chair. "There's nothing here you can't look at or ask about. You're family, just like Michael... was."

Marcus held up a framed photograph he'd found on the mantle— David and Michael at what looked like a beach, both impossibly young and tan, David's arm around Michael's shoulders as they laughed at something outside the frame.

"Damn, you guys were kinda hot," Marcus said matter-of-factly, then grinned when David nearly choked on his coffee.

"Dude!" Aiden laughed, but he was nodding in agreement. "I mean, he's not wrong. You both look really happy and shit."

"That's gross," Noah protested from the sofa. "He's like our uncle now! You can't call your uncle hot!"

"Doesn't matter," Marcus replied, still studying the photo. "Hot is hot. When was this taken?"

"1995, I think," David said, his voice softer now. "We'd been together about three years. That was at Laguna Beach—we used to go there for long weekends when we could afford it."

"He looks fun," Aiden observed. "Like, way more outgoing than you are?"

David smiled at the accuracy of that assessment. "Much more outgoing. Michael could talk to anyone about anything. He's the one who taught me how to actually enjoy parties instead of just enduring them."

"Was he cool?" Noah asked suddenly. "Like, would he have been okay with us being here and stuff?"

The question hit David unexpectedly hard, not because it was painful, but because he knew the answer with absolute certainty.

"He would have loved you guys," David said. "All of you. Michael always said this place was way too big for just two people. He would've been thrilled to see it full of teenagers asking a million questions and eating everything in sight and leaving towels all over the damn bathroom floor."

Marcus laughed. "Yo, I totally do leave towels on the floor. My bad about that."

"Don't apologize. Michael would have done the same thing, and I would have complained about both of you." David paused, looking around at the three boys who had transformed his quiet life into something entirely different. "I think he would have been proud of what we've become. This family we've made."

―――――

Later that afternoon, David found himself thinking about Michael more intentionally than he had in months. Not the painful memories of illness and loss, but the happier ones—Michael's laugh, his terrible cooking, the way he'd gesture wildly when telling stories.

The boys had asked him more questions throughout the day. What kind of work had Michael done? (Freelance graphic design.) Did he like movies? (Only comedies and musicals, much to David's professional frustration.) What was his favorite room in the house? (The kitchen, where he'd hold court during dinner parties, charming everyone while David handled the actual cooking.)

For the first time since Michael's death, David found himself imagining what Michael would say about current situations. When he'd had that awkward but necessary conversation with Marcus and Aiden about safe sex, David had actually found himself thinking: *Michael would have handled this better. He would have made them laugh while still taking it seriously.*

The realization that he could think of Michael without drowning in grief felt both liberating and somehow wrong. Was it disrespectful to be happy when remembering someone who was gone?

His phone rang, interrupting his thoughts. Elena's name appeared on the screen.

"How are my boys?" she asked without preamble.

"Thriving," David replied. "Though I think I may have three sons now instead of just one. Marcus has fully embraced his role as big brother, and Noah seems to have adopted all of us."

"And Aiden?"

David glanced toward the pool area, where he could see Marcus and Aiden sitting by the water. Even from this distance, their body language spoke of young people falling in love—the careful way they sat close but not too close, the way Aiden's attention never strayed far from Marcus.

"Happy," David said. "Really happy. They both are."

"That's wonderful. You sound different, David. Lighter.'

"I've been thinking about Michael a lot lately," David admitted. "The boys found some of his things around the house, started asking questions. It's the first time I've been able to talk about him without feeling like I was going to fall apart."

"That's a good thing," Elena said gently.

"Is it? Sometimes I feel guilty for being happy when I remember him. Like I should only think of him with sadness, to honor what we lost."

Elena was quiet for a moment. "David, do you remember what Michael used to say about laughter at funerals?"

David did remember. Michael had always insisted that the best memorial services were the ones where people told funny stories, where joy mixed with grief in ways that celebrated the person's life rather than just mourning their death.

"He said that being happy about someone's life was the greatest tribute you could pay them," David said slowly.

"Exactly. The fact that you can think of Michael and smile, that you can share stories about him with those boys—that's not disrespecting his memory. That's keeping him alive in the best possible way."

David felt something tight in his chest begin to relax. "I think he'd love seeing how Aiden and Noah are growing up. He was so crazy about them when they were little. And Marcus... God, he would've adored Marcus. He would've been so happy about him and Aiden together."

"I know he would have. And David? I think he would be proud of the man you've become. The way you've opened your heart to these boys —that's exactly who Michael fell in love with all those years ago."

———

As evening approached, David watched from his kitchen window as Marcus and Aiden settled into what had become their nightly routine by the pool. Aiden lay back with his head in Marcus's lap while Marcus dangled his feet in the warm water, one hand stroking Aiden's hair in slow, gentle movements. Aiden's hand rested on Marcus's leg, thumb tracing absent patterns on his skin.

There was something achingly beautiful about their careful intimacy —the way they touched each other like precious things, the way they talked in low voices that carried just enough for David to hear the rhythm but not the words. It was young love in its purest form, before complications and expectations and the weight of the world pressed down on it.

David remembered feeling that way with Michael, especially in those early years when everything was discovery and promise. He found himself smiling as he watched them, imagining what Michael would say if he could see this.

Look at those two, Michael would have whispered. *They're going to break each other's hearts and put them back together about six times before they figure it out.*

And then, probably: *Should we tell them Aiden has to go home in a few weeks, or let them stay in this bubble a little longer?*

David had been wondering the same thing. Neither boy had mentioned the approaching end of summer, the return to Boston, the reality of a long-distance relationship between a seventeen-year-old and an eighteen-year-old with no money for visits. They were living in the moment, the way young people in love should, but David knew that reality would intrude soon enough.

A splash from the pool drew his attention back. Noah had appeared, apparently deciding to join the older boys for their evening routine. David watched as Marcus made room for him, the three of them settling into easy conversation.

It struck David how naturally Marcus had grown into his role as a different kind of older brother figure for Noah. More than that—he'd become someone Noah could confide in without the complicated dynamics that came with actual brotherhood. David had overheard some of their conversations lately, Noah asking questions about girls and dating and growing up that he might have been too embarrassed to ask Aiden.

"I don't know," David had heard Noah say the night before, his voice carrying across the water. "Sometimes I feel like... like everyone else has someone, you know? You and Aiden have each other, and I'm just... here."

Marcus's response had been perfect: understanding without being patronizing, honest about the complications of relationships while still validating Noah's feelings. David had found himself thinking, once again, that Michael would have loved this—would have loved seeing Marcus grow into someone who could offer guidance instead of just needing it.

———

The evening before David's return to his office at the lot, the mood at dinner felt different. The easy rhythm they'd established over the past few days was about to be interrupted, and everyone seemed to feel it.

"So," David said, cutting into his grilled salmon, "tomorrow I'll be back at the studio. I've got three meetings I can't postpone any longer, and I need to check in with my team."

The boys nodded, but David could sense their disappointment. They'd gotten used to having him around, to the spontaneous outings and lazy mornings.

"What are we supposed to do all day?" Noah asked, stabbing at his vegetables with his fork.

"Well, you've got plenty of options," David replied. "There's the pool, obviously. The mall I showed you guys is about fifteen minutes away. There's that park down the street with the basketball courts. The grocery store if you need anything."

"Sounds fucking riveting," Aiden muttered, earning a look from David.

"Look, I know it's not ideal," David continued. "But if you want to go anywhere beyond those local spots, you need to text me first. I just want to know where you are."

Noah rolled his eyes but didn't argue.

"You're boys in a city..." David started, then stopped himself, took a breath, and rephrased. "You're guys in a town that... well, it..." He paused and looked directly at Marcus. It hadn't been that long since he'd met Marcus living on the streets, and his eyes seemed to ask for help in ensuring Aiden and Noah understood it could be rough out there if you ran across the wrong person.

Marcus suddenly got his drift and his tone shifted, understanding flooding his expression. "Yeah, okay," he said more seriously. "Yeah, yeah, we get it. Text you if we wanna go anywhere."

"Thank you," David said, relief evident in his voice.

"Wait," Marcus said suddenly, his expression brightening as if trying to steer the conversation somewhere better. "Didn't you mention something when Aiden and Noah first got here about maybe showing us the studio? Like, giving us a tour or something?"

David paused, remembering the conversation from weeks ago. "I did mention that as a possibility, yes."

Both Aiden and Noah immediately perked up, their earlier sulking forgotten.

"Dude, could we do that?" Aiden asked, leaning forward. "I mean, if you're gonna be there anyway?"

"Oh fuck, yes!" Noah added eagerly. "That beats sitting around here doing nothing."

David shot his nephew a look before considering it. He'd been planning to dive straight back into work, but seeing their excitement made him reconsider. "I suppose I could arrange something. Maybe lunch and a quick tour afterward?"

"For real?" Noah's eyes were wide. "Can we see where they film stuff? Do they have actual movie sets there?"

"Wait," Noah interrupted himself, his voice climbing an octave. "Do they film *Sunset Academy* there?"

David smiled. "Yes, we do. I didn't realize you were a fan."

"What's *Sunset Academy*?" Marcus and Aiden asked almost simultaneously, looking confused.

"It's this show about a performing arts high school," Noah explained rapidly. "It's really good, and there's this actress, Lily Chen, and she's like... she's really pretty and talented and—" He paused, his face reddening. "I mean, she's... you know... hot."

"Dude's got a crush," Marcus said with a grin.

"Yeah, she's like a huge star now," Aiden agreed. "I mean, we don't really know the show or whatever, but everyone talks about her."

David laughed at the familiar dynamic. "Yes, *Sunset Academy* films on our lot. I don't know what their shooting schedule looks like this week, but I can see if there's a way for us to peek in on their set."

The noise level at the dinner table increased dramatically.

"Oh shit, really?" Noah was practically bouncing in his chair. "That would be so fucking awesome! Do you think we could meet her? I mean, not meet her meet her, but maybe just see her?"

"Easy there, Romeo," Marcus teased. "You might wanna work on talking to girls in your own zip code before you start planning to charm TV stars."

"I can talk to girls!" Noah protested, then paused. "I just... haven't had much practice yet."

David felt a familiar pang of protective affection. Noah was at that particular age where confidence and insecurity battled daily, where the desire to seem grown-up warred with the reality of still being very much a kid.

"We'll see what we can arrange," David said diplomatically. "But I should warn you—television sets can be pretty boring. A lot of standing around, multiple takes of the same scene, technical delays."

"I don't care," Noah said firmly. "It's still gonna be amazing."

David looked at the three faces around his dinner table—Marcus's quiet excitement, Aiden's genuine interest despite his greater focus on Marcus, and Noah's pure, unadulterated enthusiasm—and felt something warm and paternal settle in his chest.

"All right then," he said. "Let me make some calls tonight and see what kind of tour I can put together. But you're all going to have to promise to be on your best behavior. The studio has rules about visitors, and I don't want to get any of us in trouble."

"We promise," they said in unison, then looked at each other and laughed.

"I'll call you guys in the morning with the details," David said, already mentally rearranging his schedule.

As they filed out of his room, chattering about options and making plans, David caught his reflection in the mirror. He looked happier than he had in years, more relaxed despite the return to his professional responsibilities.

You'd love this chaos, wouldn't you? he thought, and for the first time in three years, the thought of Michael brought only warmth, no sting of loss.

Young love, came the imagined response, in Michael's familiar voice. *Get ready, David. Your quiet life is officially over.*

David straightened his jacket and headed downstairs, where the sound of three teenagers planning their day filled the house with exactly the kind of life Michael had always insisted it needed.

twenty-three
kids

DAVID PLACED his usual Sunday evening call to his assistant after dinner, settling into his study with a cup of coffee while the boys watched a movie in the living room. These check-ins weren't unusual—in his position, there really wasn't such a thing as "working hours."

"So how's the whole 'dad' thing going?" his assistant asked with obvious amusement in her voice.

David couldn't help but grin. "Better than I expected, actually. Though I think I'm learning more from them than they are from me."

He filled her in on a few highlights from the past week, then remembered his promise. "Oh, I need to ask about *Sunset Academy*. What's their schedule like tomorrow? I told the guys I'd see if we could peek in on their set."

He could hear her clicking through screens. "Let me pull up their call sheet... looks like they're just in rehearsals tomorrow. No heavy shooting. Should be fine to pop by if you want."

"Perfect. Can you see if Carlos can swing by the house to pick up the boys—" David caught himself and laughed. "I mean 'guys.' They're a little sensitive about being called boys."

His assistant laughed along with him. "I'll have him call before he heads up to the house. What time were you thinking?"

"I'll give them a call with the details. They won't know Carlos, but just have him let me know when he's on his way."

———

The next morning, the three teenagers stood at the studio security office getting their official visitor badges, excitement radiating from all of them in different ways. Noah was practically vibrating with anticipation, while Marcus and Aiden seemed more interested in taking in the atmosphere of being somewhere important.

"Thanks, Jerry," David said to the security guard as they collected their badges.

"No problem, Mr. Harmon," Jerry replied, then spotted Marcus. "Hey there, kid! How's it going?"

Marcus's face lit up with recognition. "Jerry! I'm good, man. Really good."

"Glad to hear it. You look great."

As they walked onto the lot, Aiden glanced at Marcus with curiosity. "How do you know him?"

"Long story," Marcus said quietly. "Tell you later."

Aiden nodded, but David noticed the way Aiden looked at Marcus—like he'd just gained some kind of street credibility. Which, David supposed, he had.

"Let's head to lunch," David said. "You guys hungry?"

Noah was, of course, always hungry. As they walked, Aiden and Marcus naturally reached for each other's hands, then quickly pulled away, remembering they were in public.

"It's okay, guys," David said with a smile. "Plenty of 'us' here on the lot."

They still looked embarrassed until they spotted two men walking out of what was obviously the costume department, pushing a rolling rack of garments in plastic bags. The men were clearly a couple, and equally clearly attractive.

"Damn, they're hot," Aiden whispered before catching himself, his face going red.

Marcus laughed and pretended to pout. "Should I be jealous?"

Aiden looked mortified. "Shit, I can't believe I just said that out loud."

David chuckled, watching Aiden's transformation from deeply closeted and worried to calling guys hot in public. It was progress, even if it came with some embarrassment.

————

The commissary was a testament to Hollywood's golden age—an art deco atrium with soaring ceilings and a display of Oscars won over the years. Noah immediately gravitated toward the trophy case.

"Holy shit, are those real?" he asked, his nose practically pressed against the glass.

"The real deal," David confirmed.

The maître d' greeted David warmly—clearly they knew each other well. Marcus found himself wondering how many meetings with famous people David had here as they were seated in a semi-circular booth with sleek lines that screamed expensive.

Looking around at the other diners—some in suits clearly working deals, others who looked like studio regulars—Noah seemed overwhelmed by the menu.

"Order whatever you like, guys," David said.

The boys stared at the fancy descriptions, looking lost.

"I'm having the cheeseburger," David said casually.

"Really?" Noah asked, sudden relief in his voice. "They have that?"

When their waiter approached—another person who clearly knew David—there was the usual light banter.

"Your kids?" the waiter asked with a knowing smile.

"They are for the summer, at least," David laughed. "What'll you have? Cheeseburgers for me and the boss here," he said, pointing to Noah, who was beaming.

Aiden and Marcus ordered the fettuccine, which David thought was a little heavy for lunch, but they were growing boys—men, he corrected himself mentally, which made him smile.

"Do famous people eat here?" Noah asked, looking around hopefully.

"Sometimes," David said. "But normally they're in their honey wagons when they're shooting."

"Honey wagons?"

"Their trailers. Their own little homes on wheels while they're working."

"Wow!"

A couple of important-looking people stopped by their table during lunch—the usual banter about David's instant family and jokes about whether these were new stars. The boys were polite but shy, wondering if these were famous directors or producers, though they didn't really know the difference.

What they did notice was just how important their uncle really was. Up until now, they knew he worked for the studio, and that was impressive. But seeing all these people interact with David, how everyone seemed to know him—he seemed much more powerful than the Uncle David they'd been living with for the past several weeks. It was impressive, and they would talk about it for years to come, especially with their friends when they got home.

"When can we go see movie stuff?" Noah asked as they finished eating.

"Let's pop by my office so I can check if it looks good to visit some soundstages," David said. What he really wanted was to check in with his assistant about the favor he'd called in with the *Sunset Academy* showrunner—a friend who owed David anyway. David had been instrumental in helping greenlight their production when they were shopping it around, and the showrunner had always been appreciative.

———

David's office was actually a suite—his assistant's area, then a living room-style space with sofas and a round table covered with scripts and promotional materials, and finally David's private office with its imposing desk, leather chairs, and various awards displayed on the walls.

Noah immediately bounded behind David's desk and spun around in the chair, laughing. "This is so fucking cool!"

Marcus was just absorbing it all. When David had found him that night, he'd known David worked at the studio, but he hadn't realized how important he was. It was overwhelming. How could someone this powerful even care about him? That night played out in his head—how David had come back in the dark, helped him, given him a home, didn't judge him, didn't ask for anything in return. He was genuinely caring, honest... he loved him.

David had been laughing with Noah when he noticed Aiden standing beside Marcus, who was staring at everything with tears streaming down his face. It wasn't that something was wrong—Marcus was finally letting out emotions he'd been holding since the day they met.

Not wanting to embarrass him, David poked his head out to his assistant. "Could you take Aiden and Noah down to grab some sodas for all of us? I'm thirsty, and I'd appreciate the favor." He touched Aiden's shoulder so he'd understand what was really being asked.

Aiden gave a quick nod of understanding while Noah bounded out the door following David's assistant. Aiden followed, looking back as if to ask "Is he okay?" David smiled to indicate he would be.

David simply stood by Marcus and let him weep silently before putting his hand on Marcus's shoulder to let him know he was there. Marcus swung around, his floodgates lifting, and slammed into David's chest, crying tears he hadn't been able to weep since the day his father had nearly killed him.

For several minutes, Marcus sobbed while David held him, rubbing his back, saying nothing but being present. Finally, Marcus began to calm down.

Through tears, wiping his eyes and nose, he began to speak. "Why? Why did you help me?"

"Because you needed it," David said simply. "And so did I."

"You?" Marcus looked around at the office, the awards, the obvious power. "You needed help? But you have everything."

David looked him right in the eyes. "Outside of all this—the power, the things, this office—it's nothing when I came home every night to... nothing."

Marcus immediately thought of those pictures of Michael, of his glasses he'd been holding just the other day, of the stories David had told him, of that emotional dinner at Disneyland. Of Aiden, and how he knew he loved him. And then it hit him—he couldn't imagine life without Aiden. How lonely, how miserable that would be.

"Oh God, I can't imagine Michael dying," he cried, the reality suddenly striking him.

And it struck David then too. He couldn't help but let out his own pain right there in his office. Michael was gone. He was really gone. And suddenly it was Marcus holding David, as if trying to absorb his pain.

Marcus was at the beginning of finding "his Michael" and hoped it would be Aiden, but he understood now that David had to survive without his Michael. And for years, he'd had no one to help him through it.

The two cried together for what seemed like an eternity.

Outside the door, Aiden stood watching. He knew to keep Noah distracted, so he asked David's assistant if he could show Noah some of the cool props in the hallway. The assistant understood completely.

Aiden felt so much for his uncle and realized that Marcus was the best thing that had ever happened to him. He loved him. And he wiped away a tear of his own, understanding more about love and loss than he'd ever expected to at seventeen.

twenty-four
lily

DAVID'S ASSISTANT had arranged with the *Sunset Academy* showrunner for the boys to see the sets, but they'd be in rehearsals until 2 PM, so she'd organized a golf cart tour of a couple of other soundstages first. One housed a daytime talk show that was off-season for the summer, its elaborate set looking oddly empty and lifeless without cameras and an audience. Another stage had carpenters building what looked like it would become a spaceship deck, though it was still all raw wood and cardboard.

Aiden was particularly interested in that one, given his love of anything science fiction. He knew sets were just fake, but they looked so real on screen. Being up close as they were being built really showed him how they did it, but also broke the illusion.

"Once you peek behind the curtain, you can't go back," David reminded him with a smile.

Marcus seemed to be floating along, doing much better since his breakdown in David's office, but his mind was clearly elsewhere. Aiden pulled him along enthusiastically, but Marcus would often look around at the enormity of everything and then steal glances at David, seemingly reminding himself this was real. David was more of a father to him than his own had ever been, but would this end? Once Aiden and Noah returned home, what would he do? Would David let him stay? Would he need to find a new place?

And then he realized Aiden would be leaving to go home. Shit. He'd been so caught up in the present that he'd forgotten about that inevitable future. So many emotions crashed over him, but he didn't want to be a downer, so he did his best to immerse himself in all the things Aiden was pointing out and enjoying. He had to be there for Aiden—happy, present —even if his heart and head were more confused than ever.

Noah was like a kid in a candy store when they entered the company store—basically a mini-mart on the lot where staff could grab snacks or drinks, but which also sold t-shirts and other tchotchkes with the studio logo emblazoned on them. Noah immediately found three different t-shirts and a keychain he wanted, especially for a couple of his friends back home.

"How are you gonna pay for it?" Aiden asked.

Noah looked over at David with hopeful eyes. "Uh... can I...?"

"Of course," David laughed, giving Noah a hard time until the four-teen-year-old's face turned red and he stuck his tongue out at his brother. Noah was still growing up, and David hoped he wouldn't try to do it too fast.

David's assistant whispered something in David's ear, and Marcus noticed David nodding, seemingly pleased.

"Guys," David said, "I think we can go to another set now. They're just about finished."

"*Sunset Academy*?!" Noah's excitement was palpable.

The cart took them over to Soundstage 21, and they entered through a corner door. Inside, it was quiet—really quiet. Dark except for a few overhead lights. Noah noticed they were behind sets with cross slats over plywood panels stamped "SA" on each one.

"This is sooooo cool!" he whispered.

"Yeah, plywood is cool," Aiden said sarcastically, earning a middle finger from his younger brother as they followed David around a corner. Marcus snickered—a break from his earlier seriousness. He loved his new little brother.

"Oh... my... God!"

Noah was gobsmacked. They were standing dead center in the school lobby—the very place where the opening of each episode started. This was where his favorite characters stood every week. Josh and Carly and... most especially Taylor, played by...

Lily Chen stepped out from an off-set door carrying her script, as if she was coming to an appointment with David—which she was. He had arranged it, asking if she wouldn't mind doing him a favor and just saying hi to his nephew who was quite a fan. She'd been told he was fourteen, just like her, and visiting from Boston. He wouldn't be a crazy fan, and it would be just for a minute.

Lily was naturally friendly, if a bit shy, but she liked David. He'd always treated her like she was an adult, even though she knew she wasn't yet. He wasn't patronizing, and she appreciated that he didn't try to push her into things like some in the business did.

"Sure," she'd said, chewing bubble gum. "I can stop by before I head home."

Noah was catatonic. This was Lily. THE Lily. On THE set. And he was standing right there.

"Hi David, I hope I'm not late," she said, walking over to them.

"Not at all. We just arrived ourselves. Thanks for stopping by." David smiled warmly. "I'd like to introduce you to my nephew Marcus—"

Marcus had never heard David refer to him as anyone, let alone his nephew, like he was family. It really touched him.

"—and Aiden—"

He noticed David referring to his boyfriend as his nephew as well, and it warmed his heart. Instinctively, he realized he was holding Marcus's hand and saw Lily notice. Suddenly embarrassed, he blurted out, "Marcus and I aren't related. I mean, it's not like..." He was digging a hole for himself.

Marcus stepped up. "Aiden is my boyfriend. We're not related, is what he's trying to say."

David snickered and shot Lily a look like "I'll tell you later," and she smiled, even giggled at how flustered Aiden was.

"You two look cute together," she said simply.

Aiden, who knew who she was but wasn't really a fan, suddenly became one. "We look cute together? We do? Oh my God, she thinks we look cute together!"

Marcus caught a bit of Aiden's sudden joy, and Lily laughed. "Yes, you do. Aiden and Marcus, unrelated boyfriends."

David snickered at the whole exchange.

Noah was still in shock. Normally, he would've jabbed at his brother over all that blubbering, but he couldn't believe Lily was actually here, talking to them.

She noticed and turned toward him. "And let me guess, you're Noah?"

How did she know his name? OMG, she was speaking to him.

"Noah?" David asked, stepping forward to see if he was okay.

"Uh... yeah... yeah, I'm Noah." He was instantly in love.

Lily turned to David, smiling. "Is he always this cute when he meets a girl?"

She was pushing his buttons, but she never really got the opportunity to do that with boys her age. Her life was so carefully planned—on set, on panels, in interviews.

Aiden and Marcus laughed.

David giggled, knowing exactly what Lily was doing. But he also noticed she wasn't just being "Lily the actress"—she seemed like she meant the question.

"Well, I don't know," David said playfully. "Are you, Noah?"

Noah turned redder than a tomato. Had she just called him cute?

twenty-five
discovery

"I... UH..." Noah stammered, still red-faced from Lily's question about whether he was always cute when meeting girls. "I don't really... I mean, I haven't met that many girls."

Lily smiled, and it wasn't her practiced TV smile—it was genuine, a little shy even. "Me neither. I mean, I don't meet many boys. My life is kinda..." She gestured around the soundstage. "This."

David watched the exchange with growing amusement and warmth. Both kids were clearly nervous, but there was something sweet happening between them.

"Hey," Lily said suddenly, looking at David. "Do you think we could show them around the set a little? I mean, if that's okay?"

"If you don't mind taking the time," David replied. "I know you were heading home."

"Nah, it's cool. I like showing off our world." She turned to Noah with a grin. "Wanna see where all the magic happens?"

Noah nodded so enthusiastically that Marcus snorted with laughter behind him.

"Okay, so this is obviously the main lobby," Lily said, walking backward as she talked, completely comfortable in her element. "This is where we film most of the drama between classes. You know, like when Taylor finds out that Josh has been lying about auditioning for that summer program?"

Noah nodded eagerly. "Oh yeah! That was such bullshit—I mean, sorry—that was so messed up. Taylor deserved better."

"Right?" Lily's eyes lit up. "Finally, someone who gets it! Everyone always says Josh is the good guy, but he totally played her."

As they walked, Marcus leaned over to Aiden. "Dude, your brother is actually talking to her like a normal person."

"I know," Aiden whispered back. "It's kinda amazing."

David hung back slightly, enjoying watching Noah discover that his celebrity crush was just a fourteen-year-old girl who happened to be on TV. And watching Lily light up at having someone her age who actually understood the show.

"So over here," Lily continued, leading them past the main set to a smaller area, "this is supposed to be the music practice rooms. But honestly, they're so tiny. Like, how are five people supposed to fit in here for a scene?"

"Yeah, and the acoustics would be terrible," Noah said, then immediately looked embarrassed. "I mean, I don't know anything about acoustics, but—"

"No, you're totally right!" Lily interrupted. "It drives me crazy. We're supposed to be this amazing performing arts school, but half the stuff doesn't make sense if you actually know anything about music or theater."

Noah grinned. "So you actually know about that stuff? Like, for real?"

"I've been taking voice lessons since I was eight," Lily said, then added more quietly, "though sometimes I wonder if I'd be doing it if I wasn't on the show, you know?"

There was something vulnerable in that admission, and Noah seemed to sense it. "Do you like it? The singing, I mean?"

Lily considered this. "Yeah, I do. But it's hard to tell sometimes what I like and what I'm supposed to like." She shook her head, as if clearing away serious thoughts. "God, that sounds so pretentious. Sorry."

"No, it doesn't," Noah said earnestly. "It sounds honest."

David felt his heart squeeze a little. Watching Noah navigate his first real conversation with a girl he liked, seeing him be genuinely kind and thoughtful—it reminded David of why he'd grown so attached to Elena's boys.

"Wanna see the cafeteria set?" Lily asked. "It's where we filmed that gross lunch scene last week."

"Oh man, that looked disgusting," Noah laughed. "Was it actually gross?"

"Worse. They use this fake food that's been sitting under lights for hours. By take twelve, everything looks like plastic." Lily made a face. "We all just pretend to eat it."

As they walked to the next set, Aiden noticed that both Lily and Noah had relaxed considerably. Noah wasn't stumbling over his words as much, and Lily seemed less like she was performing and more like she was just hanging out.

"So," Lily said as they reached the cafeteria set, "what's Boston like? I've never been anywhere on the East Coast."

"Really?" Noah seemed surprised. "But you're famous. Don't you travel everywhere?"

Lily laughed, but not unkindly. "It's not like that. I travel to film festivals and premieres and stuff, but it's always work. I've never just... gone somewhere to see it, you know?"

"Boston's cool," Noah said thoughtfully. "I mean, it's home, so it's normal to me. But there's all this history everywhere. Like, you'll just be walking down the street and there's a building that's older than this whole state."

"That's so cool. I'd love to see that sometime."

"Yeah?" Noah's face lit up. "I could show you around if you ever came out there. I mean, if you wanted. Not that you'd want to hang out with some random kid from—"

"Noah," Lily interrupted gently. "You're not some random kid. You're David's nephew, and you actually listen when I talk about stuff. That's not as common as you'd think."

Behind them, Marcus nudged Aiden. "Did she just call him not random?"

"Shut up," Aiden whispered, but he was smiling.

David was amazed by what he was witnessing. In the span of twenty minutes, Noah had gone from starstruck and tongue-tied to having a genuine conversation with someone he'd idolized. And Lily seemed to be discovering what it was like to talk to someone her age who saw her as a person first and a celebrity second.

"Hey," Lily said suddenly, looking a little nervous herself. "Do you... I mean, would you maybe want to exchange numbers? I don't really have friends who aren't in the business, and it might be cool to have someone normal to text with."

Noah's eyes went wide. "You want my number?"

"Only if you want to," Lily said quickly. "I know it's probably weird—"

"No!" Noah said, perhaps a little too loudly. "I mean, yes. I mean, I'd like that. A lot."

They pulled out their phones, and David watched as two fourteen-year-olds figured out how to exchange contact information like it was the most important transaction in the world.

"I should probably get going," Lily said finally, glancing at the large clock on the stage wall. "My mom's picking me up in like ten minutes."

"Yeah, of course," Noah said, and David could hear the disappointment in his voice.

"But maybe I could text you later?" Lily asked. "I mean, if that's okay?"

"That would be awesome," Noah said, his smile returning full force.

"It was really nice meeting all of you," Lily said, turning to include Marcus and Aiden. "And David, thanks for setting this up. This was way more fun than I expected."

"Thank you for taking the time," David replied. "I think you made Noah's entire summer."

As Lily gathered her script and headed toward the exit, she turned back one more time. "Hey Noah?"

"Yeah?"

"For what it's worth, I think you're pretty good at talking to girls."

And with that, she was gone, leaving Noah standing in the middle of the *Sunset Academy* cafeteria set with a grin that threatened to split his face in half.

"Dude," Marcus said, breaking the silence. "I think you just got your first girlfriend."

"She's not my girlfriend," Noah protested, but his blush suggested he wouldn't mind if she were.

"Yet," Aiden added with a grin.

David put his arm around Noah's shoulders. "How do you feel?'

Noah thought about it for a moment. "Like maybe I'm not as hopeless as I thought."

"You were never hopeless," David said gently. "You just needed to meet the right person to talk to."

As they made their way back toward the golf cart, Noah couldn't stop grinning. He had Lily Chen's phone number. Lily Chen thought he was good at talking to girls. Lily Chen wanted to be friends with him.

Maybe being fourteen wasn't so bad after all.

twenty-six
fumble

DAVID PULLED into his garage around 8 PM, exhausted from a long day at the lot. Since he'd spent the morning and early afternoon with the boys, he'd needed to stay late to catch up on everything that had piled up. As he walked in from the garage, he could hear the boys giving each other shit somewhere in the living room—obviously another video game competition, judging by the trash talk interspersed with laughter and plenty of razzing, especially directed at Noah.

"What's the matter, loverboy?" he heard Aiden give his brother grief, followed by a retort from Noah that Aiden could promptly fuck himself, quickly followed by Marcus saying, "I bet you wish you could fuck someone..." and loads of laughter from Marcus and Aiden at Noah's expense.

David shook his head. Was this what parenting was? Stepping in to stop it? Or letting it play out? It seemed like they were just being boys, but...

"Hi guys, miss me?" he yelled from the kitchen, surveying the nearly empty pizza boxes and a couple of half-empty two-liter bottles of Coke. Typical. "Did you save me any?" he called out at the empty boxes.

Marcus ran into the kitchen, switching tone from his prior trash-talking self. David was at least happy he was in a better mood than he'd been earlier at the lot.

Noah followed with a less than happy disposition, but David realized it wasn't that he was mad at Marcus or Aiden—he was mad at himself for fumbling the video game. He was normally the king master.

Aiden appeared around the corner just after his brother, running up to David and giving him a hug.

"What was that for? I like it, but..."

"Just welcoming you home. And... well... thanks for taking us around today." Aiden looked suddenly like a little kid happy to see his dad home from the office, and David's heart warmed. God, he wished Michael were here.

"Well, thank you. Have a good time?"

"Yeah, the sets were really cool, but I think the best part was watching Noah meet his future wife!" Aiden laughed, enjoying teasing his brother.

"Noah and Lily sitting in a tree," Marcus sang horribly, "K-I-S-S-I-N-G!" Aiden joined him in taunting their little brother.

"Shut up! She's not my..." Noah's face was red.

Ah, that's the issue with Noah, David realized. No wonder he was fumbling at the video game. He's "in like" with Lily. He's too young to be in love, so... in-like it is.

Michael, he thought, would've nudged him and called bullshit. Noah was perfectly old enough to fall in love, even if he didn't know what it meant yet. So treat it seriously—this is a pivotal age, Michael would've demanded.

David reprimanded himself and asked the boys to help him clean up the pizza mess while he asked Noah if he'd do him a favor. Really, he didn't need anything, but he wanted a moment alone with Marcus and Aiden.

"Would you run out to my car and grab the box that's full of papers in the trunk, please? I've got something I want to show you."

Noah shrugged and started toward the mudroom.

"Noah? You'll need these," David said and threw him the keys, but even those Noah fumbled, nearly tripping as they fell to the floor. Aiden and Marcus pointed and laughed.

"What's the matter, Noah? Thinking about Lily?" they teased.

"Shut up!" Noah reddened again and grabbed the keys.

Once he left, David looked over at the boys.

"Listen, I know it's funny to poke at him, but he gave you two your space when he caught you falling for each other."

Marcus and Aiden stopped in their tracks. They hadn't really shared that Noah had caught them almost kissing and suddenly wondered just how much David knew. But he made a point—teasing your little brother was a requirement in the job description of being the older brother, but this was new territory for Noah.

"Besides," David continued, "Noah doesn't have any experience meeting someone like Lily, and she, honestly, doesn't either."

"What? Meeting a dork like Noah?" Aiden laughed, but David remained serious and he quickly stopped.

"I'm serious. She's just a kid, even if she's a star on display for the world. She doesn't have many friends, and I think it's sweet they got along. So can you two help him rather than tear him down, please? At least for me?"

Marcus looked down, his conscience kicking in. Aiden followed suit. "Yeah, I'm sorry. Me too."

"Don't need to be sorry to me. It's Noah that matters."

They nodded just as Noah slammed the garage door shut and appeared carrying a huge cardboard banker's box. He slammed the weighty box on the counter and set David's keys down.

"Thank you, Noah. That was kind of you. Now, let me see if I can find it..."

Everyone gathered around the counter, watching him dig through what looked like boring paperwork.

"Ah, here it is." David pulled out a slender binder with a plain light blue cover and a title: *Sunset Academy, Season II, Episode 14 - The Great Food Fight.*

He handed it to Noah. "Here. After you left, I stopped by and picked this up."

Noah's eyes were as wide as oranges. "How did you g—" He couldn't finish.

"What is it?" Marcus asked from across the counter.

"Just the greatest thing EVER!" Noah interjected.

"I thought Noah might like a copy of the script from the episode he and Lily were talking about earlier."

Aiden looked impressed. "Wow! That's really cool."

Noah suddenly looked a little embarrassed holding the script, seeing Marcus and Aiden gawking at him and expecting more shit from them.

David noticed and gave both of them an eye nod, indicating perhaps it was time they had a little chat.

"Well, I'm going to get out of this suit and then find something for dinner." David excused himself before anyone could say otherwise.

Aiden was the first to speak: "Uh, Noah, sorry for teasing you." Marcus joined in.

"I think it's really cool that you got to meet Lily. She seems really nice," Marcus added.

"Shut up, you guys. You're just gonna be assholes again." Noah said, sure this was a ploy to prank him.

Aiden crossed around the counter and came to his brother. Aiden was older and an inch or so taller, but Noah was making ground. Nonetheless, he had to look up to see his older brother eye to eye.

"Noah, I'm legit sorry. I mean, well, you couldn't really give Marcus and me shit when you, uh, well, caught us..."

"Tongue fucking?" Noah spit out, still unsure if they were trying to prank him, but starting to calm down.

Marcus giggled and looked down, feeling caught.

Aiden choked back a little laugh of surprise at the phrase. Noah had always been the one to curse more than him, but that was a little sharp. Still, he probably deserved it.

"Listen, you little shit, I'm trying to apologize." Noah looked up at him just like the older brother/younger brother dynamic required.

Marcus intervened, pushing between the two and putting his arm around Noah, feeling how tense he was. Damn, he thought to himself, he really is upset. He hadn't realized how much their stupid shit-talking had affected him.

Marcus squeezed him a bit, and after a moment of Noah tensing, he began to loosen up. Something about the contact made Noah realize Marcus was being genuine.

"Listen, Noah, I'm sorry. I really am. No pranks. No bullshit. I'm a stupid asshole sometimes and I was just giving you shit. But seriously," he turned Noah and bent down to be on eye level, "I think it's way cool you got to meet Lily, and whatever I can do to help you, I will."

"How?" Noah was warming up but remained skeptical.

"Well, I dunno. If you ever wanna talk about her or something..."

"What would you know about a girl? You're gay."

Aiden laughed—typical Noah. He stepped in to tag-team takeover for Marcus.

"Remember when you were talking to me about Marcus a couple of weeks ago?"

Marcus didn't know anything about this and was eager to hear.

"Uh, yeah."

"And you did something that really helped me."

"I did?" Noah was now puzzled, all his anger gone.

"Yeah, you made me feel like it was okay to be myself, and you didn't care."

"Like, gay?"

Aiden blushed a little but nodded. "Yeah."

"Like that's any big deal. So you like dick. Who cares?"

Marcus laughed, not expecting that. Aiden stifled his own laugh but continued.

"Well, yeah, I guess. But you helped me feel okay about being Marcus's boyfriend."

"So you're officially boyfriends now? I mean, like you both said it?" Noah grilled.

Marcus looked over and stepped up behind Aiden, grabbing him by the waist as he leaned over to look at Noah. "Yes. Aiden is my official boyfriend." And he kissed Noah's brother on the cheek, causing him to blush. Talking with Noah about it was one thing, but to have Marcus kiss him right in front of him was another, even if it was a simple kiss on the cheek.

Noah didn't bat an eye this time—no pretend gross-out or covering his eyes and laughing. Noah just smiled, happy for both of them.

"Lily was right," he said aloud softly without realizing he had.

"What?" Aiden asked.

Typical Noah would normally respond "Oh? Nothing..." and change the subject. This was pretty "serious" stuff, not some joking kids' conversation. However, his mind went back to earlier that day and hearing Lily say that his brother and his boyfriend looked good together. They did, he thought. So he decided to tell them: "She said you two look good together, remember?"

Both Aiden and Marcus smiled and looked down a little embarrassed. This time Noah spoke up again: "You do look good together. Seriously."

Aiden nearly wept but held it together.

Marcus, who still held Aiden from behind, rested his head on Aiden's shoulder.

Aiden finally said, "Noah, we won't tease you anymore, because we think you and Lily look good together too."

Noah scoffed. "I'm like just some dumb kid from Boston. She's like a star and all that."

"I don't think so," Marcus said politely. "Didn't you see the way she was looking at you?"

"She was?" Noah was clueless but now a little hopeful.

"Totally," Aiden added. "She was like so comfortable around you, and—"

Marcus took over. "Remember, she wanted to keep showing you around, talking to you and all that."

Noah did remember and wished she could've stayed.

"And she's already asked if you'd like to come to a taping of the next episode," David interjected from the doorway. He'd been watching and listening and marveling at how tender and lovely this whole thing had been.

Noah spun to him. "What?!"

"Tomorrow. Starts at 9 AM. You'd need to go to work with me early, if you'd like. Just an option."

"Oh my GOD, yes! That's... that's..." He couldn't speak, he was so excited.

Aiden and Marcus had broken free of each other and were walking over to David, all smiles.

"You two can go as well, but again, it can be boring. Lots of waiting while they do another take or set up lights, but you're welcome to go if—"

Aiden almost yelled out "yes" as loud as his younger brother but then saw the scene as it might play out in a split second. He and Marcus would be "in the way," playing big brothers, interrupting Noah with Lily—if Noah could even see her again. She would be working.

"Uh," Aiden said, turning back to Marcus and giving him eyes that said "follow my lead," "that sounds really cool, but Marcus and I had something we already planned tomorrow. I suppose we could try and move it, but..."

Marcus got it and seconded his excuse. "Oh yeah, I mean, I could call and see if we could reschedule, but..."

"What thing?" Noah asked innocently, wondering why he hadn't been invited.

"Well then, Noah, would you like to go? You can head into the lot with me, but I'll leave early."

"Uh, yeah, I would," he said, looking puzzled at his brother and Marcus, but then turned to ask David what time and if he'd attend the taping as well.

"6 AM, buddy. Sorry, but I've got work to do. Unfortunately, I will have meetings, so I won't be able to sit with you at the taping."

Noah couldn't imagine doing something as big as this alone. He was fourteen and felt old enough, but his mom would never, in a million years, let him go alone to something like that. It seemed odd Uncle David would. He knew he was a cool uncle, but this was huge. And then he thought about meeting Lily again. Maybe he'd get to talk to her? Probably not. She'd be working, and he'd probably be sitting in the audience. Well, at least he'd get to see her. And to see an actual taping of his favorite show! Wow!

"That's cool. I wanna go." He lit up again.

David winked at Aiden and Marcus, thanking them for opting out. He had another surprise for Noah, but he'd find out tomorrow. In reality, he had a surprise for both Noah and Lily.

twenty-seven
lights, camera...

NOAH FOLLOWED David as they walked from his car in the garage over to his office. He remembered the way from yesterday. As they passed a few people, he kept noticing how others would address his uncle by saying "Good morning, Mr. Harmon." It seemed weird when he just called him Uncle David.

David checked his email quickly and then took them over to the commissary for breakfast. A quick meal of fruit and coffee for him while he suggested the fresh-made waffles for Noah, who eagerly agreed. Loads of syrup and blueberries followed by a Coke. How he could put away that stuff this early in the morning puzzled David, but he enjoyed spending time with just the two of them. Aiden and Marcus were still sleeping when they left, but he was sure they'd keep each other company today... and his mind immediately went back to their safe sex talk. Oh well, he exhaled. He had to trust them and put out whatever hijinks they were bound to get themselves into would be alright, and resisted checking in on the security cameras around the property.

"Noah, this is where I'm going to leave you. I've got an important call to make with New York. I'll plan on picking you up later today, okay?"

Noah nearly panicked. "Uh, where do I go? I mean, where is the taping?"

David smiled. He expected this, quietly excited about it. He only wished he could be there to witness. Noticing Sara pop in the commissary doorway, he motioned toward her. "Remember Sara from yesterday?" Noah followed his hand and caught sight of her, at least recognizing the face.

"She'll take care of getting you to the taping. It's not scheduled to start for another couple of hours, but she can get you settled, okay?"

Noah was a little hesitant. This was him doing this day alone. Was he old enough? He felt he was, maybe, but this was new.

"Okay, but do I come here for lunch?"

"Sara will get you squared away. I promise. And you can text me if you have any problems. I'll be in meetings, but I'll reply when I can."

Noah seemed nervous, and David didn't want to scare him too much. "It'll be okay. I'm just in my office over there," pointing in the general direction they had come from. "And if you forget everything, just text me, okay?"

Noah just nodded, a little uncertain.

"You've got this. I trust you."

Those were the most magical words Noah had heard. David trusted him? A little kid? Was he a little kid still? He perked up, his confidence building.

"Noah! Nice to see you again," Sara said. "How was your breakfast?"

He smiled. It was nice she remembered his name. "It was good."

"That's great!"

"Well, I'll leave you to it then." David excused himself and winked at Sara, who knew the itinerary today.

"Hey Noah, I was thinking you might be able to help us out a little. It's still a few hours before taping, so do you mind?"

"Uh, sure." He was uncertain what he was supposed to do.

Sara took him in a golf cart to a building just down from the soundstage he remembered meeting Lily at yesterday. It felt good to ride in the golf cart, just him with Sara driving.

"So, we were wondering," as they got out of the cart, "if you'd like to be an extra today? We need another boy who is in the classroom scene."

"WHAT?"

Sara was all smiles. "Yeah, you don't need to do much, just sit at one of the desks in the back and do homework as the cast has a scene in front."

"Are you serious?"

"Totally."

Noah could only nod. He was going to BE ON THE SHOW? His mind was going to explode.

"Great. Well, we've got to get you to hair and makeup and then wardrobe."

"Really?" This was all... this had to be a dream. Hair and makeup? Him?

The next two hours were a blur. He sat in a chair as a stylist brushed and sprayed his hair to be more "California surfer meets skateboarder meets boy-next-door" looking. Then someone put makeup on him. The hardest part was whatever they were doing to his eyes, because the brush tickled. There were a couple of other guys his age sitting in the chairs next to him, but everyone seemed so caught up in their looks, the only people who talked were the stylists.

Someone came and introduced themselves as an assistant and walked the three down to another room where a couple of hangers of clothes awaited them. "This one is for you, Noah," she found his name on a clipboard, and then handed the others out to his fellow extras. "Change into these and I'll come get you in a few minutes."

Noah could not believe he was dressing up to be on set. Just wait till his friends heard about this back home. Heard about it, he thought, just wait till they SEE him on TV!

The three extras were taken into a different door of the soundstage he was on just the day before and told to wait in a small room with a fridge, some chairs and a sofa. Lots of mirrors and lights around them flanked one wall while a radio played somewhere softly, although no one paid attention. They all seemed excited to be doing this.

An eternity seemed to go by. Occasionally the assistant would pop her head in and ask how they were doing... it'd only be a little bit... But Noah didn't mind. He couldn't wait to do whatever it was he was going to do.

Finally, the production assistant took them to the set. It was so different than yesterday, all lit up. Cords and cameras and wires everywhere. There were actually those folding chairs with people's names on them just like in the movies, and behind was an entire crowd of people watching the set and the TVs hanging from the ceiling. This was so weird.

A man with a backwards ballcap came over and spoke to the three extras. They were to sit in the last three classroom desks and pretend to be working hard on homework, flipping through textbooks for answers, writing things down, paying no attention to the action up front. Start when they hear 'Action' and keep going until they hear 'Cut'. Simple. Think they could do that? Everyone nodded eagerly. Great! Why don't you go take your places?

Noah sat on the rightmost desk in the back, recognizing the classroom. He'd watched this very classroom many times on the show before, but now it was real... and he was in it. Not just in it, but he was a Student!

Just then, the crowd erupted in applause and he heard someone speaking over a microphone, although it was hard to hear from the set. Something about welcome back, now they're ready to shoot scene 3, classroom trouble, and give it up for... and then Noah saw the three main stars walk out, including Lily, although she had her back to him. He gulped. I can't believe I'm here. This is impossible.

The stars waved and then went to take their places. The camera moved in and the sound guys seemed to swoop out from the ceiling. The lights were bright, the audience quieted, and suddenly he heard "And... Action!"

Noah began to "study," writing on his paper tablet in front of him the word "Lily" and little hearts, then remembered to pretend to look up something in his textbook, so he flipped the pages, scanned something and then began to write again. He wanted to watch so badly, but kept to his chore, flipping the page and then he noticed a shadow. Someone was walking his way and then...

Lily looked at him in near excitement.

Someone yelled "Cut!" and Lily looked at him. Surprised doesn't even begin to express... "NOAH? What... what... how?"

"Hi!" He had no idea what to say. She was so pretty.

Someone mentioned to reset the set and let's pick it back up at the crossover, whatever that was.

Lily looked at him with a thousand questions, but smiled, just coming out of her professional actor persona enough to say "I'm so happy to see you" before mouthing "be right back" and then taking her spot on stage.

"And... Action!"

Noah almost forgot to pretend to study, but picked up his pencil and began to write Lily's name again. He could hear the dialogue between the stars up front and then the shadow again, and there was Lily, right in front of him, acting.

Her character was saying something about she'd rather go out with anyone but him.

The other character retorting something like "Oh yeah? Like who?"

"Whom," she corrected and then turned and pointed directly at Noah, who was still "studying."

"Him!" she said. Noah shot his head up instinctively. Was she still in character as Taylor or was this actually Lily speaking? He suddenly remembered he had been told to keep his eyes down and pretend to study, so he put his embarrassed and red face back into his notebook and looked overly serious in his study. It was comical and the audience laughed aloud. Lily nearly giggled, but kept in character.

"Cut!"

That wasn't supposed to happen and Lily spun around and finally let out a laugh. Noah apologized as the production assistant came up to remind him he was supposed to not look up, but someone else popped by. Lily spoke with him and then walked over and introduced Noah to him—the director. The writers loved what he did as did the audience. Would he mind doing it again? This time, perhaps a little bigger so the camera could really see.

Noah's mind was blown. Lily and the director both looked at him as if willing him to do it. "Of course, sure."

Lily leaned down and whispered "That was fantastic! You're a real pro" and winked.

"Reset everything. Quiet audience. And... Action."

Noah studied, writing things, but this time he was paying extra attention to the dialogue. Suddenly he saw the shadow from the lights. Lily was walking his way.

"Him!" she said and pointed. Noah's head shot up, eyes bulged in surprise more than even before and he mouthed "Me?!" in mock shock. The audience roared and he could see in Lily's eyes her holding back a laugh. She kept her dialogue going and the scene ended.

Lily came back to see him. "OMG that was sooo funny!"

Noah was suddenly shy. "You think? I just wanted to help."

"I gotta run to get ready for the next scene. You're staying, right? Let's meet up after, okay?"

Noah could only nod, and she ran off, looking back at him before she disappeared around the set.

Noah got up to follow the production assistant off stage when the director pulled him aside.

"No..." he'd forgotten his name.

"Noah," he offered meekly in his costume.

"Yeah, Noah. Uh, this is Charles and Linda. They're the writers here."

Noah shook hands as he'd been taught long ago and they smiled, clearly busy, but seemed to want something.

Linda spoke first. "How would you like to help us out one more time?"

"Uh, sure. I can pretend to do my homework..."

Charles interjected. "We'd like you to do just a tiny bit more, if you're okay with that?"

"Uh, sure. Like what?"

"Are you a SAG member?"

Noah had no clue what that was. "I uh..."

Linda and Charles spoke softly with the director when they saw the look on his face, but he somehow remembered Uncle David mentioning if he needed anything to text. He didn't have his phone, but spoke politely, interrupting the three.

"My uncle David works here. He probably knows." He had no clue what they were talking about, but figured David would.

The director repeated "Your uncle works here?"

"Yeah. David, uh, Harmon."

The three stopped as if Noah had turned into an alien.

After a moment, the director asked if Noah wouldn't mind sitting down for a moment. "Here, take my chair." It was the fold-out chair for the director. Noah was sitting in the director's chair! This was too much.

Phone calls and whatever the people around him were doing, he just watched as someone was telling jokes to the crowd and reminding them of the next scene coming up soon.

Noah looked over and there was Uncle David walking onto the set, people seemingly stopping to notice him there, like he was some powerful man walking in their presence.

The director grabbed his hand and shook, thanking David for stopping by before they all stood before a made-up Noah in costume sitting in the director's chair wondering what he did wrong.

"Well, it looks like you got yourself in this one now, Noah," David said but through smiles.

"I didn't do anything, I swear! They just asked something about a swag or something and I didn't know what they were talking about. I promise! Am I in trouble?"

David's heart nearly broke. "No, no, nothing like that. What they want is to have you do a scene with Lily. But you need to be a member of the acting union. Of which I can arrange."

Noah's eyes went wide. "You're kidding, right?"

"No, they're serious. But we don't have a lot of time, kiddo. Normally, I'd call and ask your mom, but... well, would you like to?"

"What?"

"Do the scene? With Lily?"

"Really? You're serious."

"Well, Roger seems to want you," waving the director over followed by the writers Linda and Charles.

"Roger, what would Noah here need to do?"

Linda stepped in. "Well, here's what we have in mind and we think the audience will love it!"

The next two minutes, they explained his role. Small, but it would be impactful and set the tone of the story better than what they had planned originally.

Noah couldn't believe it. "Sure, I'll do it. Just tell me what to say and do."

"Fantastic!"

"Roger, I'll get Sara to give Susan a call over at SAG and we'll get it cleared. Go ahead."

"Perfect!"

"Noah, why don't you follow Priscilla back to makeup for a touchup, but we'll need you back here in five, okay?"

He could only nod. This was crazy. All around him was activity—crews setting up lights, the crowd was being warmed up and laughing. Someone was moving the desks on the set and he was following Priscilla, the same production assistant who originally got him in the first place, back to makeup. He was sure he was in a dream.

twenty-eight
mornings

MARCUS AWOKE BEFORE AIDEN, but he didn't get out of bed until the need to pee couldn't be pushed away. Looking at his clock by the bed, it was already 10:13. For a moment, he had forgotten that Noah would be heading in early with David, but it popped in his head just as he was putting his shorts on to head downstairs. He dropped the shorts back on the floor and walked out into the hall, turning left to head down to find breakfast. Pausing, he realized there were no sounds to be heard other than the muted sound from the outside hills that seemed to be omnipresent. No toaster pop, no microwave beep, no television rabble... Aiden must still be asleep.

He debated waking him. They had settled into a nightly routine of sitting poolside talking about this and that and nothing more than just to be together. Often, Aiden would wind up laying his head on his lap, playing circles on Marcus's legs with his thumb as they told old jokes and shared stories of days gone by.

David and Noah aren't here... why not go wake him up? They had intentionally decided they weren't going to sneak around—no popping into each other's room at night to... well, to be honest, have sex. Although they desperately wanted to... desperately... and had begun talking openly about it, but only at night around the pool when there were no ears to hear. But David's talk with them a while back about safe sex and being responsible... well, it resonated. They somehow felt they'd be letting him down if they pretended they weren't doing anything yet fucking like bunnies at night behind closed doors.

To be honest, Marcus thought, he wasn't entirely sure how to go about it. Like, he knew the basics, but like... what was he supposed to do? Whisper into Aiden's ear "let's fuck!" He laughed to himself. Could you imagine? He thought and smiled. He paused... maybe he could imagine. Instead of turning left, he made a right and walked down to Aiden's room. It was only a couple of doors down. He'd been there what seemed a million times. But now it seemed like a doorway to another dimension. Something seemed naughty, yet enticing, like he was going to be "an adult" if he walked in there, yet there was also something that tempered his expectations. He didn't really want to "just fuck." He wanted... he shook his head just thinking the words as they seemed corny as hell, but they were the only ones he could conjure in his brain... he wanted to make love. He let out an audible gasp, more a stifled giggle than anything. What was he? Sixty-seven? Isn't that how old people talked about fucking? Somewhere in his head, he could hear David correcting him... making love with another is different than fucking someone... just think about it.

Marcus slowly turned the handle and opened the door. He didn't know why he hadn't done this a long time ago, but then realized if he had, Noah or David would bound to see him... or he'd be worried about getting caught. David didn't say they couldn't have sex, but he spoke to them honestly about what that meant, both physically and emotionally. Marcus didn't feel like he'd be disappointed in them, but he'd really want them to mean it if they began having sex.

Geesh, he thought, still holding to the handle to Aiden's room. Where the hell did my conscience come from? He smiled. Truth be told, he was a regular scaredy-cat, honestly.

Aiden's room was dimly lit, the light from the late morning sun filtering through the modern shade that was almost blackout, but not quite. Aiden liked keeping his room cold—not cool... cold. Like it was freezing in here and it was in the eighties outside. Maybe it was because he was from Boston and used to the winters? Whatever the reason, he was bundled under a thick down duvet that was off-white, just like everything in the room. This was a guest room, of course, but Aiden had a few little touches that made it his, especially some of his junk he'd bought since they arrived: a small painting he picked up for ten dollars from a street vendor in Hollywood of the LA skyline, a couple of magnets meant for a fridge, but he had them stuck to the metal desk legs (the only place he could in the room) that he picked up for his friends back home while they were down in Disneyland. He had his Jansport backpack in the corner that he kept his socks and underwear in still, even after washing it in their laundry rather than packing it away. Marcus asked about it once and he replied that's how he had them back home in Boston. Marcus guessed he didn't have any drawers.

But what caught his eye was the kangaroo stuffed animal he got at Disney—part of Winnie the Pooh's family. He bought it saying it reminded him of growing up... he'd always bounce. Marcus imagined a young Aiden bouncing around and smiled when he heard. It was endearing.

Marcus closed the door quietly and walked in the semi-dark room over to Aiden's queen bed. Sitting down on the edge, he looked at his boyfriend asleep... his hair tousled... his face beautiful... breathing peace-fully... looking so content. God, he could watch him forever... and he wondered if somehow, Aiden could stay in California. It was a stupid thought, but... God, he loved him.

Marcus couldn't help himself. He had pushed aside the thought. He couldn't love him. He was leaving soon. They'd say how they'll make it work, they'd FaceTime and all that. And maybe he could find a job to save money to fly out once in a while. But Aiden was still finishing up high school. And Marcus... well, he needed to finish. And if he had a job, he wouldn't be able to take time off to actually see him... and...

His mind raced a myriad of thoughts, always jumbling itself.

"What are you staring at?"

"Huh?"

Aiden asked again in his sleepy voice. Marcus hadn't noticed he'd woken and was still clinging tightly to his duvet, unable to break free of his cocoon.

"I was... well..." Marcus realized he didn't have a good response. He'd violated Aiden's space and was sitting on the edge of his bed staring at him.

"Do you always break into guys' rooms and sit on their bed in your underwear staring?" He smiled a sleepy smile.

Marcus suddenly realized he was sitting there with practically nothing on and became embarrassed. "Uh... no... I uh..."

"I'm just teasing. Wanna snuggle?"

Aiden opened up the duvet enough to let his boyfriend join him, cuddling up behind him like a spoon and bringing the duvet back to protect them both.

This was heaven. Marcus never realized how wonderful it felt just to be held... to feel safe... to feel the warmth of his boyfriend's body behind him... his arms enveloping him, holding him tight.

"What do you want to do today?" Aiden whispered in a soft sleepy tone, both their eyes had closed again as they lay somewhere between sleep and love.

"I dunno... be with you."

"Already am..."

"Then let's just stay in bed..."

"Sounds good to me," Aiden replied softly and hugged tighter, melting Marcus into his chest.

A moment later, Aiden suddenly pulled away from the covers and slipped out of bed. "Gotta pee."

Marcus didn't even open his eyes for the minute that he was alone in Aiden's bed, but he definitely felt the void of the absent boyfriend. Just as he heard Aiden coming out of the bathroom, Marcus turned and realized his boyfriend was naked. His eyes quickly opened and he had no control over their zeroing in on Aiden's body...

He'd seen him of course while swimming, but... they hadn't even seen each other in their underwear... well, he guessed Aiden saw him a moment ago considering that was what he was wearing... but to see Aiden... "You're... naked," Marcus said more as a question, but it came as a statement.

Aiden was still sleepy, but didn't even think about it until Marcus mentioned it. Suddenly, he became shy, covering himself and jumping back under the duvet and sliding next to Marcus. "Uh... I forgot... sorry..." clearly embarrassed.

"I don't care... really... but..." Marcus turned to look at his boyfriend, both face-to-face, "you're hot," and smiled that devious, sexy smile indicating he meant it.

Aiden clearly woke up now—bashful and terribly embarrassed. He slept naked since he'd been in tenth grade, it being so natural anymore he hadn't even considered it when he got out of bed earlier. Of course, he never had someone in bed with him while he was sleeping.

Marcus pulled him over so they were practically kissing, that close their lips were. "Listen," he practically whispered, "you're beautiful. And don't get shy on me, because you are... I love how you look."

"Really?" Still shy.

"Really." And he kissed his boyfriend slowly, tenderly, with a hint of something more.

Aiden pulled from the kiss out of breath. "I... I love how you look, too," he replied through exhalations.

Marcus shielded his eyes, pretending to be bashful, but Aiden pulled his hand away, which led to Marcus pulling it back, which led to Aiden trying to pin Marcus's hand down so he could look at his face, but Marcus put up a play fight. Before they knew it, both were trying to practically wrestle the other, tossing back and forth, pushing the duvet in their gyrations, until Marcus had Aiden pinned, sitting on his knees on Aiden's chest, his boyfriend's hands held above his head, both laughing. Marcus looked down at the naked Aiden and leaned in to kiss his boyfriend. "I really do love your body," he nibbled into Aiden's ear, causing white sparks of electricity to go down his spine.

"I really love... you," Aiden whispered back.

Marcus paused, pulled up to look at Aiden in his eyes, just a few inches away.

"You do?" He said so tenderly he could've joined hearts across seas.

"I love you, Marcus."

Marcus couldn't hold back. He kissed Aiden so aggressively, Aiden had to beg for breath. It was so sexy, so passionate, so...

"I love you, Aiden. I couldn't love anyone else..."

Aiden bit his lip, a once-in-a-lifetime smile.

"Marcus?"

"Yeah," he said, his breath still sporadic.

"Can you... uh..."

"What?" He asked as he leaned in to kiss Aiden's neck which added to the spine tingles.

"Can you... take me?" Aiden could barely get out the words before

Marcus was biting at his earlobe and nearly made his eyes roll up under his power.

"Aiden?" He asked between kisses.

"Yeah?" He barely exhaled.

"I... want you..."

"Please..."

That morning, the two learned what it meant to give themselves over to each other. Passionate, yes, but there was something else, some connection, something that made it more... made it love.

twenty-nine
audience

DAVID LEFT the stage after clearing the director to allow Noah to act, even if it was a bit part. He'd been in a call with NY when his assistant waved his attention from his office door, looking hesitant to bother him, but certain to wait.

"Hang on, Charlie—What is it?"

He smiled to himself when she gave him the lowdown. He'd thought allowing him to be an extra somewhere on the show would be a fun surprise... sort of like opening up the drum set on Christmas morning that the parents had forbidden, but he, as uncle, could give. But he'd had no idea that whatever it was Noah did would resonate not only with Linda and Charles, but apparently, the audience.

Having settled the matter, he asked Sara to get Charlie back on the phone before stopping her. He probably should let Elena in on this. Being a SAG member, while a big deal, was just a formality from his perspective. Noah was going to get a small day rate... it wouldn't be enough to even warrant a 1099, but she still needed to know what was going on.

"Sara, hang on. I need to call Noah's mom."

"What is it? Everything okay?" She called back a few minutes after he left a voicemail, in between the classes she taught. He never called her during the day so this was bound to be a problem.

"Everything's fine," he said without even a 'Hello'... "I just needed to bring you up to speed on something that seemed to just happen this morning..." And so he gave her the cliff notes... Noah meeting Lily on the set the day before... the two clicking... him taking Noah to watch a taping... getting him as an extra...

"I can't believe you did all that for him. I bet he's beyond thrilled. And isn't she some big Disney star or something?"

David laughed. He knew Elena well enough that the last time she watched television was probably with him and Michael... and that was only because she was squeezed between the two of them with a popcorn bowl on her lap that she couldn't move.

"She's on our lot. Walt wishes he had her," he joked as an industry insider would and then switched back to the matter at hand. "There's something else..."

"What did Noah do?" She automatically assumed a 14-year-old would have done the worst.

"Apparently, made the audience love him..."

"What?!"

David explained his request to come to set... the ask by his friend the director as well as the two writers to use him as they adapted a scene...

"You what?"

"But," he continued, "he needs to be a SAG member to be on set like that..."

"SAG?"

"It's the actors union... for Noah, it'll be a formality..."

"Union? MY Noah?"

"I cleared it... just so he can get paid..."

"Noah? Paid?"

"It'll be a day rate... nothing big. But, I thought you should know."

She had a million questions about finances, taxes, responsibilities for Noah... all of it were minor or non-existent, he assured her. More important, however, was he would be on television and in a speaking role...

"Noah will be... on TV?"

"Assuming you're okay with that. I'm told it's really a bit role... nothing more than a few seconds... so don't get your gears going, El... I know how you can get."

He did know her. She'd already started to go down the route of what to do about paparazzi...

"And how is Noah?"

"I think he's more thrilled to see Lily than anything."

She'd almost forgotten about his new "friend"...

"God I wish I were out there."

"Well, El... in some ways, it's good you're not."

"Why?" She feigned offense. Although David and her both had too much history to ever be offended by the other. There was too much dirt and tears they had on each other.

"You're such a drama queen, El!" He laughed alongside her. "But, yes... Noah... well... he's learning something about himself, I think... he's... figuring out what it's like to... well... like someone."

"OMG, David... first Aiden and now Noah! I'm missing out on everything!"

"Well... I think that's actually good for them at least for now. Helicopter mom isn't hovering... you know?"

"I'm not a helicopter!" She protested through lying teeth and she knew it.

"Right. Of course." He yawned overtly to piss her off. It worked, but she laughed.

"Okay okay... I get it. Mom needs to get the hell lost while uncle David gets all the fun."

"And responsibility, remember? What did someone tell me the other night..."

"Don't use my own words against me, David. I'll bitch slap you through this phone," she laughed and so did he. Michael and her would always gang up on him, but he knew it was always in love mixed with humor.

"Okay," she finally said. "I get it. But, David..."

"Yeah, El?"

"Keep an eye on Noah. Aiden is older. I still worry about him, but he's got a good head on his shoulders."

"As does Noah."

"Yeah... but he's still learning."

"As is Aiden."

"Goddammit, David, I'm trying to be convincing sounding here!" She laughed as did he.

"Okay okay... prattle away..." he snickered.

"You dick! Anyway," she continued, "just... well... he's my little boy... don't let some celebrity crush ruin his heart."

David paused and reflected before commenting.

"El... I understand... and I am already on the same page. But, I know Lily... and I'm learning more about Noah... and at this point in his life... I don't think that's too much of a concern. But I will obviously keep you in the loop. Okay?"

She exhaled. "Okay. Fair enough."

"Now, I gotta run. I'm already late for another call."

"David..."

"Yeah El?"

"Thank you..."

"You're welcome, but for what?"

"For doing this... for my boys..."

"I feel like I've got a stake in them, too, now."

"You do. You always have."

David smiled, reflective... Missing Michael more than ever.

"So did Michael," he practically whispered.

"Yes... yes he did... still does."

"Have fun in class."

"Have fun being a big shot."

Noah found himself finished with a touch up in makeup and following Priscilla quickly back to set. The director waved him over to the other two in the scene, Lily and her on-screen boyfriend, played by Tyler Matthews, a teen celebrity that Noah was also familiar with and a little star struck. Tyler fist bumped Noah and seemed really welcoming.

"So, Noah..." Linda stopped up beside him with a hastily re-written page of the script. "We want you to be the 'new boyfriend' for Taylor here," pointing to Lily, who had already had time to read her new lines and was obviously thrilled that Noah was now her "new boyfriend." Tyler was playing jealous and Linda had written Noah as the funny guy who seemed smooth as silk while Tyler's character was tripping over himself out of jealousy. Noah's character name was "Ryan" now and he was to act like he didn't even know what was going on, which endeared him to Taylor even more. It was just half a dozen lines and all he had to do was stand there with the other two looking back and forth at each. In the end, Lily would put her arm around his and walk off leaving Tyler's character wondering what happened after the last joke.

"Think you can do that?"

"Uh... sure..."

The director put his arm around Noah and pointed out towards two cameras, two guys holding big poster boards of lines. "Since you haven't had any practice, there's your lines on those cue cards, right? Just don't look right at the camera."

"Got it..." he was a boy of a thousand words apparently, but everyone moved on. Time was ticking.

Lily reached over and whispered: "Just pretend you're my new boyfriend, and take your time. Don't rush your lines."

Noah's heart wouldn't let his brain think about all the cameras, the lights, the audience... it was now focused solely on being Lily's boyfriend... er... he meant Taylor's... this was acting... right?

"Places... and... Action!"

Lily had the first line, followed by a brief retort from Tyler and then Noah realized it was his turn. He was supposed to play as if he didn't know what was going on... which was actually the truth... so he shrugged his shoulders and looked confused before delivering the first big laugh:

"Uh... who are you?"

The audience burst into laughter and Lily's eyes locked to his, telling him that was perfect. The scene played out before the last laugh line, which was Noah's:

"I didn't steal her - I just made a better offer than 'Netflix and actually chill.'"

The crowd erupted and Tyler looked stunned. Lily put her arm around Noah's and they walked stage left, Noah looking smitten... which he was.

"And cut!"

The director came up and said it was perfect. No need for another take. "Everyone feel good about that?"

Lily smiled and nodded. Tyler slapped Noah on the back and said he was a natural.

Noah felt most happy that Lily still had her arm around his...

"Great! Let's move on. Noah, if you want, you can hang in the green room."

"Sure..."

"Uh... bye," he waved a little wave to Lily... she gave him a quick hug and whispered that she'd see him once they were done. And with that, Noah's life was changed.

thirty
convergence

NOAH RAN EXCITEDLY into the house, not waiting for David to retrieve his things from the car, in search of his brother.

Aiden and Marcus looked up from their perch on the pool deck, both looking relaxed like they'd been there for days.

"OMG OMG OMG!" he yelled out, trying to catch his breath.

"What?" Aiden asked, sitting up. "Calm down!" He was a little annoyed by his little brother's dramatic entrance cutting off the perfect day he and Marcus had.

"You'll never guess what I did today!"

"Annoyed everyone?" Aiden retorted and giggled, leaning back against Marcus, clearly more comfortable about being connected with him and he didn't care who saw.

Noah flipped him off, as usual, but still was excited.

Marcus took the bait.

"What happened, Noah?"

"I... am going to be on TV!"

"Bullshit!" Marcus laughed, typical older brother type banter.

"Bull-True!"

Aiden laughed alongside Marcus. Noah came over and sat down in front of them alongside the pool cross-legged and continued his story, so excited he could barely form sentences.

"Hold up hold up," Marcus raised his hand confused between Lily, Tyler, Taylor, Ryan, Linda and whomever he was spitting names out...

David appeared at the doorway still in his suit, but his tie had clearly been loosened and he was smiling watching the two try and decipher the spurts and fits that were Noah's story. His eye wandered and realized something was different with Aiden and Marcus. Something subtle... but... even though they were both volleying back and forth to get Noah to calm down, as he'd expected, there was something... closer... more relaxed between them.

They'd become more comfortable and, bold if he admitted, in showing physical affection in front of him over the past week or so, but this wasn't just because Aiden was leaning back into Marcus or the way Marcus's arms draped around Aiden's waist. It was something unseen, yet more connected like a binding had pierced the other and pulled them taut.

He could hear Michael's voice... *They've taken a leap today...* and he knew. He knew this would be a day that would stick with them forever, regardless if they remained together or not. He wasn't surprised. In fact, if he were honest, he expected it. But it still hit him a little... in the way perhaps a parent might knowing their little boy is now really a man... still he was happy for them. Firsts are called that for a reason. And he hoped it was as tender and loving as possible.

Noah's continued excitement drew his mind back to reality. Marcus and Aiden still seemed confused so he stepped outside, sat his briefcase down and took over for Noah—if nothing but to help him catch his breath. He looked like he ran from the studio back home.

"I think what Noah is trying to say, guys, is that he was asked to be on Sunset Academy for a small role."

"Like, on TV?"

"Yes."

"For real?" Aiden shot up from Marcus's chest and looked right into his brother's eyes.

"Yes!" Noah spat out proudly.

"Wow!" Aiden and Marcus both shared... clearly impressed. They thought he was just going to watch.

"How?"

"Why don't we get changed and have some dinner and Noah can tell you all about it? Sound good?"

Noah ran up to his room followed by Aiden, Noah telling him bits and pieces while his bigger brother was asking questions, clearly interested. David put his arm around Marcus as they walked back into the house, following.

"How was the day?" David gently asked.

Marcus couldn't help but feel caught, like somehow David knew. His red face betrayed him and that was all David needed to understand.

"I'm glad you two had a good day today," he simply responded to Marcus's non-answer, making Marcus blush even more.

David stopped briefly just before the door from the pool into the house and turned to look Marcus directly.

"Aiden's a sweet boy and he's lucky to have you, Marcus."

Marcus couldn't look at him, not necessarily embarrassed, but this was the first time David and he spoke this directly about Aiden alone together. David understood Marcus was still young and developing... these talks weren't meant to embarrass or shame, rather to impress upon him the normalcy of expressing feelings and being a good partner... one who relies on others to help in their own development and health of their relationships.

"He is, Marcus. You're a good man. I see it. And, I'm glad you were his first."

Marcus felt like he was going to melt into the concrete. But David continued.

"Look at me, Marcus." He asked gently... Marcus lifted his gaze under what seemed the weight of the world.

"I'm serious. I'm happy you two have each other now. And I'd like to think you'll feel comfortable with me to know you don't have to keep all your feelings to yourself. The heartiest relationships take work and help from friends and other people that love us... Elena was that for Michael and myself..."

Marcus quickly thought of Aiden's mom and then what he was learning of Michael.

"You think she'll be mad?" Marcus finally asked.

"About what?"

He couldn't bring himself to say it and just cast his eyes down to the concrete as if his bare feet from swimming earlier were somehow relevant to the conversation.

"That you and Aiden are... intimate?" David chose his words carefully. He didn't want Marcus to lock up, already embarrassed. This was a day of firsts for him, including being an adult about these things...

He nodded.

"No, I don't think so. But it's none of our business... hers nor mine."

"But she's his mom and..."

"And she has her own life to worry about. She obviously will want to protect Aiden. He's her son... but she's not stupid... and she knows that you two are boyfriends..."

"She does?!" Marcus hadn't realized she knew anything.

"Yes. She does."

"Oh my god. Is she mad?"

"Why would she be?"

"I dunno... I guess... I just figured..."

"Marcus... what your father did to you—trying to hurt you, throwing you out—that isn't normal. Most parents don't react that way. Elena loves Aiden and she's happy for you both. Really."

The mention of Marcus's past hadn't been in the forefront of his mind, but David calling it out certainly brought it into the spotlight. He hadn't realized that he felt like being "caught" with Aiden was going to always result in harm or pain or...

His eyes began to water, but David put his hands on Marcus's shoulders and looked at him like a father would any son who was growing up.

"Listen, Marcus. It'll take time. Don't push yourself too much, but realize... there are those of us who are rooting for you... me included. I want you to be as happy and healthy as possible."

Marcus shook his head, trying to control his watery eyes.

"And..." David continued... "I love Aiden as my nephew as much as I love you as if you were my own son."

Marcus's tears burst and he pulled David into a hug he never wanted to let go of. David just embraced him and let his emotions flow as they would, rubbing his back slightly and allowing nothing more than the sounds of the pool fountain and Marcus's crying echo around them.

. . .

Noah pulled Aiden's arm down the stairs, having both changed to head to dinner. They'd no idea where they were going, but didn't care. Aiden caught the gist of Noah's story from the day and was both impressed and excited for him, if not a little jealous. He couldn't believe his little brother was going to be a star!

Noah corrected him. "I'm not anything... it was just something... fun... but..." then lit up again talking about Lily and how afterwards she and him spent some time together and she asked if he would like to come by again and maybe they could have lunch or something...

"Smooth! You've got a date with a Hollywood star, Noah!"

He became shy. "Nothing big deal," he said... "just... food."

They both stopped in their tracks at the bottom of the stairs... looking through the kitchen at the sight of Uncle David consoling Marcus in front of the pool. This was the second time Aiden had seen Marcus break down and his uncle try and calm him, but Noah had no clue what was going on.

"Is he... alright?" Noah suddenly forgot about his exciting day.

"He... he will be, I think."

"What's wrong?"

"It's complicated. I don't know everything... but... his dad... kicked him out."

"Why?"

Aiden paused... it wasn't his story, but Noah's questions were innocent enough... "Because he found out Marcus had a boyfriend."

Noah thought for a moment and then wrinkled his brows in confusion. "That's stupid. Who cares?"

"I guess his dad did... he... uh..."

"What?"

Aiden didn't know if he should say it, but something compelled him forward... "he tried to... uh... kill him." Aiden's voice trailed off.

Noah stopped his heart for a moment before speaking next... "I... I can't imagine dad..."

"Me neither."

Both had an awkward relationship towards their father and remained dealing with their own emotions about him, mostly unspoken, but to imagine him trying to kill one of them... Noah immediately wondered what their dad would do if he found out about Aiden and Marcus.

Neither knew what to do next... but it stirred something in them that suddenly connected them more than simply being brothers.

Marcus released David and they heard their uncle say something to him, getting him to smile while wiping his eyes. Aiden's heart melted, wanting to run out to him and kiss him... to make it all better...

"You love him, don't you?" Noah asked quietly.

Aiden just nodded, a tear forming in his eye.

"I do."

thirty-one
best laid plans

IT'D TAKEN considerable effort to work through all the logistics, but David thought he had pulled it off.

He hoped.

After that last call with Elena the day of Noah's on-screen debut, and the subsequent emotional conversation with Marcus later that evening, he lay in his bed staring at the ceiling wishing Michael were here to help navigate all this. He nearly broke down when Marcus did, feeling completely out of his depth about how to help the boy heal while simultaneously wanting to throttle any father who could throw such a sweet kid out.

Just be there for him, he kept hearing Michael's voice whisper.

But it was harder than it sounded. Not just being present... but doing it without backup.

Then again, he didn't have to go it alone, did he? Elena was kicking herself for missing out on everything... she was probably rearranging her entire life right now, canceling her mother's visit and all that. And honestly... he just wanted his friend here. She was Michael's closest confidante, and maybe... well... it might feel a little like the old days when she'd conspire with Michael during their card games... or when Michael would methodically remove every onion from his salad just so she could steal them.

So he called her the next morning. Was she interested? He'd cover the flight. She'd have to shuffle some things around back there... but it would be an adventure... and then she could escort the boys home... the whole thing.

She was game. She'd figure it out and call him back. Neither of them considered how the boys might feel about her sudden appearance... or whether her being there to "collect them" might complicate things.

───────

By Friday evening, the household had settled into new rhythms, though each carried its own complexities. Noah had become David's shadow at the studio each morning. After Lily invited him for lunch Tuesday, he'd been asked to film another small scene Wednesday—the final shooting day of the week. Over lunch, the director mentioned they were considering expanding Noah's role for the rest of the season, if he was interested. David stayed noncommittal, knowing Noah was supposed to return to Boston the following week. He'd need to discuss it with Elena... among other things.

Noah had taken to spending afternoons in Lily's trailer with her mother, Diana, who found him refreshingly genuine—completely unaware of industry politics and utterly uninterested in leveraging his connection to Lily for personal gain. His complete ignorance of how Hollywood worked amused her, Diana confided to David later. She simply enjoyed watching her daughter light up around him. Still, she worried they might be getting in deeper than two teenagers could handle, especially with their obvious mutual attraction. They were both so young, but she wanted Lily to experience some normalcy, even in small doses. David agreed they should keep communicating... and suggested Diana might enjoy meeting Noah's mother. She'd love that, she said. Another perfect reason for Elena's surprise visit.

Meanwhile, Aiden and Marcus had grown bold in their newfound intimacy. Since David's gentle acknowledgment of their relationship, they'd begun spending nights together—not just the stolen hours by the pool, but actual sleeping arrangements. They maintained the pretense of separate bedrooms initially, but inevitably one would migrate to the other's bed in the pre-dawn hours. Something about preserving their individual spaces felt important, even as they craved each other's presence. Marcus had adopted Aiden's preference for sleeping without clothes, and they'd often wake before sunrise to make love quietly before drifting back to sleep entwined. During the day, they'd taken to swimming without suits, living out their youth with the abandon that comes from being desperately, completely in love. They'd venture out on their bikes—exploring the mall, grabbing lunch in Beverly Glen—but always returned by five to resume their poolside vigil, properly clothed this time, awaiting David and Noah's return from "the office." Both were "breadwinners" now, they joked.

Elena called back the following day. After considerable juggling, she had it sorted. She'd catch the 6 AM flight to LAX Friday, arriving around 10. David would arrange a car... Terminal 4, American Airlines... simple enough. She'd come straight to the studio where she could freshen up and maybe nap in one of the vacant bungalows before they headed home. "Noah will be there," he mentioned, suddenly uncertain about orchestrating the surprise.

"Why don't I just appear on set?" she suggested, mischief creeping into her voice.

"They don't film Fridays, but he'll definitely be with Lily..."

"Oh, wait!" An idea struck him. "Diana would love to meet you. What if I arranged a late lunch? Gives you time to recover from the flight... we could do the commissary?"

"Perfect. What's she like?"

David spent ten minutes briefing Elena—Diana's protective instincts, her desire for Lily to have normal teenage experiences, her genuine fondness for Noah. As they talked, the plan crystallized. He'd participate in the surprise, starting at the studio, then bringing Elena home to shock Aiden and Marcus. Even better... what if he sent those two out for dinner somewhere walkable? Somewhere casual that wouldn't arouse suspicion... he'd figure something out. This was going to be absolutely delicious!

Elena was practically bouncing through the phone. "I feel like I'm plotting to sneak out in high school all over again."

"You snuck out? I had no idea!"

"Darling, there's plenty you still don't know about me."

"Slut!"

"Homo!"

They dissolved into laughter, and for a moment it was exactly like old times—the three of them scheming and giggling over some ridiculous plan.

Except now there were only two.

The silence stretched just long enough for both of them to feel Michael's absence like a physical ache. David could almost hear him chiming in with some perfectly timed joke or gentle correction to their plotting. Michael had always been the heart of their triangle, the one who made David laugh and kept Elena grounded.

"He'd love this," Elena said softly, reading his thoughts.

"Yeah," David whispered. "He really would."

thirty-two
unlikely allies

"IT'S SO nice to meet you. David has said wonderful things."

"Uh oh! I guess I'm in for it, then!" Elena jested and everyone laughed. David intentionally chose the same semi-circular booth he and the boys had shared during their lunches, but this time he wanted Diana and Elena to have space to connect. In fact, it should be any moment before...

"I'm sorry, David... but there's a slight... ahem... problem." His assistant Sara arrived right on cue.

She leaned in and whispered, "Was that convincing?" and winked.

"I'm sorry ladies... duty calls," he offered his apologies along with assurances they should take as long as they liked and order whatever they wished. Stopping by the maître d', he signed something that would clearly cover any expense and was out the door, followed closely by his assistant.

"Mr. Big Shot," Elena gestured toward his retreating figure as she turned back to Diana. "He's always been that way—perpetually busy," she said in her transplanted Boston accent.

"How long have you known each other?"

And with that, the two began what would ultimately become a life-long friendship. Diana found Elena's unfiltered humor and sharp wit refreshing in the carefully orchestrated world of Hollywood. Elena was charmed by Diana's candor about raising a young star and her honest admission that she sometimes craved ordinary life—for both her daughter and herself.

Both discovered their shared single motherhood. Both confessed their worries about children growing up too quickly. Both understood the delicate skepticism surrounding young love and swapped stories from their own adolescence—Bobby Stevens for Elena in seventh grade when she had braces and her mother still insisted on pigtails; Tommy Sanderson for Diana in ninth grade when her mother pressured her to abandon her heritage and "become white" to fit in. Before they knew it, Diana was confessing she'd never been allowed to curse while Elena couldn't remember a day she hadn't. They shared how they'd ended up as single parents, how Lily had stumbled into the business, how Noah sometimes struggled in his older brother's shadow, how David had woven himself into both their lives... and Michael.

Diana hadn't known about him. David remained fairly guarded with most people, Elena being the notable exception. Diana suddenly saw him through completely different eyes—more depth, more humanity. He'd always been courteous, even kind, but now she glimpsed the real man behind the professional facade. She found herself wishing he'd find someone who could restore his happiness. Michael had clearly been that person—Elena's stories of initially interrogating David when Michael first brought him around, the adventures the three had shared, the devastation of his death, the careful existence David had maintained these past six years.

"I had no idea," Diana murmured, somehow finding herself welcomed into their extended family without realizing it.

"It's partly why I encouraged the boys to visit this summer. They're old enough that I didn't worry about them flying alone... well," she paused, "and there's Aiden..."

"What about him? Your eldest, right?"

"Yeah... well, between us..."

She sketched a brief history—her concerns about Aiden growing up, her suspicion he might be gay but struggling with it, her hope that Uncle David might provide guidance... and then he'd met Marcus.

"Marcus?"

Elena offered an abbreviated version of his story as she understood it, which admittedly wasn't much. But Diana's heart clenched when she heard how David had literally rescued him from the streets, tears gathering in her eyes. "I... I had no idea. It's so..."

"Tragic? Heartbreaking and heartwarming that David would even consider helping..." Elena couldn't finish the thought.

"But what about your son? How does he factor in?"

"Well, David tells me the two have... how shall I put this delicately... a budding romance."

"What?" Diana's face lit up. "Let me understand this correctly—you have two sons, both visiting their uncle for the summer, and both are falling in love?"

Elena nearly giggled with the nervous energy of a mother contemplating her sons' romantic lives. "Well, I don't know if it's love exactly, but essentially, that's what David's reported."

"Are you comfortable with that?"

She considered the question, taking a sip of the cocktail they'd both ordered—it was Friday, after all. "Yes. I trust David's judgment, and I know he's monitoring the situation carefully. But more importantly, I trust my sons."

Diana nodded, recognizing similar maternal instincts.

"They're teenagers, of course, so I know they're bound to screw up royally," Elena continued. Diana laughed and waved dismissively, encouraging her frankness. "But they're fundamentally good kids."

"Young men," Diana corrected with a smile.

"Right! They don't consider themselves boys anymore, apparently. But they'll always be my babies."

Diana smiled knowingly. Girls seemed easier in some respects, at least to her. She could relate to Lily's experience of finding a boy special, particularly when he wasn't "one of them"—she air-quoted—meaning another aspiring actor. "Lily describes Noah as 'like a normal, cool guy,'" she mimicked her daughter's voice, "whatever that means." Both women laughed.

Their conversation continued to flow, Elena eventually revealing the surprise she'd orchestrated with David. The boys had no idea she was in California.

Diana's eyes sparkled with mischief. "Oh, can I help? This sounds delightful!"

"You know what? Absolutely! Noah's with Lily right now, isn't he?"

"Yes... oh, I see exactly where this is heading."

And with that, both women began scheming like sorority sisters plotting the most deliciously perfect surprise.

thirty-three
mothers and girlfriends

LILY AND NOAH sat opposite each other at the banquet table in her trailer parked down the block from Stage 21. Her mom had said she had a "business luncheon" to attend and expected both to be on their best behavior—the usual mother-daughter "I'm giving you an opportunity to prove you can behave with this boy" talk without explicitly saying it. She understood. Even Noah understood. Truth be told, he was too nervous to try anything anyway. Lily was obviously the more mature in these matters.

"Yes, mother."

"I should be back around 2. We've got that dinner event, remember, and then of course, you need to study. So Noah, unfortunately you'll need to head back to your uncle's office after my return."

"Yes ma'am," he replied, disappointed but obedient. He was nothing if not polite to adults, especially mothers of girls he liked.

Lily gave him an "I'm sorry" look but he replied it was fine with his eyes.

A quick kiss on Lily's head and her mother was off.

Lily blew out a breath of relief and sighed. "Sometimes being fourteen really sucks," she said and Noah laughed in agreement. "My mom is worse," he said. "She yells!" They both laughed.

They continued their card game, something Noah was teaching her if he could only remember all the rules. It didn't matter—they were having fun.

What seemed like fifteen minutes turned into a couple of hours, so intense had the cards been. They'd discovered they were both competitive, full of "Oh yeah? Well, beat that!" and "You're going down, Chen!" and "Read 'em and weep, loser!" It was all playful, and the more time they spent together just being... well... themselves... the more it felt like they'd been friends since forever.

"Lily, darling, I'm back."

They both darted their eyes to the doorway, followed quickly by checking their phones, unaware of how much time had passed. "That was quick!"

Noah looked up at her mother staring a hole through him and suddenly felt uneasy. He actually gulped like they do in cartoons. Lily became alarmed—her mother's demeanor seemed to transform instantly.

"Mr. Walsh," Diana said sternly, "I've learned something about you that... well... I'm afraid before you can continue to visit with my daughter, you'll need to speak with your mother."

Lily shot a look at her mother followed quickly by one to Noah. "What thing? What happened? What's wrong with Noah?"

Noah couldn't understand what just happened. He scanned his memory lightning fast trying to figure out if he'd accidentally said or done something... he didn't think so, but... oh my god! I'm in trouble.

"I... uhh... uh..." He stammered and it took all the strength and acting prowess Diana could muster to keep in character.

"But... but... but I... my mmm... mom?"

"Yes, Mr. Walsh. I suggest you speak to her immediately!" She said probably a little too sternly and felt a little guilt for the charade.

Noah looked like he was about to cry. Lily was not too far behind.

"Ooo... okay... I'll... ccc... call..." he was actually tearing up now. Lily suddenly reached to grasp his hand, unaware of her actions, her heart suddenly breaking.

Diana noticed and felt daggers in her soul.

"You don't have to... she's..."

"Right here!" Noah's mother quickly stepped into the doorway and announced herself.

Diana quickly smiled and apologized. "Sorry Noah... it was just a little joke."

Noah burst into tears—somewhere between frightened and relieved.

"Oh, honey! Come here. We were just playing a trick on you! Everything's fine." Elena ran over and sat down giving him a mother's hug, which felt terrific, but then he became suddenly embarrassed—he was crying in front of his girlfriend... well... not girlfriend... but... Lily.

For her part, she was alternating between looking at her mother and Noah's, then to her boyfriend—yes, her boyfriend, she realized. She crumpled her face and gave her mother "the look" for making her boyfriend cry, but quickly melted back to somewhere between heartache and sweetness watching Noah's mother calm him down. Diana came over and sat down next to her daughter, giving her the "I'm sorry" look before Elena spoke up.

"Hi Lily! I'm Elena, your mom and I just met for lunch," she offered her hand to shake across the table as she was releasing Noah to wipe his eyes and embarrassment.

"Hi Mrs. Walsh. I'm Lily... but... you probably already know that..." She suddenly felt slightly embarrassed and shy—uncharacteristic for someone who performed in front of cameras and audiences, but something about meeting Noah's mother made her feel like just a regular girl again.

Diana noticed and thought she must really like this boy if meeting his mother makes her this nervous. Elena caught the same thing and gave Diana a quick knowing glance before speaking.

"Honey, I'm sorry. We thought it might be a funny way to surprise you that I'm here."

Noah had calmed down and was getting over his embarrassment when he started to process what had just happened.

"You... that was..." he couldn't finish his sentence, but Lily did for him.

"Terrible!" she said, and both mothers winced with guilt.

"But," Noah interjected, his excitement building, "it was totally epic! I can't believe I fell for it! I really thought..."

"Me, too!" Lily added. They were now both assessing the quality of the prank. The mothers were slightly amused at how they went from upset to impressed in seconds.

"I mean... I really thought I wasn't allowed to see you anymore!" Noah said.

"Me too! I mean... that was like..." Lily made a face that conveyed fear and anger more than any words she could offer.

"Really?" Noah suddenly questioned, as if he was realizing she was just as upset at the thought of them not being able to spend time together.

"Really! I mean," Lily then turned to her mom, "that was really mean! I would've been like... crushed!"

Noah processed what he was hearing. Lily really did like him—enough to be upset at the thought of not seeing him anymore.

Diana and Elena exchanged meaningful glances. Definitely something to discuss over their next coffee, they both thought.

"Well, again... we're sorry," Diana offered before Elena added, "If it's any consolation, you can help with how we're gonna surprise your brother."

Noah's eyes lit up. Anytime he could prank Aiden, he was in!

"Can Lily help, too?" He asked before even consulting her, then realized and stopped. "I mean, if you'd like to, of course," he became shy again.

"I'd love to! Sounds fun!" She practically bounced in her seat and they high-fived across the table, but didn't release hands after the clap. For a few seconds they just held on, both suddenly aware that their mothers were watching. The realization hit simultaneously and they pulled back, faces flushing. Holding hands! In front of their moms!

Diana had to stifle a laugh and Elena looked away to give them a moment. The sweetness of young love—they both remembered those butterflies.

"Then, let's figure out a plan, shall we?" Elena asked, clearly on board with planning Mission: Prank Aiden.

Diana reluctantly chimed in. "Unfortunately, Lily has a dinner event tonight and schoolwork..."

The air deflated from the room.

"Unless..." Diana then spoke, as if her mind was concocting a plan of her own.

"Unless what?" Elena asked, Noah and Lily both following her gaze to Diana.

"Let me make a few calls... be right back." She got up and left the trailer, her office normally being her iPhone just outside the trailer or soundstage.

Elena gave a shoulder shrug to indicate her wonder at what magic Diana was making and turned to look at the two fourteen-year-olds.

"How did you get out here, mom?" Noah suddenly asked.

"I hitchhiked," she said in her characteristic sarcasm. Lily laughed and Noah rolled his eyes. Yep, this was his mom.

"Your uncle David flew me out."

"Uncle David?" Noah asked.

"No, your other uncle David." Again with the sarcasm and Lily actually laughed. She liked Noah's mom. She was funny. And had a funny East Coast accent.

"Mom!"

"Well, you asked!" She smiled and nudged her son sitting next to her.

"I mean... I thought you couldn't come out."

"Well, I couldn't, honey. But David and I spoke last night and... here I am!" She gave a "Ta-Da" jazz hands wave which again made Lily laugh.

"You're so corny!" Noah said, rolling his eyes again.

"I think she's funny," Lily corrected him.

"See! She likes me!" Elena pushed Noah again, enjoying his embarrassment in front of his girlfriend.

"So, sweetheart," Elena said gently, "are you two having a good time together?"

"Mom!" Noah protested, but there was warmth in his embarrassment —secretly, he was glad she was here to witness this.

"Yes, Mrs. Walsh... Noah's really funny... and sweet..." Lily's usual poise faltered slightly as she spoke to his mother.

Noah was turning red as a fire truck, which Lily found endearing and Elena found absolutely precious. She wanted to freeze this moment forever.

"You two are ganging up on me!" He laughed, mortified but secretly loving every second of it.

"Of course we are, honey," Elena said and gave him a side hug. "It's not often I can embarrass you in front of your girlfriend!"

"She's not my girlfriend!" Noah quickly corrected, feeling utterly hopeless and looking for a rock to crawl under.

"I'm not?!" Lily turned and seemed offended.

"I mean... well..." Noah fumbled. "I uh..."

"Well, are you my boyfriend or not?" She wasn't giving up—despite her usual composure, this mattered too much to let slide. Elena admired a girl who knew what she wanted.

"Well... uh... if you want me to be..."

"I do!"

Noah's embarrassment suddenly began to shed away as a deep smile began to curl at his cheeks. "Really?" he said hopefully.

"Of course!" Lily reached across and took Noah's hand, then became a little more tender. "If you want to."

Noah could only nod, overwhelmed by the moment. Elena nearly teared up—she was witnessing something most mothers never get to see. Usually she was lucky if Noah grunted about his day, but here she was watching him take this huge step.

"I want to," Noah replied as shy as a six-year-old.

"Then that's settled. You're my boyfriend!"

Noah couldn't wipe the grin off his face. "And you're my girlfriend!"

"Well, congratulations!" Elena said softly. Both kids turned to her, having momentarily forgotten she was there. They looked slightly embarrassed at having such a private moment witnessed, but somehow it felt right too—like she belonged there.

Diana had just opened the door and asked, "What are we congratulating?"

Lily suddenly was the one who turned red-faced—this was her mother. Noah kept quiet—he wasn't sure what the rules were with mothers-in-law.

Elena handled it perfectly. "These two were just telling me a little about themselves and I was congratulating my son on his acting debut, thanks in large part to his girlfriend."

Diana noted the word but smiled warmly. She knew Elena's history with David after their afternoon together, but to Lily and Noah, their mothers were still relative strangers who had somehow conspired together.

"Don't forget his uncle probably played a big hand in it, too," Diana added.

"Oh David? Pssh... He's just a minor character!" Elena laughed and Diana joined in, sharing the inside joke from their earlier conversation.

"So... I think we can make all this work. Lily needs to make an appearance at this dinner, but it's not until 7:30... and... if you're agreeable Noah... you can be her date. Then..."

"Date?!" Noah gulped. "Like..."

"Well, it's nothing big, just show up and shake hands. Lily can show you. It's just a DGA session. You don't need to eat... and..."

"DGA?" Noah had no idea what that was and looked over at Lily who loved the idea. She usually had to go alone—well, with her mom, but this would be way cooler!

"Yeah," Lily said. "Just follow me. It's easy!"

Diana continued, "And I've told Damon—Lily's publicist," saying that part to Elena to bring her up to speed, "that we have another commitment at 8 so we'll need to make this work. He's on board."

Elena looked a little confused about what all this was, but trusted Diana had it covered. Besides, David was sure to understand. One question she did have: "Do you want me to attend? I haven't brought anything for such a formal..."

Diana quickly answered, sparing her any formalities. "You don't have to Elena, but you're welcome. I can call over to Wardrobe and see if they have something for you, if you'd like. They owe me a favor anyway." She paused. "Now that I think of it, I'm betting you don't have a suit, Noah." She didn't wait for his response and continued. "I'll call right now and see if they can get something for him." Then stopped. "Where are my manners? This is a bit much on such late notice... we can just meet you both somewhere after if..."

"I'd like you to go!" Lily said, grabbing Noah's hand across the table again and then realizing everyone was watching and pulling back. "I mean, if you'd like."

That was the clincher. Noah nodded and said he'd go. Could they find a suit for him to wear that soon? Elena was moving her head like a Wimbledon match and landed back on Diana.

Diana smiled and exhaled. "Sorry, Elena... I'm just so used to taking care of these sorts of things..."

"No need to be sorry. I'm impressed!" She laughed causing Diana to as well.

"Now, there's the matter of your schoolwork," Diana turned to Lily.

"What grade are you in, if I may ask?" Elena spoke up.

"Eighth. But I have to do the work mostly alone because... well..."

"Oh, I can imagine," Elena responded. Turning to Diana, she said: "Perhaps this is where I can help?"

Diana looked questioning for a minute as did Lily. Noah suddenly understood and smiled. Lily's mom had been "coordinating and doing her thing" but now it was his mom's turn, he realized and was kinda proud.

"I teach both seventh and eighth grade! In Boston. In fact, your boyfriend here is in one of my classes." Elena smiled as if solving a problem for everyone.

"You do? He is?" Lily shot up.

Diana remembered her mentioning she was a teacher, but they hadn't gotten that far in their discovery of each other. "I didn't realize, Elena... do you think..."

"I could help Lily with her studies? Of course. But just as a tutor... I'm only licensed in Massachusetts."

"I'm sure you'll be fine... probably more than fine." Diana seemed relieved. Apparently, the dozen tutors in as many months just didn't click with her daughter. They only seemed to want to treat her education as a side gig rather than what it should be—a real education.

"I'd be delighted! That is, of course, if you're willing to work with me Lily."

"I'd love to! But..." she turned to Noah.

"Is she tough?" Lily made a show of it.

"The worst!" Noah grinned and his mother swatted his shoulder making him laugh.

"Hey! I'm fair! Just disciplined!"

Everyone laughed. Diana offered: "A little discipline might be exactly what we need," and looked right at Lily. "Sometimes, assignments are..."

"A little tough getting finished?" Elena knew the routine.

Lily looked embarrassed. Noah understood and gave her an 'I'm there with you" look.

"Well then... why don't you and I have a look at your assignments and material, Lily... and Diana, you and Noah can take a trip to Wardrobe to see about a suit? Sound like a plan?"

The kids nodded and Diana asked if Elena might like to join them that night. If so, she could pop over and see if they could find something for her.

"If it's fine with you, Diana... why don't I spend some time with Noah's brother and his boyfriend. They don't know I'm here yet and maybe we could meet up after?"

"OMG, I forgot about Aiden!" Noah added. Lily smiled, enjoying his enthusiasm and ease at just being himself. This felt like a family. It felt... nice.

"I think that sounds perfect," Diana said. "We can talk about logistics after we return then."

"Maybe you can pop by Mr. Big Shot's and see if his important 'thing,'" using air quotes, "is finished." She laughed as did Diana. "Maybe he'll have an idea about plans."

"Shall do. C'mon Noah... Let's go get you a suit," Diana said.

Noah nodded and scooted out of the banquet seating after Diana. Elena sat back down while she watched her son and... well... future daughter-in-law head off to Wardrobe. The thought made her smile.

"So, Lily... where shall we begin?"

She pulled out a stack of books and an iPad with some notes on an app. Midway between explaining what she'd been learning and her assignments, Lily paused.

"I like you, Mrs. Walsh. You're nice."

"Thank you! And I like you too."

Lily smiled. This was nice. It felt like family.

thirty-four
the perfect
surprise

"KNOCK KNOCK..."

David spun his chair around toward Diana standing in his office doorway.

"Diana, what can I do for you?" He rose to greet her and noticed Noah standing just behind her in a tuxedo, looking more handsome than he probably ever felt, stopping David in his tracks.

Whistling, he took in the sharply tailored fourteen-year-old. "Wow! What are the fancy duds for?"

"I called in a favor with Jerry. Noah's going to be Lily's date tonight at the..."

"You're going to the DGA thing," he finished for her. "I forgot about that."

"You're not going? I thought you..."

"I begged off, sending Susan in my place. Figured the boys were here and with Elena..."

"About that," Diana cut him off. Noah laughed at all the times they interrupted each other. "She's over tutoring Lily now."

"She's what?" David looked surprised. "I thought you two were..."

"Scheming some way to surprise her children with her visit? Well, we did... at least with Noah."

David could see him visibly flinch remembering it.

"Didn't go quite as planned, but at least Noah can say he was surprised."

Noah was nodding vigorously, but David got the hint and didn't ask for an explanation.

"So... tutoring?"

"Long story, David, but here's the gist: I called Damon and bumped us to 7:30. Said we just had to be out by 8."

"Right..."

"And Noah agreed to take Lily as his date to attend..."

"She's taking me," Noah corrected, and David smiled. He looked like a young James Bond. Diana grinned and continued.

"So we had to get something for him to wear..."

"Okay..." David wasn't sure what this had to do with surprising the boys with Elena's arrival.

"But Lily's behind on schoolwork..."

"She is?" David was concerned. The law was pretty clear on what child actors could and couldn't do, and education was up there.

"Don't worry, David. Elena is apparently a teacher."

"She's tough!" Noah interjected and both David and Diana grinned. He was so cute.

"Anyway, she's back in the trailer having school now and we stopped by here."

"I think I get it. But... what about the boys and her surprise?" This was becoming so convoluted.

"Well, that's where you come in, David."

"Yeah!" Noah agreed.

"What am I getting myself into?"

Aiden and Marcus had ridden their bikes up the hill in the heat of a 2 PM sun and decided to strip and jump in the pool right then and there. It felt freeing to just do as they pleased—no worries of being caught, no parents to get after them to pick up their clothes off the kitchen floor, no one to yell at them for being naked together. It was heaven. Until Aiden's phone buzzed somewhere in the pocket of his shorts. He almost didn't hear it, the buzzing being muffled ten feet away.

The call went to a generic voicemail message and David hung up. He doubted Aiden even knew how to listen to messages—he'd rarely heard him on the phone. He'd try Marcus next. Same. Where could those two be? Probably just busy, didn't hear the phone. But after a couple more tries, he couldn't help himself and logged into the outside security cameras to see if they were around. Nothing on the front door, drive, garage, or back yard against the hillside. But the pool... Bingo. David quickly logged out after his initial relief at knowing they were alive and well at the house was replaced by a sudden sense he was invading privacy when it was clear neither were wearing swimming suits. He smiled, remembering when he and Michael used to skinny dip in the pool, which they did mostly at night to unwind. Still, the plan he'd come up with Diana and Noah earlier meant he'd need to get their attention somehow.

It dawned on him he could remotely ring the doorbell. That'd get their attention. A moment later, he logged back in and saw Aiden opening the front door wearing a towel. Time to call, he laughed.

"Hey Uncle David."

"How's it going Aiden? You two doing anything fun today?"

"Oh, nothing... just swimming."

David smiled. Swimming was always fun, especially naked with your boyfriend, he thought, but dismissed it from his head. Time to execute his plan:

"Listen, Aiden... It's been pretty crazy here today and Noah's been pulled into another thing so we'll be a little late tonight. Do you mind meeting us for dinner down the block later at Bruno's? Say 8:30?"

"Isn't that the place you took us when we first got here?"

"Yes, that's the place."

"Do we have to dress up or something?"

"Not really, but no shorts. Think you two can handle that?"

He heard Aiden half-snicker. "Uh, yeah, I think we can wear jeans or something."

"Good boy."

Aiden grinned through the phone and David heard Marcus say something in the background, Aiden whispering he'd fill him in a minute.

"Oh, and Aiden..."

"Yeah?"

"Lily is coming. With Noah."

"She is?" He perked up. "Like, his date?"

"Well, it's just burgers, but don't make it a big deal, please."

"Uh... sure... we wouldn't..."

"Tell Marcus... and... no socials, fine? We don't need chaos there."

"Uh... yeah... yeah... of course. I get it."

"Good boy..." Aiden giggled.

"I'm not a dog..."

"Yes, I know... Good boy!" David laughed.

"You're pretty corny, Uncle David."

"So I've been told. Tough crowd!" And he laughed again, this time alongside Aiden.

"I'll see you at 8:30... and remember, please keep this to yourselves."

"I promise..."

"Good..."

"Boy," Aiden said in his place. "Yeah yeah yeah, Uncle David," causing both to laugh.

"Oh... Aiden, before I forget..."

"Uh huh..."

"Remember, there are security cameras out by the pool. Just sayin'... See you tonight!" David almost laughed before hanging up. He was pretty sure Aiden would probably be petrified after he realized the cameras had been on them this entire time. Later, he'd tell them no one had seen them, including him (well, except for the five seconds he was trying to find them), but letting them squirm a little was fun. This parenting stuff could sometimes be a blast.

Lily was the most gorgeous thing Noah had ever seen when she walked out of her bedroom in the trailer dressed in a sophisticated gown appropriate for the event. Diana was in a formal evening gown and carrying a bag of other clothes for later, she said.

Noah could not stop staring at her, but had no words to describe how absolutely stunning she looked. How did this happen to him? How did some random kid from Roslindale end up here? Elena watched standing next to David like her son was taking his date to prom. In a way, she guessed he was. Who knew what would happen to a couple of four-teen-year-olds, but if they lasted... Her heart simultaneously beamed and ached. Her baby was growing up, and she wasn't sure she was ready for it.

"So," David clapped his hands together, "everyone remember the plans?"

Lily and Noah forgot themselves for a moment and both shouted "Absolutely!" at the same time, laughed and then "Jinx!" again at the same time, laughter only teens could muster. Diana and Elena rolled their eyes and said they hoped it would work.

"It will. I've given extra time."

"Just think, all of this for lil' ol' me?" Elena exaggerated and Diana laughed. "Honey, surprising your son traveling across the country is much more interesting than any stuffy industry dinner. Besides, how long has it been?"

She looked over at Noah and thought. "Since the beginning of summer. The longest I've ever been away from them was summer camp, and that was only a week."

"This will be a wonderful night," Diana added, "for everyone." She caught Elena's eye and smiled warmly. It had been so long since she'd had a real friend, someone who understood both the joys and challenges of motherhood. Noah looked at Lily and knew it already was the best night of his life.

"Great. Time to go. I'll see you three at Bruno's at 8:30. Remember, back entrance. I've already worked it out. Oh, and Noah..."

"Yeah, Uncle David?"

"Make sure you change back into your jeans before you head inside."

"Where am I going to change?"

No one had thought about that. "Hmmm," David wondered. Elena said he could change in the car they were being driven in.

"In front of..." Noah almost seemed panicked and Diana and Elena exchanged knowing smiles. A fourteen-year-old changing clothes was completely innocent, but Lily would be there, and Noah was still figuring out how to be around the girl he was falling for.

"Well, how about you slip in and change in the men's room at Bruno's quickly? That'll work?" David offered and Noah nodded. He liked Lily, but changing in front of her was way too much to even consider. Maybe when he was much older... like seventeen or something.

. . .

Since it was only 7:20 by the time David and Elena arrived at the restaurant, they popped into the bar. A nice cocktail and some appetizers helped both of them. It'd been a long day for flights, conversations and scheming. Elena wouldn't have traded it for the world, but she was tired, more than her usual late-night self. It also gave the two of them downtime to simply talk.

"Excited to see Aiden?"

"You bet your ass! But I'm more excited to see Marcus. I feel like you've told me everything and yet I know almost nothing."

"Well, just don't be yourself and scare the hell out of him, like you did me."

"What? I did no such thing!"

"Your third question the night I met you—and remember, I was trapped in that booth at Michael's favorite terrible restaurant—was, and I quote, 'So how many times have you two slept together?'" David could barely keep a straight face as he sipped his drink.

Elena burst into laughter. "I was protecting Michael!"

"From what? My charming personality?"

"From heartbreak, you ass! I'd seen too many of his boyfriends come and go."

They both laughed, and David felt that familiar warmth of friendship he'd missed so much. "I'm glad you're here, El. It's been too long since I've had someone to really talk to."

"I'm glad you flew me out. And David?" She paused, suddenly serious. "I've missed this too. Having an adult conversation with someone who gets it."

"Least I could do. Besides, I wanted you to meet your new son-in-law."

Elena choked a little on her drink and David patted her back.

"You fine?"

"Yes... yes... just went down the wrong way..."

He picked up another olive and popped it in his mouth.

"You think those two really are in love?"

"Undeniably."

On the phone, David was a bit more cautious, reserved with his commentary. In person and a couple of drinks at a bar, he spoke his mind. This was the David she missed and rarely got to see anymore given their distance across the country.

"I... I'm happy for Aiden if they are."

"Are you? You don't sound too excited, El."

"I AM," she made a show of it, but he could tell she was worried.

"Mmhmm," he mumbled and took another sip of his cocktail.

"I'm just worried..." she paused, gathering her thoughts. "Aiden and I... we live in Boston. Marcus is here. And they're seventeen and eighteen, David. At that age, everything feels like forever, but..." She trailed off, staring into her drink.

"But what if it is forever?" David asked gently.

"Then I lose my son."

The words hung between them. David reached across and squeezed her hand. "Elena, you raised an incredible young man. Trust him. Trust what you've taught him."

"It's not about trust. It's about distance. About growing up too fast. About watching them build a life that doesn't include me." Her voice caught slightly.

David was quiet for a moment. "When I was Aiden's age, all I wanted was to get away from my family. Not because they were bad people, but because I needed to figure out who I was without their expectations weighing on me."

"And did you? Figure it out?"

"Eventually. And you know what? The farther I got from home, the more I appreciated what they'd given me. The more I wanted to share my life with them." He smiled softly. "Love doesn't diminish with distance, El. It just changes shape."

Elena took another sip and listened to his words. She wanted to meet Marcus... to see her son... and she wanted it more than ever. It'd been quite a day to see Noah earlier... and in the course of his short time out here, he'd matured a million years. Forget the celebrity girlfriend, just how he seemed to be growing up before her eyes. Her little boy was still there, but now... she was so proud.

But now Aiden... sweet, tender Aiden... The one who she first brought into the world... The one who was more sensitive than his brother... the boy who she worried over and spoke to David about in late-night phone calls... she wanted to see him... really see for herself.

"Almost time," David said looking at his watch and finishing the last olive. "You ready?"

Elena was unusually quiet, like she was nervous. This was her kid, not some long-lost family member, he thought. But he looked over at her and for the first time ever, his empathy kicked in, catching the most profound mixture of protectiveness, fear, worries and sorrow for anticipated lonely days ahead, yet pride beyond anything he'd ever witnessed, bittersweet joy and what seemed like anxiety over being there for... for her children.

"Are you fine, David?" She knew this look in him from the past... it wasn't often, but she and Michael would speak of it sometimes.

David rubbed his temple and shook his head out of it. "Yeah... I... uh..."

She looked up at him... and David spoke one last time before they walked over to their booth. "I'm always here for you, El. I'm not going anywhere."

She wanted to cry, instead gripped her lips and nodded, willing herself to keep it together. Aiden and Marcus would be here soon. She needed to be on top of her game. Besides, she started to loosen up... she'd get to see her baby!

"Lily! It's so lovely to see you!" Some important-looking woman fake-kissed her cheeks like they do in movies, Noah saw. "And who is this dashing young man?" Noah blushed, but extended his hand as he'd been taught.

"This is my boyfriend, Noah Walsh. He's from Boston."

"A Boston boy! Hear that, Harold. He's from your neck of the woods," the lady in the fancy dress and diamonds said to an older guy with wire-rimmed glasses and an equally fancy-looking glass full of some clear drink in his hand.

"Really? I'm a Harvard man myself. What part of town you from?"

"Roslindale, sir."

"Hear that, Rose? He's from my old neighborhood!"

"What a coincidence! Looks like you've got quite a catch there, Lily. Keep him close and don't let him get away," she continued in the way fancy women in movies did, Noah thought.

Lily played along with the older woman's theatrics, laughing and drawing Noah close, pretending to put a protective arm around him. "Don't worry, I'm not letting this one get away." The comment made Noah's heart skip, even though he knew she was just being charming for the crowd. He loved how she could command any room, yet still made him feel like the only person who mattered.

The woman clapped her hands together. "How delightful! Young love is so precious." As they moved away, Noah whispered to Lily, "Do you actually mean any of this stuff you say to them?"

Lily glanced around to make sure no one was listening, then leaned closer. "Some of it's just what you're supposed to say. But..." She looked directly at him. "Not the part about not letting you get away. That's real."

Noah felt like he might float away right there in the middle of the party.

"Noah! I didn't know you were coming tonight." Noah remembered him as the director of Sunset Academy from the other day.

"Hi," he smiled, unsure if he should say anything else. Lily came to his rescue by saying he was her date.

"Really? Wow! I didn't know..." Noah thought he could see him looking back and forth like he was planning something. "Well, good for you! Good for you both! Enjoy the night."

As they walked away, Noah whispered in her ear, "What was that about?" Lily simply said he's probably making notes for another episode or something and moved on.

"Think we'll be finished by 8? There are a lot of people here."

"We will. Mom will ensure it," and they walked directly her way.

"You two just about ready?" she said for the benefit of three important-looking men surrounding her, drinks in hand. They turned as Lily replied politely that they had met so many wonderful people tonight and did they have to go? He was confused. They all agreed to leave by 8. Diana seemed to be smiling the entire time, something in her voice was slightly different... more... not polite, but it was different than Noah remembered.

"As much as I'd love to, sweetie, we've got another engagement, remember?" Diana said to her daughter but looked at the three older men around her.

"Oh yes... well, more to come," Lily said turning to look at Noah and he smiled, figuring not saying anything was the best approach.

"Lily, are you going to introduce this sharp-looking fellow?" one of the men asked.

"Oh, where are my manners? Mr. Spielberg, everyone... this is my boyfriend, Noah Walsh, from Boston."

"Noah? Boston, eh? Boy, it's been a long time since I was in Boston. I remember when we shot Jaws out off the cape... God... what, 50 years ago?" he asked one of the other men standing there and laughed. "Has it been that long? Wow! We're really a bunch of old guys, aren't we?" and they all laughed again.

Noah laughed along and then it suddenly hit him. He was standing here, in a tuxedo, holding hands with the most beautiful girl he'd ever met, talking to Steven Spielberg. Three weeks ago he was just some kid in Roslindale whose biggest worry was passing algebra. How did this become his life?

"So, first time in Hollywood?"

"I'm sorry?" Noah snapped out of his daze.

"First visit to Los Angeles?"

"Oh... yes, sir. I'm here visiting my uncle David..."

"David Harmon, Steven," Diana interjected quietly.

"David's your uncle?! Well, I'll be a... I've been meaning to call him... you tell your uncle he needs to have you out more!" He laughed and everyone followed, including Noah.

"If I have anything to say about it, he will," Lily added charmingly, just as her mother taught her and everyone laughed again. Noah thought he saw Diana flash a look of pride in her eyes.

"Hear, hear! You should! Well, nice meeting you Noah from Boston..."

"Very nice making your acquaintance, Mr. Spielberg."

"Call me Steven, Noah. And I look forward to seeing you around."

Noah was officially in some alternate universe. This was beyond anything he could have imagined when he got on that plane in Boston. How do you go back to being normal after this? How do you sit in homeroom and pretend you didn't spend a week dating a TV star and shaking hands with movie legends?

Diana guided them toward the exit, exchanging the usual pleasantries and air kisses that seemed to be the currency of these events. Soon they were in the back of a black SUV, the kind Noah had only seen in movies.

"That was something else..." Lily said, settling back into the leather seats.

"Noah, you were perfect," Diana added with genuine pride. "You handled yourself like you'd been doing this for years."

"I... I still can't believe any of this is real," Noah said, staring out at the city lights.

"That you met Steven Spielberg?" Lily asked, though she already knew the feeling. She remembered her first big industry event, the over-whelming sensation that she'd somehow wandered into someone else's life.

Noah nodded, still processing it all.

"You know what I love about you?" Lily said quietly, taking his hand in the darkness of the car. "You're still amazed by all this. Most people I meet either act like they deserve it or like they're too cool to care."

Noah looked at her, this incredible girl who could have anyone, who moved through that world of celebrities and executives like she belonged there. "And you picked me."

"I picked you," she confirmed, squeezing his hand.

Noah dashed into the men's room from the kitchen entrance where the owner met them. It wasn't unusual to have notable people show up in the back, looking for privacy. Quickly changing into his jeans and a polo shirt, he felt weird stuffing the tuxedo into the brown paper bag Diana gave him from Gelson's... whatever that was... and walked back out to see Lily and Diana coming out of the ladies' room. In the span of five minutes, they went from looking like a billion bucks to casual, normal. Was this Hollywood life? he wondered.

David walked up to Diana and gave her those fake kisses he saw everyone giving back at the party and then leaned down and asked him and Lily how it went.

"Steven said he was going to call you," Noah said like he was simply a messenger.

David looked puzzled before Diana added "Spielberg" and David smiled. Noah was already living it up with Hollywood royalty. "Well, Mr. Important," he teased. "I'll have you help me on his next salary negotiation!" And everyone laughed, although Noah wasn't entirely sure if he was joking.

Turning the corner, they saw Elena already seated in a large circular booth David had specially reserved. It was in the back, secluded and dimly lit with a simple tea light and spillover from the bar, perfect for some privacy.

Elena got up and embraced both Noah and Lily warmly. When Diana approached for the typical Hollywood air kisses, Elena pulled her into a real Boston hug instead. Diana was surprised for a moment, then melted into it gratefully. It had been so long since someone had hugged her like that—like a real friend, not a business contact.

"I'm never going back to those fake kisses," Diana whispered, and Elena laughed.

"Welcome to how we do it on the East Coast," Elena replied.

"Are they here yet?" Lily asked.

"Should be anytime. I guess we should go up front. C'mon Noah. You ready?"

He beamed. This was going to be fun.

Walking down the block, Aiden kept telling Marcus to hurry up. It was almost 8:25 and he didn't want to be late. Marcus was learning some of his boyfriend's idiosyncrasies, being punctual near the top.

"Fine, fine... geesh! Hungry or something?"

"Starved!"

They'd grabbed some leftover pizza around 6 when Aiden complained he was getting hungry. Marcus had smirked—"Shit, babe, all that fucking really worked up your appetite, huh?"—which made Aiden turn completely scarlet. But Marcus loved that reaction, the way Aiden could be so bold when they were making love yet still get mortified when Marcus talked about it afterward.

"Jesus, Marcus!" Aiden hissed, looking around even though they were alone. "You can't just say stuff like that!"

"Why not? It's true," Marcus grinned, pulling Aiden close. "Besides, I love making you blush."

"I hate you," Aiden muttered, but he was smiling despite himself.

"No you don't. You love me," Marcus said, suddenly more serious. "Even when I'm being a complete asshole."

"Especially then," Aiden admitted, still amazed that someone wanted all of him—the shy parts and the bold parts alike.

They were almost at the restaurant when Aiden spotted David and Noah out front.

"Hey!" Aiden called out, then turned to hurry Marcus along. "Come on!"

David smiled watching them approach. There was something different about how they moved together now, a kind of certainty that hadn't been there before. They'd found their rhythm as a couple.

"How did the things... uh... go?" Aiden couldn't remember what things they had to do... he'd been... distracted when David called... and then remembered his comment about cameras and suddenly became embarrassed just thinking about it.

"Dude, what's wrong? You're like all red," Noah asked, perplexed. Marcus and David caught each other's eye and nearly laughed, David turning to pretend to cough into his hand.

"Uh... just a long walk... Anyway, shall we eat? I'm starving!" Aiden recovered.

Noah was "on" according to the plan. He was to lead his brother in while David kept Marcus back a few paces.

Noah took to his acting job like a natural... "Dude! Like you won't believe what happened to me today!"

"What?" Aiden was hooked, wanting to know what the latest install-ment of "His little brother is dating a movie star" would be when Noah turned the dark corner and there was their mom.

"Excuse me, can you tell me the way to Hollywood?" she said to Aiden who, for a moment, didn't recognize her in the dimly lit restaurant before it kicked in.

"MOM?!"

thirty-five
everything on display

UNDERSTATEMENT.

There's no getting around it—Aiden was mortified. His mother was standing right there. Looking right at him. Right through him. Everything. All of it... his life here in California was now on full display... Marcus... his new confidence... his "screw it, I'm finally myself" spirit... the way he and Noah had grown closer... his... God, his virginity was gone... his love... love for Marcus... love for himself, finally... And it was all exposed in this very second.

For years, he'd perfected the careful dance around his mother—watching every word, every gesture, every glance. He'd planned to have the entire flight back to Boston to slip back into that carefully constructed version of himself, the one she expected. The dutiful son who never caused problems, who kept his secrets buried deep.

But here she was. Right now. And there was no time to rebuild those walls, no chance to hide who he'd become. Everyone was here, he saw, scanning the dimly lit space... Lily and, he guessed, her mom... and his brother... David... Marcus... where was Marcus? The panic was building, years of carefully maintained composure cracking apart. And then...

"Mom?!"

"Hi sweetie! Miss me?"

The room tilted. Every secret, every moment of freedom he'd found this summer, every kiss with Marcus, every night they'd spent together—

it all crashed over him at once. The boy who'd spent years hiding was suddenly, brutally exposed. His vision blurred, the restaurant spinning into fragments of light and sound, and then...

Passed out.

Marcus lunged to catch him.

Elena looked completely mortified, unable to break free from herself, glued to the ground.

David's eyes bulged trying to comprehend what was happening.

Noah was closest and instinctively reached to grab his brother.

Lily began to open her mouth as if to scream out for help.

Diana's motherly instinct thrust her forward, but she came crashing into the edge of the table.

Noah took the worst of the fall, having grabbed Aiden's sides and tumbling down with him.

It all happened in mere seconds. David knelt down, immediately reaching for Aiden's pulse.

Marcus was already on the floor, reaching for his boyfriend's head to cradle it in his lap.

"Don't touch him!" David snapped and Marcus froze. "He may have hurt his neck."

Diana ran to Elena, but she was already in tears, kneeling down to help both her boys.

Lily had swung around looking for Noah, who was trapped partly underneath his brother, stunned but otherwise fine. Lily grabbed his free hand and he held on, not wanting to move after David's orders.

Someone had called an ambulance.

"I just wanted to surprise him..." Elena was inconsolable.

David gave Diana a look to get her back to the booth.

"He'll be fine. He just fainted," she held onto her new friend, but thought she'd be the same if it had been Lily.

David took a cloth napkin and dipped it in a water glass and began to cool Aiden's forehead.

"Aiden... Aiden, son... Are you awake?"

Slowly, Aiden began to open his eyes. Where... where was he? Why... why was he on the floor?

Marcus's face looked down at him, tears streaming. "Are you okay, babe?"

"Yeah," he croaked out as if he was waking up for the day. "Why... what's wrong?"

Marcus choked back more tears.

"Aiden, are you hurt? Do you feel fine?" David was hovering over him now. Why was he asking if... he felt stiff like he'd hit his side and then realized Noah was lying there and he... Aiden rolled over off of his brother, wondering what happened. Lily pulled Noah's hand and helped him up, immediately looking him over for bruises or cuts.

"Aiden, you must have fainted and fallen. Do you feel hurt? How's your head?"

Aiden felt fine... he thought, and began to sit up.

"Hold on, buddy," David said. "I want someone to check you out first."

A small gathering of restaurant patrons from the other room were starting to cluster in the passageway, but the owner quietly asked them back. Just someone fainting... nothing to worry about.

Diana, for a brief moment, wondered if she and Lily should disappear before someone called one of those tabloid photographers, but put it out of her mind. This was about Elena's boy, not her daughter. She felt a tinge of guilt for even thinking it—so jaded she'd become in the business.

Two paramedics had been escorted from the back entrance and asked everyone to move away. Aiden heard David saying something to one of them as the other—a man who looked in his twenties with short-cropped hair, a tan and a handsome face—asked him basic questions like what day it was and who was the president while poking and prodding.

"Can you tell me how many fingers I'm holding up?" he asked, looking directly into Aiden's eyes, and Aiden responded correctly.

The other paramedic looked around his neck and asked if he felt pain anywhere. "No, why all the fuss?" Aiden looked over and saw Marcus hovering, still with tears in his eyes. "Why are you crying? I'm fine." But even as he said it, Aiden felt the crushing weight of embarrassment settling over him. He'd fainted. In front of everyone. In front of his mother. Like some fragile kid who couldn't handle a surprise.

"Can you sit up?" the attractive paramedic asked.

"Yeah..." Aiden raised up slowly. His back was slightly tender, but the physical pain was nothing compared to his humiliation.

Aiden looked over at Marcus, who was practically vibrating with worry, and felt something shift inside him. Marcus didn't care that they were in public, didn't care who was watching. He was completely focused on Aiden, his face streaked with tears, his hands shaking slightly.

"I'm okay. Really I am, babe."

The word slipped out so naturally, so easily. *Babe.* In front of his mother. In front of everyone. And for the first time since he'd opened his eyes, Aiden didn't feel the urge to take it back.

The attractive paramedic looked over at Marcus and back to Aiden, having finished checking his pulse for the umpteenth time. "He your boyfriend?" "Yeah, that's Marcus." "You two look good together," and winked. Aiden began to smile, a blush coming.

The two paramedics spoke with each other and then the handsome one told Marcus he could help his boyfriend to his feet... which was all he needed to hear. Marcus was immediately at Aiden's side, kissing his face and asking how he felt.

"Why all the fuss?" Aiden kept asking, thinking this was no big deal, but appreciating the kisses. Marcus didn't care where they were or who saw them... this had scared the hell out of him... he loved Aiden so much and to see him hurt... it was death times ten.

The attractive paramedic smiled and leaned in to both in a hushed voice: "He'll be fine, but just take care of him tonight, okay? If he feels off... take him to the ER, okay? I don't think he has a concussion, but just be careful..."

"I'll take care of him," Marcus said immediately, his voice firm with conviction. The paramedic smiled at the obvious devotion.

"You two really are cute." He turned back to his partner, but not before adding quietly, "He's lucky to have you."

From across the small space, Elena watched this exchange with growing amazement. She'd worried about Marcus being too young, too damaged, too unstable for her son. But there was nothing unstable about the way he hovered protectively over Aiden, nothing immature about the tears he didn't try to hide, nothing uncertain about his immediate promise to care for the person he loved.

This wasn't some teenage infatuation. This was real.

"Yes, we will," David conveyed his understanding to the paramedic who advised he must have fainted and to keep an eye on him the next 24 hours. "Of course." His partner nodded his head towards Marcus and suggested he was in good hands before they packed their medical case and headed back through the rear entrance.

Thanks to Diana's steady presence beside her, Elena was beginning to calm down. She'd never dealt with so much as a broken bone with either of her boys, but this... this had terrified her.

But watching Marcus with Aiden now—the gentle way he kissed his face, how he'd taken the wet napkin from David and was carefully wiping Aiden's brow, the protective circle his arms made around her son—Elena felt her earlier fears beginning to crumble. She'd been so worried about heartbreak, about distance, about losing Aiden to someone who might not truly care for him.

Looking at them now, she realized how wrong she'd been. Marcus wasn't going to break her son's heart. He was going to protect it with everything he had.

The tears that had been subsiding returned, but now they were different. Bittersweet. Because she was watching her little boy being loved— truly, deeply loved—by someone who would move heaven and earth to keep him safe. And she was also watching that little boy love someone back with the same fierce devotion.

He wasn't her little boy anymore. He was a man, choosing his own family, his own future. And maybe... maybe that was exactly what he was supposed to be.

After consulting everyone about whether they'd rather call it a night, it had been Aiden who overruled that thought. He was hungry. Really hungry now. And he wanted to stay. So, everyone did... hesitant at first. Marcus was treating him like a precious item to be delicately handled and everyone kept looking at him like he was going to faint again.

"Would everyone just... eat already! I'm fine. Seriously. I just..."

"We just wanted to make sure that..." David began.

"He'll be fine. He has Marcus to look after him." Elena's voice was quiet but decisive, her eyes still fixed on the menu. The voice of a mother who understood that the natural order had shifted. She'd have time later to talk with her son, to process everything she'd witnessed. Right now, he needed to just be part of the family—this new configuration of family that included the young man who was now his anchor.

Aiden looked at his mother with a mixture of surprise and terror, bracing himself for questions he wasn't ready to answer, for disappointment he couldn't bear to see in her eyes. This was the moment he'd been dreading—when all those carefully maintained walls would come crashing down and she'd see exactly who her son really was.

But instead of interrogation or rejection, she'd simply... accepted it. Quietly, matter-of-factly, as if Marcus had always been part of the family. Most people probably didn't even catch the significance of her words, but Aiden did. He heard everything she wasn't saying: *I see you. I understand. This is okay.*

Something inside him began to unknot. Maybe he didn't have to be that carefully constructed version of himself anymore.

"So, Marcus..." Elena turned to look directly at him for the first time. "Want to split an appetizer with me?"

It was such a simple question, but Aiden heard everything in it. *I see you. I accept you. You're part of this family now.*

And with those words, years of careful pretense finally crumbled away. Aiden felt himself breathe fully for the first time since walking into the restaurant.

The evening gradually found its rhythm after the initial chaos. Elena found herself studying Marcus throughout the meal—not with the suspicious eye she'd planned, but with genuine curiosity. The way he made sure Aiden ate something substantial. How he deflected attention when Aiden still looked embarrassed about the fainting. The protective way he kept one hand on Aiden's back, casual but constant reassurance.

David had been right. This wasn't just teenage hormones or summer romance. This was the kind of love that weathers storms, that shows up when it matters most. The kind she'd hoped her son would find someday —she just hadn't expected someday to be now, and here, with this particular young man who'd already survived more than most adults ever would.

When Marcus joked to Lily that "at least your boyfriend didn't faint," and Noah shouted "Drama queen!" from across the table, Aiden's laughter was genuine and unguarded. This was who her son was when he felt safe to be himself. And Marcus was a big part of why he felt that safety.

Watching them together—really watching them—Elena felt her last reservations dissolve. She'd been so focused on protecting Aiden from potential heartbreak that she'd almost missed something wonderful: her son was genuinely, completely happy.

And somewhere in all that laughter and warmth and chaotic family joy, Aiden caught his mother's eye across the table. In that moment, they both understood. This was family—messy, complicated, chosen family that didn't look like anything she'd planned for, but was exactly what it needed to be.

thirty-six
mother and son

"WELL, I'm wiped out. I'll see you all in the morning."

David walked from the pool into his home as if nothing extraordinary had happened that day... just another evening.

Noah had already gone to bed, having spent a few precious moments with Lily in the restaurant's back entry hall while waiting for their car. Diana and Elena had given them some space while still keeping watchful eyes. He'd wanted to kiss her, but with the moms right there, they'd just talked the way fourteen-year-olds do. "I'll text you tomorrow," Lily had said before giving him a kiss on his cheek. Elena and Diana had turned to look away, both smiling like schoolgirls themselves. This was the fun part of motherhood—reliving those magical moments.

Noah was on top of the world and Elena could tell. But she kept it to herself. Let him enjoy the feeling. No need for mom to bring him back to reality tonight.

They'd decided to walk back to David's home, just a short stroll up the hill. Aiden and Marcus had already gone ahead, and David met them at the corner in front of the restaurant, the three of them talking as they walked. Actually, Noah was pointing things out to his mom proudly—David and Elena catching glances at each other, knowing that Noah was in his element, proud of his independence and knowledge of his summer neighborhood.

"Goodnight David... oh... David..." Elena remembered.

He turned from within the kitchen.

"Thank you."

He threw up his hand and turned to head to his suite.

Elena had been sitting with her feet dangling in the pool while Aiden reclined on one of the loungers nearby. The soothing sound of the fountain and the blue lights from under the water created a spa-like mood as Elena looked out over the LA skyline west toward the ocean. She'd been here many times before—as Michael's best friend, as David's chosen family—but never like this. Never as the mother watching her son become a man.

The last time Aiden was here, he was still small enough to need her help with everything. And then there was Michael's funeral, when this house had felt too heavy with grief and memory. She'd wondered then how David could bear to stay here, surrounded by reminders of what he'd lost.

But maybe that was the point. Maybe David stayed because love didn't end when someone was gone—it just changed shape, found new ways to exist. Looking at her son now, she realized she was learning the same lesson in reverse. Love didn't end when someone grew up, either. It just had to learn to let go.

"Where's Marcus, honey?"

"He's up in his room... said he wanted to give us our space... or something..." Aiden was staring up at the sky as if daydreaming.

"I like him. He's good for you."

Aiden didn't say anything. What could he say? He felt it, too.

After a moment of quiet, Elena turned to look up at her son still staring into the stars. "Aiden, honey..."

"Mmm..."

"I'm sorry I surprised you."

"It's fine. I'm sorry I fainted. I still feel stupid."

"Don't. I would've done the same."

"Really? Fainted?"

"Well... it was a shock... and... I think I know why."

"It's fine, mom. I'm okay."

"Aiden... let me say this, right?"

He nodded, not taking his eyes off Polaris.

"I know you've been struggling... and I can't say I know exactly why, but I want you to know how incredibly proud I am of you."

Aiden swallowed hard. Here it came—the lecture he'd been dreading. The careful, loving explanation of why this couldn't work. Boston versus LA. School. His age. All the practical reasons why his mother, no matter how much she liked Marcus, would have to be the adult and put a stop to this before it went any further.

"And I'm really impressed with your boyfriend."

She used the word. Aiden's breath caught. *Boyfriend.* Not "friend" or "that nice boy" or any of the careful euphemisms he'd expected.

"Marcus is wonderful, and I hope I can get to know him better... But..."

There it was. Aiden braced himself for the gentle disappointment, the reasonable arguments, the loving but firm boundaries his mother would have to set.

"But, I don't want to interfere with you two like some hovering mother. I want you to love him as hard and fast and give everything you have to each other."

Aiden looked at his mother in complete shock. This wasn't the conversation he'd expected. This wasn't the gentle letdown or the practical concerns about distance and age and all the reasons why teenage love couldn't last. This was... permission. Encouragement, even.

"When you fainted tonight," she continued softly, "I watched Marcus with you. I've seen people in love before, Aiden, but I've also seen people who think they're in love. What I saw tonight..." She paused, her voice catching slightly. "That boy forgot everyone else existed. The only thing in the world that mattered to him was making sure you were okay."

"What?" Aiden asked softly.

"Let go of themselves... trust you..."

Aiden sat up straighter, seeing his mother not as the authority figure who set rules and boundaries, but as someone who understood things he was just beginning to learn. Someone who had watched love stories unfold, who had her own experiences with friendship and loss and letting go.

"I trust you, Aiden. And while I'll always worry—I'm your mother, that's what we do—" she laughed, and he found himself smiling back.

"What I saw tonight between you and Marcus... it reminded me of something. Of the night I first met David."

"You were friends with Michael first, right?"

Elena's expression softened with memory. "We were inseparable. Best friends since high school. If he'd been straight, he probably would have been your father." She laughed, and Aiden grinned. He'd heard stories about Michael, but never understood the depth of that friendship.

"But he was gayer than Christmas morning, so instead we became the kind of friends who tell each other everything. Until David."

"Why were you worried?" Aiden asked, genuinely curious now.

She turned to face him fully, and he saw something vulnerable in her expression—not his mother the authority figure, but Elena the young woman who'd once been afraid of losing her best friend.

"Because I knew David would take him away from me. Not intentionally, not meanly, but... when you find the person you're supposed to love forever, everything else shifts. It has to." She paused, looking out at the water. "I was terrified I was going to lose the most important person in my life."

"Did you? Lose him?"

Elena smiled sadly. "In some ways, yes. Michael became part of something bigger than just our friendship. But you know what I learned? Love doesn't actually take people away from you. It just... expands the family."

She gestured toward the house, toward the lit window upstairs. "Marcus is up there giving us space because he knows you need this conversation with me. But in a little while, you're going to go up to him, and he's going to ask how it went, and he's going to care about the answer because how I feel about him matters to you." She reached over and squeezed his hand. "That's not losing you, honey. That's gaining a son."

Aiden looked slightly embarrassed the way any son does when his mother says things like that.

"It's true. And one day, you two might have children..."

Aiden looked as if he was going to debate her, but she stopped that politely.

"No, it's true. You never know. And if you do, you'll understand. You want them to grow up with everything you didn't... to protect them from harm and all sorts of things... to never get sick, never hurt from some asshole calling you names on the playground..." (Aiden giggled—he loved when his mom was herself and calling a kid an asshole was proof she was in her zone now). "The point is, Aiden... you spend years wanting to be so much to your child that one day, you realize they are an adult... and it's time you quit being 'mom' and turn into being not their friend, but a different kind of mother... the kind that allows them to live their lives the way we wanted to live when we were their age... supportive, perhaps nagging sometimes," (Aiden laughed), "but full of love for them when their lives are going well and even more when they're not."

Aiden felt tears prick his eyes. He'd expected logistics and limitations, not this deep understanding of what love could mean.

"David was right," Elena said quietly, looking up at Marcus's window.

"About what?"

"You're fully in it. Real, honest-to-God, change-your-whole-life love." She looked back at him. "And that boy up there? He's your David, isn't he?"

Aiden followed her gaze to the illuminated window, thinking of Marcus probably lying in bed worrying about this exact conversation. "We're just—"

"Don't you dare say you're just boyfriends," Elena cut him off. "I've got eyes, Aiden. I've been where you are. What you two have... that's the real thing. I could feel it the moment I watched him catch you when you fell."

Aiden was quiet for a long moment. "I don't know how David survived losing Michael. I can't even imagine..."

Elena's expression grew soft and proud. "The fact that you can put yourself in David's shoes, that you understand what that kind of loss would mean... that tells me everything I need to know about how deeply you love."

They sat in comfortable silence, watching planes line up for LAX in the distance.

Finally Elena stood, stretching. "Alright, I'm dead on my feet. It's been one hell of a day."

"Mom?"

"Yeah, sweetheart?"

"Thank you. For coming out here. For... all of this."

She smiled. "Thank you for letting me see who you've become."

As she started toward the house, Aiden called after her. "Mom? There's something I need to say officially."

She turned back, eyebrows raised.

"I'm gay."

Elena's face broke into the biggest grin he'd ever seen. "No shit, Sherlock. I've known since you were twelve and asked me to take down the Sports Illustrated swimsuit calendar in the garage because it was 'gross.'"

"Mom!"

"What? You think I'm blind?" She was laughing now. "Honey, I've been waiting for you to trust me enough to tell me for years."

Aiden was mortified and relieved and laughing all at once. "You could have said something!"

"And rob you of the chance to come to me when you were ready? Not a chance." She started walking again, then called back over her shoulder, "Now get your ass upstairs to that gorgeous boyfriend of yours before he thinks I scared you off!"

Aiden stood there grinning like an idiot as her voice echoed from inside the house: "And use protection!"

"MOM!"

Her laughter floated back to him, and he realized he'd never loved her more than he did right now.

thirty-seven
a brilliant idea

AGAINST HIS BETTER JUDGMENT, David arrived back at the studio Monday morning to find his desk buried under a mountain of emails. He'd considered taking another day off to play tour guide with Elena and the boys, but there wasn't much left to show her—she'd been exploring LA since before her sons were even a thought. Besides, they'd spent a quiet weekend at home, much needed after Friday's emotional whirlwind. Noah had been sulking because he and Lily could only text— she was tied up with weekend commitments, and Elena had claimed Sunday for herself with her boys. David had tactfully taken Marcus on a quick day trip to Solvang, giving Elena the space she'd never ask for but desperately needed. Marcus missed Aiden, of course, but the Danish village proved a welcome distraction. Besides, the kid needed to learn that love meant both togetherness and independence.

Sara appeared with her usual stack of messages, sorted with the precision that came from years of knowing David's priorities. At the top sat a cryptic note: Roger had called with a "brilliant idea" he wanted to discuss. David's eyes rolled automatically. In his experience, directors' brilliant ideas usually translated to budget requests. Still, he had genuine respect for Roger—they'd worked together for nearly a decade, ever since David took a chance on him as an unknown. Michael had been the one to convince him that night, snatching the portfolio from David's hands as he lounged on the sofa. "I like him!" Michael had declared after his nosier-than-necessary review. "Hire him for the picture." Sometimes Michael's instincts were better than David's own analytical approach. That portfolio had been headed for the rejection pile.

David reached for his phone and decided against it.

"Sara, I'm walking over to Roger's office."

A few minutes later in the morning sun, he pulled off his sunglasses and walked in, not bothering to knock. David was generally very polite and prided himself on not living up to the reputation of a studio executive, but some perks he kept for himself—and walking into someone's office without feeling like he needed to be asked to cross the threshold was one. He wasn't a vampire.

"David! I... I didn't expect to see you... at..." he looked up at the wall clock, "8:30. I didn't think anyone arrived here until after 10."

David just looked at him with a polite smile. He wasn't necessarily a big talker, and definitely not early in the morning. Still, he did like Roger. They weren't truly friends, but he enjoyed his work and they held mutual respect for each other.

"So, how much do you need?" David asked with a small grin.

"What? Oh..." he laughed. "Nothing like that... well... maybe." David lifted a brow of inquiry.

"Say... your nephew..."

"Noah?"

"Yes. Have you seen the fine cut with him?"

"I didn't realize you had one ready."

"Hang on..." He pulled up a window on his laptop and spun it around.

David watched Noah's scene play out, his nephew transitioning from background student to scene-stealer with an ease that was both impressive and unsettling. The kid's surprise looked completely genuine—because it was. His delivery of the Netflix line felt natural, unforced. Hell, Noah could probably roll out of bed and walk onto set without missing a beat.

"Not bad," David admitted.

"Linda and Charles think he's got real potential. But there's something else..." Roger spun the laptop back toward himself and pulled up a new window. "Take a look at the audience feedback."

David leaned over Roger's shoulder, scanning the responses:

The new kid steals the show I LOVE Ryan!
Never watched before, but this Ryan guy has me hooked

"It goes on like this for pages," Roger continued. "The kid's testing through the roof. I think he'd be perfect for a recurring role. Start small, see how it develops, but write him in properly. Linda's already brainstorming storylines for the rest of the season, and if we get renewed for another thirteen episodes..."

"Thirteen?" David straightened up. The business side of his brain engaged automatically.

"We need to hit at least a 3.5 to 3.7 in the demo, and with Noah... honestly, David, he could bump us a full point, maybe more."

David felt the familiar weight of adult responsibility settling on his shoulders. "Roger, he's fourteen. He's supposed to start high school in Boston in a few weeks."

"Look, I know it's complicated. But this is the kind of opportunity that doesn't come along often. And after the DGA event... David, everyone's already talking about him and Lily. Steven Spielberg specifically asked about Noah's experience, mentioned some project he's developing..."

David knew exactly which project Roger meant—they were deep in negotiations on it. The business implications were staggering, but all he could think about was Noah's innocent excitement that night, how unprepared he was for the machinery of Hollywood fame.

"I appreciate you coming to me directly," David said finally. "But I need to think about this. More importantly, I need to talk to his mother."

Roger nodded, understanding. "Of course. Just... don't think too long, all right? These windows don't stay open forever."

David was already moving toward the door. He'd heard enough to know this was real, substantial, potentially life-changing. He also knew it was the kind of decision that could destroy a kid if handled wrong. Noah needed protection from this industry, even from opportunities that looked golden on the surface.

"Uncle David!" The boys practically jumped on him as he walked in the house. Elena stood in the kitchen cutting celery in Michael's old apron. He hadn't seen anyone wear it since... well...

"How was the office, *Dad*?" Elena sarcastically asked over the boys' voices, causing them to laugh.

"It was a long day, *Mom*!" He gave it back to her and they laughed again. "What in the hell are you doing?"

"Applying for a mortgage!" she spat almost instantly. "What the hell does it look like? Are you going senile on me, David? I'm cutting celery." The boys loved to see the two of them razz each other, grown-ups being kids for their amusement.

"Uh... and *why* are you cutting celery, Your Highness?"

Elena put the knife down, turned to open the cabinet, pulled out a jar of peanut butter, made a dramatic show of opening the jar and shoving one of the newly cut stalks right into the middle of it. Pulling out the peanut butter-laden celery stalk, she shoved it in David's face. "This! This is why. Happy?"

Noah practically rolled laughing at Uncle David's expression. But David, without flinching, bit a big chunk off right from Elena's hands and walked into the living room to drop his things. The boys yelled and laughed and David thought he heard Elena call him a dick, but what else was new.

"How about," he turned and said, "we all go out tonight for dinner?"

"So, no celery?" Elena asked deadpan.

"For dinner?"

"No, to shove up your ass."

Noah finally lost it, followed quickly by Marcus. Aiden tried to keep it together, but finally succumbed to the giggles.

David looked at Elena and asked, "Are they always like this?"

"Just around you."

The two of them were perfect for each other.

"I cannot believe I let you all talk me into this."

"I don't know, David... it's sort of fun in a..." Elena pulled her finger along a sticky residue on the table they were sitting at, "...gross way."

The boys were off playing video games at the Shakey's Pizza Parlor a ten-minute drive away while everyone waited for their Sausage and Pepperoni and large order of Mojo potatoes to arrive. A birthday party full of grade-schoolers sat opposite their table alongside a few families in booths here and there. This most definitely was not Beverly Hills.

"Listen, El... I had an interesting conversation this morning with the director of that show Noah was an extra on."

"Yeah?" She took a sip of her Pepsi in a red plastic tumbler that probably had more mouths on it over the years than a porn star, and grimaced.

"What's wrong?"

"CO_2 is out. This... is shit."

David giggled as she reached for his water. He knew better when they ordered.

"So, what about the director?"

"He wanted to talk about Noah."

She perked up. "Noah? What about him?"

David spent ten minutes explaining Roger's proposition—the audience numbers, the storyline possibilities, even Spielberg's interest in Noah for future projects.

"Noah?" Elena's voice went up an octave. "My Noah? The kid who still asks me to cut the crusts off his sandwiches?"

David nodded solemnly.

Elena stared at him for a long moment. "I... David, this is..."

"Overwhelming. I know."

"He'd have to stay in LA, wouldn't he? I mean, he couldn't commute from Boston for television work."

"Elena, he's fourteen. I wouldn't put a kid through that kind of travel schedule. Besides, if this takes off, there'd be promotional work, appearances, interviews..." David watched her face pale. "Look, I told Roger that Noah has school, a life in Boston. I can easily shut this down if it's too much."

"But what if we're crushing his dreams? What if this is his one shot and we're too scared to let him take it?" Elena's voice cracked slightly. "God, David, what kind of mother says no to her kid's dreams because she's too chicken to figure out the logistics?"

"But then there's Aiden," she said, staring into the distance. "God, David, I can't just drag him back to Boston and away from Marcus. Not after everything that boy's been through. Not after seeing how happy they are together."

"So we're back to the same problem."

"Exactly. How do I give one son his dream without breaking the other son's heart?" Elena reached for David's water glass and took a sip. "A month ago my biggest worry was getting Aiden to open up to me about anything. Now I'm trying to figure out how to juggle two kids' entire futures without screwing up either one."

David reached for his glass back and took a drink, but the ice shifted suddenly, splashing water down his shirt.

"Serves you right for hogging the only decent drink at this place," Elena laughed.

David grabbed some napkins to clean up the mess, and Elena's expression grew more thoughtful.

"But what about Noah again?"

"What about him? Roger wants him to do a regular part on the show."

"How long would that take?"

"Well... they've got 8 more this season and, if it gets picked up for 13 more next year, he'd have a break around Christmas and then back at it probably in February."

"When will they know if it gets the extra 13?"

"Well... that depends..."

"On what?"

"If I decide to pick them up again."

"Oh, so you, Mr. Big Shot, have a role in this, I see." She smiled, loving to dig at him as the important executive, but was the only one since Michael was gone to truly know him... as the guy who has water all over his shirt at a Shakey's Pizza. He laughed.

"Listen, El... I won't bullshit you. This is big time. The show's a real winner in the 13-17 demo. And from the data I saw today, Noah really is a natural, even though he doesn't know it."

"You're shitting me."

"No bullshit, El. I wouldn't do that to you... or Noah."

"So... if Noah does this... this thing... he'd need to be here, I suppose."

David nodded and reached for his glass again, this time being careful of the ice.

"Are you ready to be a full-time parent, David? Really ready?"

The question hit him harder than expected. David looked over at the arcade where the three boys were clustered around a racing game, Noah trash-talking while Aiden and Marcus laughed. It had been wonderful having them visit—like playing house with the family he'd never imagined having. But this would be different. Real responsibility. Real consequences.

"I honestly don't know, El. Having them for the summer has been amazing, but you're right—this would be completely different. Daily homework battles, teenage attitudes, actual parenting..." He paused. "But maybe it's time I tried. Maybe I'm ready to stop living like Michael's ghost."

"And then there's Marcus."

The words stopped David cold. Marcus. Of course. He'd been so focused on Noah's opportunity and Elena's concerns about Aiden that he'd temporarily forgotten the most important fact: he was already parenting. Marcus wasn't just staying with him temporarily anymore—somewhere along the way, David had become the closest thing to a father that kid had.

"Jesus, you're right. I'm already responsible for him. School, college applications, his entire future..." David felt the weight of it settling over him. "When did I become a parent without noticing?"

"The minute you decided to love him," Elena said quietly.

"But El, I've watched you pace the floor every night worrying about your boys being three thousand miles away. How could you possibly consider letting Noah move to LA permanently?"

"Because maybe..." she took a shaky breath, "maybe the best way to protect them isn't to keep them close. Maybe it's to make sure they're surrounded by people who love them enough to do the right thing, even when it's hard."

"So what are you saying?"

"I'm saying we need to figure out how to protect Noah's dreams without destroying Aiden's happiness. I'm saying maybe there's a solution we haven't considered yet."

"Like what?"

Elena was quiet for a moment, working through possibilities. "If Noah did this show, and Aiden stayed to finish senior year with Marcus, they'd need supervision. Real supervision, not just you checking in between meetings."

"Of course. Diana's been invaluable with Lily, but Noah would need..."

David stopped mid-sentence. Elena was watching him with that expression she got when she was waiting for him to catch up to her thinking.

"Oh," he said quietly.

"Yeah. Oh."

"The studio needs qualified teachers for all the young actors, not just Lily. Noah, if he joins the show, plus kids from other productions... Elena, you could oversee the entire educational program."

"I don't have California certification."

"So get it. The studio would cover the costs, the time off, everything."

"And housing? LA isn't exactly teacher-salary friendly."

"You'd live with us. Michael's house has plenty of space, and frankly..." David's voice softened. "I think it's time that house was full of family again."

Elena stared at him. "You're serious."

"Dead serious. You could keep the Boston house, spend summers there, Christmas... but your base would be here. With your boys. With us."

"David, I can't just uproot my entire life because my kid might want to be on TV."

"Can't you? Elena, you moved to Boston for Tom. You built a whole new life there for love. Why not build another one here for your sons' futures?"

The silence stretched between them, punctuated by the distant sounds of arcade games and children's laughter.

"I need to think," Elena said finally.

"Then think. But El? Don't think too long. Roger was right about one thing—windows like this don't stay open forever."

"Suck on this, losers!" Noah yelled as he ran back to the table, interrupting their conversation.

"Noah! Don't say that!" Elena chastised him, looking around at the other tables as if they'd heard and disapproved.

"Sorry, Mom," he said then turned back towards his brother and Marcus who were walking their way. "Suck on this, dickheads!" And laughed.

David spat out his water, causing more puddles to fall on his shirt, re-wetting the already drying spill from earlier.

Elena yelled out "Noah!" but laughed after seeing David's spit take.

Aiden and Marcus practically fell into each other laughing at it all.

Just then the pizza and Mojos arrived. Everyone was laughing so hard, all David could do was wave his hand in acknowledgment to the waiter.

"Welcome to Shakey's!"

thirty-eight
reality check

AIDEN WALKED into Noah's room, pushing aside assorted clothes scattered on the floor with his foot and sat down on the bed at his brother's feet. Noah was too busy on his phone, propped up against the headboard with his knees bent to support his marathon texting session, to even notice.

"Lily?"

"Huh?"

"You texting Lily?"

He simply nodded, not bothering to even look at his older brother.

"What are you gonna do when we have to go home next week?"

"Huh?" Noah grunted as Aiden caught a smile develop from whatever message he'd just received.

"When we go home..."

"Go home... where?" Noah's sole focus was whatever was going on in the virtual conversation he had going with Lily on the other end of the ether.

Aiden threw a pair of shorts that had been lying on the floor at him, bringing him into reality.

"What the fuck!"

"Only way to get your attention away from your wife for two seconds, you dickhead." They'd spoken like this to each other for what seemed like since they could walk, so neither took offense.

"So..."

"So, what?" Noah balked, wanting to get back to his girlfriend.

"I said... we have to go back home next week... you remember?"

"Next week?" Noah suddenly snapped his concentration back into the room with his brother and sat up from the headboard. "Really?"

"Yeah... school starts in a..." Aiden pulled his own phone out and swiped, looking for something. "Two weeks from Thursday."

"Really?!"

"Yeah, sucks, right?"

"Big time!" And then he looked at Aiden and smiled. "I mean..."

"I know what you meant." Aiden smiled.

"So, what's your plan with Lily? 'Cause I'm fucking clueless about Marcus."

"What do you mean? Like you'll still be boyfriends, right?"

"Well... yeah... but..." Aiden's voice got quieter, more serious. "Bro, I'll be three thousand miles away. Different time zones. Different lives." He looked out the window, his usual confidence cracking. "How the hell do you make that work when you're seventeen?"

"Three thousand miles?" Noah's phone was forgotten now, the reality hitting him. "Jesus... that's..."

"Yeah. That's like... everything changes." Aiden's voice was barely above a whisper.

Aiden looked at his brother for a long moment. The kid who usually bounced off the walls with excitement was actually thinking this through. "Doesn't Lily know you have to go home?"

Noah's expression shifted, guilt creeping in. "We... we haven't really talked about it. I mean, she knows I live in Boston, but..." He trailed off.

"But you've been living in denial land, just like me." Aiden's voice was kind but honest.

"Think mom would let me stay longer? Like, finish the summer or something?"

Aiden gave him a look. "*Teacher of the Year Elena Walsh*? The woman who made us pack our bags three days early for this trip?" He shook his head. "Dude, she probably only came out here to personally escort us home."

Noah's face fell. "Shit. You're right."

"This whole thing fucking sucks," Noah said finally, putting his phone down.

"Yeah," Aiden agreed quietly. "It really does."

———

"Lily, I was wondering if I could ask you something?"

Roger caught her in the hall at the production office on her way somewhere. Stepping into an empty conference room, he said it'd be quick. He and Linda and Charles all had been looking at the numbers and how things went with Ryan's character... Lily had to quickly remember which character was Ryan and then landed on Noah's impromptu lines on set.

"Yeah?" She learned to keep her eyes and ears open, opinions to herself long ago from her mother. Roger was always nice to her, but business was something Lily was still figuring out.

"Yeah. He's testing really well and I spoke with David about..."

"David?" She interjected and then caught herself, apologizing for interrupting.

"Yes, he and I spoke about the possibility of... well, that's what I'd like your opinion on."

"My opinion?" she thought. While she knew she was one of the stars and the face of Sunset Academy, she also knew that she did as she was told. Opinions were for writers and producers. At least at her age.

"What would you think if we wrote Ryan's character into the series more?"

"Really?" She allowed herself to become eager for a moment before remembering her place and turning the indifference switch back on. "I mean, if you think that will work for the show."

Roger smiled. He knew she would love it. And he got his answer. He'd figured as such, but wanted to ensure there wasn't any weird friction that could develop between her and Noah. After all, they were fourteen. They could be just "going out" for a week or two, like he used to do when he was their age. Hell, he'd had five girlfriends before the end of eighth grade.

"Yes... we're looking at making him a semi-regular to start... see how it goes. If he tests well, he could move into a weekly."

"Really?" This time she didn't care and allowed herself to nearly screech with excitement. "You're serious?"

"Well, we still need to clear it with him, of course."

"Wait! He doesn't know?"

"No, not yet. David wanted to ensure we've covered all the bases."

"Does his mom?"

"I haven't spoken to her yet, but Dav..."

"OMG, I need to..."

"Lily, if you don't mind, I'd prefer you keep this to yourself for now. There's a lot at play and not a lot of time, so while I know it's exciting for you..."

Lily turned professional again. Roger could visibly see it. "I get it. I won't say anything, Roger."

"Good. But... it would be fun, wouldn't it?" he rebounded to a more upbeat tone.

"I think it is an interesting proposition," she remained professional. Roger smiled. Diana was teaching her well.

———

"Where are the two lovebirds?" Noah asked, making exaggerated kissing sounds to tease his brother and Marcus.

Elena rolled her eyes as she set the table. Fourteen-year-old boys and their constant need to be obnoxious. "Grab the forks and help me," she redirected. "They went out for the evening. It's just us three."

"Ooh, a date. Bet they're getting busy," Noah grinned, knowing exactly how to push buttons.

Elena reached over and flicked his ear. "Behave yourself, you little shit."

Noah cackled. Nothing was better than getting his mom to swear.

David walked into the kitchen, having changed from his suit into shorts and a polo. He made the mistake of dipping a spoon into Elena's marinara sauce for a taste test.

The coughing started immediately. He lunged for a water glass, eyes watering.

"Jesus Christ, El! What's in this? Liquid fire?"

"A little Boston spice," Elena sang, completely unapologetic.

"Mom goes psycho with the cayenne," Noah warned, too late. "I learned that lesson when I was like eight."

"You could have mentioned that before I burned off my taste buds," David gasped, downing more water.

Elena put on her most innocent expression. "I thought you liked things hot."

"Food, Elena. I like hot food. Not napalm."

Noah was cracking up, watching the two adults banter like old friends. This was what he loved about being here—seeing his mom relaxed and happy, trading insults with David like they were siblings.

A few moments later, the three sat near the glass wall overlooking the pool, chatting about their day before David gave Elena a look which said "you want to start?"

"Noah, honey, there's something we need to discuss," Elena said, breaking apart a piece of garlic bread.

Noah's fork stopped halfway to his mouth. The universal parental tone that meant either he was in trouble or his life was about to change in some major way.

"Jesus, El," David laughed. "Why don't you just say 'Your father and I are getting divorced, you're adopted, and your dog has cancer' while you're at it?"

"What?!" Elena shot back. "All I said was we needed to discuss something."

"Right. And I might as well have said 'Son, your mother and I have something very important to tell you...'" David mimicked a serious parental voice.

Noah burst out laughing. "Dude, yes! I was like, oh shit, what did I do now?"

"Well, Mr. Expert-on-Teenage-Psychology," Elena said, reaching for more sauce, "why don't you tell him?"

"Tell me what?" Noah's curiosity was fully engaged now.

David set down his fork, considering his approach. "All right. Direct approach. Roger wants you to—"

"Who's Roger?" Noah interrupted.

"The director from *Sunset Academy*. He wants to talk to you about—"

"Wait, what? The director? Like, THE director?"

"Yes, the director. He wants to—"

"Holy shit! What's he want? Am I in trouble? Did I mess something up?"

"Noah, if you'd let me finish—"

"But why would he want to talk to ME? I'm nobody! I just stood there!"

"Can I please get through this without twenty questions?" David asked with mock exasperation.

Elena grinned. "I thought you were the one who understood how kids communicate these days, Mr. Hollywood Executive."

David flipped her off without looking. Elena gasped dramatically.

"Hey! That's my signature move!"

Noah was laughing despite his curiosity. These two were like an old married couple, and somehow it made everything feel safer, more normal.

"Anyway," David continued, trying to regain control of the conversation, "Roger thinks you're a natural. He wants you to come back and do more work on the show."

Noah's fork clattered onto his plate. "No fucking way! Are you serious?"

"Language, Noah," Elena warned, but she was grinning.

"Sorry, but... REALLY? Like, for real real?"

"Yes, really."

"OH MY GOD! This is insane! Wait till I tell Jake and Connor and—"

"Whoa, slow down there, Speed Racer," Elena interrupted. "There's more to discuss."

"More? What more? I get to be on TV with Lily! This is like the best thing ever!"

David and Elena exchanged a look. "It's not that simple, bud."

"What do you mean? I just show up and act, right? How hard can it be?"

Elena snorted. "Oh, honey. You sweet, naive child."

"What's that supposed to mean?"

"It means," David said, "that you'd have to live here. In LA. Full time."

Noah's face went blank. "Live here? Like... forever?"

"Well, not forever. But for as long as you're on the show."

"But what about home? And school? And my friends?" The questions tumbled out without filter.

"What about mom?" Noah asked, suddenly realizing the implications.

Elena took a breath, then dove in. "I'd move here too and become your on-set teacher."

"You'd be my teacher?!" Noah looked horrified. "Oh hell no. That's like having a prison guard who also makes your dinner."

Elena flicked a piece of bread at him. "Prison guard? I'll show you prison guard, you ungrateful little—"

"But I'd be famous! Famous people don't do homework!"

David laughed. "Famous fourteen-year-olds absolutely do homework. It's the law."

"That sucks! What's the point of being famous if you still have to do algebra?"

"The point," Elena said dryly, "is that you don't end up being one of those child actors who can't string a sentence together by the time they're twenty."

Noah slumped in his chair. "This is way more complicated than I thought."

"Welcome to the real world, kiddo," Elena said. "It always is."

"What about Aiden?" Noah asked, suddenly remembering. "Would he have to come too?"

Elena's expression got more serious. "That's... complicated. This would affect his whole life too."

"But he's got Marcus! He'd probably WANT to stay!"

"It's not that simple, Noah. Aiden's got his own life to think about."

"Yeah, but Marcus is here, so duh, obviously he'd—"

"Noah." Elena's voice had an edge that made him shut up. "Nothing about this is obvious. Your brother gets a say in his own life."

David jumped in. "And there are other things you need to think about, kiddo."

"Like what?"

"Like no more posting whatever you want on social media. Like people following you around. Like not being able to just be a normal kid."

Noah's enthusiasm flickered. "What do you mean?"

"I mean," Elena said bluntly, "that if you do this, your privacy goes out the window. People will know who you are. Some of them will be nice. Some of them will be creeps. Some will hate you just because they can."

"That's..." Noah looked uncertain for the first time. "That's kinda scary."

"It should be," David said. "This isn't a game, Noah. This is your whole life changing."

Noah was quiet for a moment, his teenage brain trying to process adult-sized consequences. "I... I want to talk to Lily about it."

"Smart move," Elena said. "She's been living this for a while. She'll tell you straight."

"How long do I have to decide?"

"Not long," David admitted. "TV moves fast. Maybe we talk again tomorrow?"

Noah nodded and pushed back from the table. "Can I go call Lily?"

"Go ahead, baby."

As Noah bounded up the stairs, Elena looked at David. "Think we scared him enough?"

"Think we scared him just right. Kid needs to know what he's getting into."

"God, I hope we're not about to ruin his life."

David reached over and squeezed her hand. "He's got your brain, El. He'll figure it out."

thirty-nine
opening up

NOAH STARED at his phone for the third time, thumb hovering over Lily's contact. They texted constantly, sure, but actually calling felt... bigger somehow. More serious. What if she was busy? What if her mom was around and thought he was being clingy?

But the dinner conversation with his mom and uncle was still spinning in his head. The director wanted to offer him a real role on the show —not just background extra stuff, but an actual character. Lily's boyfriend. And Uncle David had suggested that Lily might be able to help him understand what that would really mean, what he'd be getting into.

He needed to hear her voice. Needed to know what she really thought about all this.

He pressed call.

"Noah?" She picked up on the second ring, sounding a little out of breath. "Hey! You're actually calling me? What's up?"

"Yeah, I'm fine. Sorry, I just... Mom and Uncle David told me something at dinner tonight, and I needed to talk to you about it."

"Hold on." He could hear her moving around, then a door closing. "Okay, I'm in my room now. What's going on?"

"The director wants to offer me a real role on the show. Like, as your boyfriend character. Not just extra stuff."

"Oh my god!" There was excitement in her voice mixed with relief. "Noah, this is so cool! I've been dying to talk to you about this."

"Wait, you already knew?"

"Roger asked me about it today, but he made me promise not to say anything until he talked to your uncle first. I've been going crazy keeping it secret!"

Noah felt a little weird about that. "So you knew before I did?"

"I'm sorry! I wanted to tell you so bad, but... well, this is kind of exactly the stuff I need to warn you about."

"What do you mean?"

"Like, they asked my opinion about whether I thought you'd be good for the show, and whether we'd work well together as scene partners. But they didn't want me telling you in case it didn't work out with the grown-ups, you know? It's all very... political, I guess."

"That's so weird. What did you tell them?"

"That you're amazing and I'd love to work with you more!" Her voice got brighter. "But also that I thought it would help the production, you know?"

Help the production. The words sat heavy between them. Noah had been thinking about this like some amazing dream opportunity, but Lily was already thinking about ratings and storylines and business.

"Help the... production?" he repeated.

He heard her shift, probably sitting down. "Noah, it didn't surprise me that they want you. You're like... a natural. You could play that role without even trying. But... there's something you need to understand."

"What's that?"

"It's all fake."

His heart stopped. "Being... being your boyfriend?" His voice cracked on the words.

"Oh god, no!" Her response was immediate and emphatic. "You're *definitely* my boyfriend. I didn't mean that at all."

He exhaled, not realizing he'd been holding his breath.

"No, the whole business side... it's... well, you just have to be careful."

"I know that."

"No, Noah. You don't. I didn't either when I started. I'm still learning."

This was a different Lily than the one who texted him about homework or laughed at his dumb jokes during lunch. Her voice carried a weight that made her sound older, more experienced. Professional.

"Sometimes people really do want your opinion," she continued. "But we're fourteen. What Roger really wanted to know was whether we'd get along as scene partners."

"Get along?" Noah was confused. "You're my girlfriend."

"Yes, but think about it," she said, suddenly sounding much more mature than him. "How many of your friends back in Boston have girlfriends?"

Noah thought about his classmates. It seemed like they were always talking about some girl one week, then a completely different girl the next week.

"And if we didn't get along, or broke up, or had drama... that could really mess up the show, you know?"

He found himself nodding even though she couldn't see him.

"You understand?"

"Yeah." Though honestly, he preferred just thinking about the fun parts—being on TV, getting to act with Lily, maybe becoming famous.

"So I said what he needed to hear. I *want* you on the show, if that's what you want." Her voice brightened, becoming his girlfriend again instead of a seasoned actress. "And I think you're really talented. Seriously."

Noah felt his cheeks warm. For once, he was glad they were talking instead of FaceTiming—he didn't need her seeing him blush like an idiot.

But somehow, she knew anyway. She could hear it in his voice, the way it got softer when he was embarrassed. It made her smile. This was what she loved about him—he was so genuinely himself.

"Noah?"

"Yeah?"

"I'm also really happy you might be here more often. I mean, if you decide to do it. Because..." She trailed off, suddenly tongue-tied herself.

"Admit it!" Noah's confidence returned with a grin. "You like me!"

"Keep telling yourself that," she shot back, but he could hear her smiling.

"Uh huh! You liiike me," he sang into the phone.

"No way."

"Way!"

They dissolved into giggles, and for a moment they were just two fourteen-year-olds being silly on the phone, the weight of the industry and adult decisions forgotten.

The front door opened with its usual squeak, followed by the sound of Aiden and Marcus's voices drifting through the house. David could hear them chatting about some skateboarder they'd seen at the beach—something being "epic" or "insane" in that particular way teenagers described everything. He'd long since stopped trying to decode their language.

"Uh, Aiden?" David called from the kitchen. "Could we chat for a minute?"

The voices stopped abruptly. David could practically feel the shift in the house's energy.

"And yes, I know how that sounds," he continued, walking into the living room where both boys had frozen by the door. "But we do need to talk. You and your mom."

Aiden's face went pale. "Is... something wrong?"

Marcus mouthed "What the fuck?" behind Aiden's shoulder, looking equally nervous.

"Marcus, this won't take long," David said, not answering Aiden's question directly. He headed toward his office, hiding a small smile. Sometimes this quasi-parenting thing was more entertaining than he'd expected. He wondered if his own parents had enjoyed watching him squirm this much.

Aiden followed him like a man walking to his execution, shoulders tense, mind clearly racing through every possible disaster scenario.

Inside the office, Elena was waiting on the sofa, looking much more relaxed than her son expected.

"Come sit, sweetie," she said, patting the cushion beside her.

Aiden perched on the edge, still wary. He glanced between his mother and uncle, trying to read the situation.

Elena noticed David's expression—what she privately called his "resting bitch face"—and realized why Aiden looked terrified.

"For fuck's sake, David!" she said, swatting his arm. "Now *you're* the one who's scaring the hell out of my kid!"

"What?" David gave an innocent shrug.

"It's okay, Aiden," Elena said, turning back to her son. "You're not in trouble. We just want to talk about Marcus."

"Marcus?"

The single word opened floodgates in Aiden's mind. They didn't approve. They thought he was too young. They'd figured out he and Marcus were sleeping together. They were going to make him choose between his family and his boyfriend. They were going to send him home early. They were—

"Aiden." David's voice cut through the spiral. "Aiden!"

Aiden snapped back to the present, meeting his uncle's concerned gaze.

The moment their eyes connected, David felt it—a rushing wave of his nephew's emotions that nearly knocked him backward. Fear, yes, but so much more. Crushing worry about disappointing everyone. Guilt about being happy when others might be struggling. The exhausting weight of trying to hold everything together, to be the perfect son who never caused problems, to carry everyone else's happiness on his shoulders while his own needs got smaller and smaller until they barely existed at all.

David's chest tightened. His breathing became labored. Every muscle in his body contracted as Aiden's emotional burden became his own—years of carefully suppressed feelings hitting him all at once.

"David!" Elena was beside him instantly.

"What's wrong, Uncle David?" Aiden shot to his feet, panic replacing his earlier anxiety.

David waved them back, struggling to break the empathic connection. "Just... give me a second," he managed, forcing himself to breathe.

"Aiden, get him some water," Elena ordered.

As Aiden ran from the room, Elena knelt beside her best friend. "What just happened? That looked intense, even for you."

"I never realized..." David accepted the glass Aiden thrust at him, drinking deeply. "I never realized how much he carries."

Elena looked at her son, who was hovering anxiously nearby. There were layers here she didn't understand, some communication between David and Aiden that spoke a language she didn't know.

"Sit down, Aiden. Please. You're making me more nervous than I already am."

Aiden reluctantly returned to the sofa, but his concern was genuine. David could feel it—cleaner now, less overwhelming, but still there.

"You're a good person, Aiden," David said finally, his voice steadier. "You carry so much, and you do it quietly, trying not to burden anyone else."

Aiden looked surprised, then bashful. "I... thanks, I guess."

"But I want to ask you something directly, and I need you to be honest. With me, and with your mom."

The old tension returned to Aiden's shoulders. Elena watched her son transform from a seventeen-year-old back into someone much older, someone who'd learned to hide everything behind careful control.

"It's okay, honey," Elena said softly, reaching for his arm. She felt him flinch reflexively before catching himself, embarrassed. The reaction cut through her like a knife.

"Are you in love with Marcus?"

The question hung in the air. David already knew the answer—he'd felt it, lived it, been overwhelmed by the depth of it. But Aiden needed to say it himself.

"I... fuck..." Aiden's voice broke. He wiped at his eyes, frustrated by his own emotion. "I don't know why I'm crying. This is so stupid."

Elena started to speak, but David caught her eye and shook his head slightly.

"Marcus... well... he's been through a lot of shit, you know?" Aiden kept going, not looking either in the eye. "But, like... I see how much he, like, really lights up, and well... I don't know... it's like he trusts me... like really."

Aiden's composure wavered.

"But summer's almost over."

That did it. Aiden looked down, shoulders shaking with the effort of holding everything in. This was the conversation he'd been dreading—the one where they explained he had to leave Marcus behind, go back to Boston, pretend this summer had never happened.

Noah was the strong one, everyone knew that. Aiden had always been too sensitive, too emotional. So he'd learned to pack it all away, to be the good son who never caused problems, who carried his own burdens and everyone else's too.

The room fell silent except for Aiden's quiet, desperate breathing.

"I fucking love him," he finally whispered, the words barely audible through his tears. "God, I love him so much and I don't know what the hell I'm supposed to do about it."

Elena's heart broke. She reached for him again, but felt him tense against her touch—not rejection, but overwhelming emotion that couldn't bear physical contact right now.

David leaned forward, deliberately catching Aiden's eye. This time, instead of fighting the empathic connection, he invited it—offering to share the burden, to take some of the weight Aiden had been carrying alone.

For a moment, nothing happened. Then Aiden felt something strange—like his pain was being lifted away, redistributed, made manageable.

"I love him."

The words came again, but not from Aiden's mouth. Everyone turned toward the doorway where Marcus stood, having heard enough to understand what was happening.

"I love him," Marcus repeated, walking straight to Aiden and pulling him up into his arms.

That's when the dam broke. Years of held-back emotion poured out of Aiden—not just love for Marcus, but all the fear and worry and desperate need to be perfect that had been eating him alive. His whole body shook with the force of it, but Marcus held him steady, rubbing his back and murmuring reassurances.

Elena sat transfixed, watching her son finally let go of whatever invisible weight he'd been carrying. She'd seen their connection that night she'd surprised them at the restaurant—the way Marcus had lunged to catch Aiden when he fainted, the protective panic in his eyes. She'd known then this wasn't just some summer romance. But this... watching Marcus hold her son while years of bottled emotion poured out... this was beyond words to witness.

David felt the shift too, the way Aiden's emotional load lightened as Marcus took some of it willingly, naturally. This wasn't just teenage infatuation. This was love in its truest form—the kind that made space for the other person's whole self, pain and all.

As Aiden's sobs gradually quieted, still safe in Marcus's arms, Elena finally understood what David had been trying to tell her. Some decisions weren't really decisions at all. They were just recognizing what had already become true.

Family wasn't just blood. Sometimes it was who showed up when everything fell apart, who made room for your messiest, most broken pieces, who helped you carry what you couldn't hold alone.

Sometimes family was a boy from the streets who loved her son enough to catch him when he finally stopped trying to catch everyone else.

forty
debut

"DO YOU NEED ANY HELP, EL?"

Elena turned to Diana, gesturing toward the two large bowls of popcorn. It was nice to hear her name mentioned so casually. Michael used to call her that, and David had adopted it soon after they met. But now Diana seemed to have just naturally landed there too. It'd been a long time since she'd had a proper friend—well, other than David, but he was family.

In high school, she'd been one of the most popular girls around, but as she got older, the true friends seemed to fade away with their own lives and dreams. It always seemed so damn difficult to make new friends as an adult, and she wondered if anyone else felt the same.

Seeing Diana help with the snacks... it was silly, really, she thought... but this was a friend just for her. Not one of Noah's friend's mothers, or someone at work she'd grab lunch with once in a while. Diana was... well, she hoped she was... a real friend.

"C'mon, Mom!" she heard Aiden call out from the living room where everyone had gathered. She snapped back to the task at hand, grabbing another 2-liter and the seasoning salt before walking in to see the crowd before her.

David sat in his usual chair—Michael's chair, really. She remembered one of the few fights he and David ever had over that hideous piece of furniture. David had thought it was an eyesore and wanted nothing to do with it being in the house. The more David bitched about it, the more Michael had loved it. Now, David wouldn't let anyone else sit in it. She smiled at the memory.

Aiden and Marcus were practically lying on top of each other on the floor, cozied up with a couple of pillows from the sofa. Diana stepped over them to set one of the popcorn bowls on the coffee table. Sitting next to each other, but not quite as close, were Noah and Lily. They were still at the age where having their moms witness them even holding hands was gross. Elena saw Diana nod toward them and wink before she plopped down on the edge of the sofa and patted the spot next to her.

Elena took her seat after handing Noah the soda and reached for a handful of popcorn from Diana's bowl before passing it to David.

"Where's our popcorn?" Noah asked with typical fourteen-year-old indignation.

"On the coffee table. This is for the adults!" Elena shot back with a laugh. "Think of it as the kiddie table at Thanksgiving."

Just then, Marcus reached up from the floor and retrieved the bowl to sit in front of him and Aiden, causing Noah to look between the two and back toward the parents.

"Uh! No fair! We're like the stars of this thing and we don't even get any!" He pouted, but Lily giggled.

"Be a good little star and start the show while you're up there," David teased.

Noah frowned but reached for the remote, making a dramatic show of diving his hand into Marcus and Aiden's popcorn bowl, spilling kernels everywhere but at least getting a handful. Plopping back onto the sofa, he held out his clump of popcorn for Lily to share.

"Such a gentleman," Elena laughed, eating another piece of popcorn.

Noah pressed play on Hulu and *Sunset Academy* began. The theme music played and everyone clapped when Lily's name came on screen, much to her embarrassment. She'd been in the business for several years, but it still felt weird to have everyone focused on her, even though you'd never know it judging by her press appearances.

Then came the credit everyone was really waiting for.

And introducing Noah Walsh as Ryan.

The room erupted in hoops and hollers, with Lily being the loudest. Elena watched her youngest son's face transform from embarrassment to pride to something best described as pure joy in a matter of seconds. She had to admit she stole some of his pride for herself. How many mothers got to witness something like this? She glanced at Diana, who was cheering along with everyone else. Well, Elena thought, Diana obviously knew exactly what she was feeling. It dawned on her that not only was Diana turning into a real friend, but she knew firsthand what it was like to navigate this weird world Noah was finding himself in.

"Shh!" Aiden was quick to quiet everyone. "The show's starting and I want to see my little brother's breakout performance. I've only heard about this shit—watching it on screen is totally different."

Lily reached over without thinking and grabbed Noah's hand as her character walked back into the school cafeteria...

Aiden was the loudest when Noah looked up and delivered the impromptu performance that had sealed his fate as a budding star. Everyone laughed, Marcus even sitting up on his knees, completely captivated. Lily squeezed her boyfriend's hand and he smiled awkwardly. It was weird as hell watching himself on TV, especially on something as big as this show.

"Hang on... wait for it!" Lily shushed everyone. "And..."

Noah delivered his Netflix line and the studio audience erupted, but no one in the living room heard it, laughing so hard they momentarily drowned out the TV. Even Noah giggled at himself. Lily, caught up in the moment, forgot her mother was on the other end of the sofa and gave him a peck on the cheek. They both laughed as Elena nudged Diana to look, but Diana just wiggled her eyebrows and gazed over at David, who was enjoying watching everyone else more than the show itself.

Aside from business meetings, this was the first time David had actually watched the show for fun—he rarely watched anything outside the office. He got a kick out of seeing how it brought everyone together. If this is all it took, he thought, he'd have the show on every night.

David caught Elena's eye and they both knew they were wishing for the same thing: Michael being there with them. He would have run over and given Noah a big hug, tickling him and embarrassing him in front of his girlfriend. David could just picture it and felt that familiar melancholy smile cross his face, but quickly pushed the thought away. Michael might not be here, but David could still learn from him.

Standing up from his chair, he asked, "Does anyone need anything?"

Only Noah bothered to respond, remembering his earlier complaint about being left out of the popcorn distribution.

David didn't know what came over him, but he seized on what he imagined Michael would have done. He reached down and hoisted Noah up over his shoulder. Noah burst into laughter, kicking his legs and demanding to be put down while Lily dissolved into giggles. Everyone else joined in—Marcus pointing and rolling on the floor with Aiden.

"Then let's get in the kitchen and make some, Mr. Movie Star!" David teased as he carried Noah off. The kid was getting a little too big to hold onto for long, but it felt good—something he never would have imagined doing in a million years.

Michael had made him do it, somehow. Even from wherever he was now, Michael was still teaching David how to be part of a family.

As their laughter faded toward the kitchen, Elena looked around at the scene—Aiden and Marcus tangled up together on the floor, Lily trying to contain her giggles, Diana shaking her head with amusement—and felt something settle in her chest.

This wasn't just a vacation anymore. This was home.

epilogue

"WHEN ARE THEY GONNA GET HERE?" Noah complained, sitting on his knees at the front window, staring out at the heavy falling snow. He'd been counting the minutes all morning and now it was past two. Snow had started last night and already caused widespread delays, but so far their flight was still coming—just not on time.

"Honey, they'll make it. Just have patience." Elena walked up behind him, placed her hands on his shoulders, and looked out the window. She grimaced. The winter wonderland outside was beautiful, but it made her worry. Still, she could see Noah's anxiety building now that their scheduled arrival had come and gone.

"Besides," she put on her best "it'll be fine, honey" face, "this is much more Christmasy, don't you think? Much better than LA."

Noah barely listened, already scanning through the snow for any car to arrive. A whole week without Lily felt like forever when you were fourteen and this was your first real girlfriend.

They were supposed to head out to Logan Airport, but when the forecast suddenly called for a snowstorm last night, Elena and David agreed she'd stay home—they'd take a taxi. Those drivers knew how to navigate this mess better than anyone.

"Mom! I still don't understand why Marcus can't just stay in my room. There's not enough space for everyone already and—"

"We've already had this discussion, Aiden. I know you two are...

close... but it's out of the question. I don't care if it's you or him, but one of you is sleeping on the basement couch."

"But Mom! We've been apart for a fucking week!"

"Language, Aiden. But nothing. Do I make myself—"

"They're here!" Noah yelled over them, causing both to rush to the door. Aiden practically barreled out into the snow in his socks.

"Aiden! Put some damn shoes on!" Elena fought a losing battle.

Noah had been in his winter coat and snow boots for hours, ever since their original arrival time. Elena watched as he ran through the snow toward Lily, who stepped out of the taxi looking like she'd never seen snow before in her life.

"Noah!" she shrieked, half laughing, half terrified as he scooped her up in his arms, spinning her around until they both nearly toppled into a snowdrift.

"Holy shit, I missed you so much!" Noah buried his face in her neck, not caring who heard him.

"Careful!" Diana yelled from the taxi, but she was already hurrying toward the house. "It's too fucking cold for this!"

David had forgotten how brutal Boston winters could be—he and Michael had only visited a few times over the years. He grabbed luggage from the taxi while calling to Marcus to help, but Marcus was already running toward Aiden, who was practically bouncing on the porch in his socks.

"Get over here, you idiot!" Aiden grabbed Marcus the second he was within reach, pulling him into a fierce kiss right there on the front porch. They'd been apart for a week—the longest since they'd gotten together—and neither gave a damn who was watching.

Elena and the boys had flown out early to spend time with her parents and get the house ready for everyone else. It was the first time they'd been back since she had organized the move to LA in September, taking most of her clothes and precious keepsakes west. Her mother looked in from time to time, but otherwise the house remained exactly as they'd left it.

In some ways, Elena felt like she was coming home to memories. This is where the boys had grown up, had their first days of school, learned to ride bikes, celebrated birthdays and holidays. Now they lived in LA with David, and it was wonderful—his house was much more modern, fancier

—but this was still home. She'd been happy when David suggested keeping the Boston house for occasions just like this.

David had seemed eager since Halloween to have everyone fly out to "El's place," as he'd begun calling it, for Christmas. It would be something different, he'd told Diana. An opportunity to really enjoy the holiday. If they were lucky, it might even snow.

Looking around now, David reminded himself to be careful what he wished for next time as he dragged the last luggage toward the house he hadn't been to since Michael was... well, for a long time. He pushed away the memory that threatened to surface. He'd been having a lot of "Michael moments" lately. Most were warm and pleasant, but some reminded him of the loneliness that used to consume him. Now that his house was always full, he was never truly alone like before. But especially at night, lying awake staring at the ceiling, he'd still miss Michael's presence, his warmth, his love.

"The house is gorgeous, El!" Diana was shaking snow off her puffy jacket—the one she usually wore skiing at Big Bear, but this was the real deal. Thank God she owned a proper winter coat.

Her attention turned to the Christmas tree in the corner by an authentic fireplace. "Is that real wood burning? I haven't seen one of those in years!"

"Indeed. I had the boys get wood from the hardware store the other day just for tonight."

"The house is so... festive," Diana continued, taking in all the decorations—old ornaments and holiday knick-knacks, snow globes and garlands.

"Pictures!" Diana's voice filled with joy. Elena had what seemed like a million framed photos on the mantel, her favorite being the boys when they were in grade school, posed together smiling. Diana smiled warmly and gave Elena that look mothers share.

Meanwhile, David was fighting with the glass storm door, Marcus having abandoned the luggage to make out with Aiden on the snowy porch. Noah was showing Lily how to pack a proper snowball when he suddenly grinned mischievously.

"Think you can hit those two idiots?" he asked, nodding toward his brother and Marcus.

Lily looked at the snowball in her hands, then at the kissing couple. "I've never done this before."

"Just aim and throw. Hard."

Her first attempt went wide, but her second nailed Marcus directly in the back of the head.

"What the fuck?!" Marcus spun around, snow dripping down his neck.

"Oh, it's on now!" Aiden wiped snow from his face and immediately started packing ammunition. "Here, babe." He shoved two snowballs into Marcus's hands. "Time to show these little shits how it's done."

"Bring it, asshole!" Noah called back, already ducking behind the snow-covered hedge with Lily.

"Did he just call me an asshole?" Marcus asked, looking genuinely confused.

"Welcome to the family," Aiden grinned. "Now throw the damn snowball!"

What followed was an all-out war. Marcus, who'd never had a snowball fight in his life, threw like he was pitching a baseball. Aiden had deadly accuracy from years of practice. But Lily—sweet, California-raised Lily—turned out to be a natural.

"Holy shit!" she squealed as a snowball exploded against the tree next to her head. "This is insane!" She packed another one with surprising skill and launched it at Aiden, nailing him square in the chest.

"Damn, girl!" Noah stared at his girlfriend with new admiration. "Where the hell did that come from?"

"I don't know!" Lily was laughing so hard she could barely stand. "This is amazing!"

"You two are so dead!" Aiden called out, preparing his counterattack.

From inside the house, Elena, David, and Diana watched through the storm door as the four teenagers pelted each other mercilessly, shrieking with laughter and cursing like sailors.

"Should we break this up?" Diana asked, watching her daughter get absolutely demolished by a snowball from Marcus.

"Let 'em play," David said, remembering his own words from months ago. "They won't get to be kids like this much longer."

Elena was watching and laughing, seeing her sons completely uninhibited for maybe the first time in their lives. "Look at them," she said softly. "They're just... happy."

Finally, soaked and shivering, the four combatants called a truce and stumbled inside, leaving a battlefield of snow and laughter behind them.

———

"Okay, Noah, I think it's your turn this year," Elena announced.

Everyone was gathered in the basement family room she'd furnished when she bought the house. It was perfect for opening gifts—big enough for the larger of her two Christmas trees, with a sofa, several chairs, a small wet bar, and a pool table she'd converted into a miniature Christmas village for the season.

Lily sat cross-legged on the floor at Noah's feet, still glowing from their snow fight. Her hair was finally dry, but she kept catching Noah's eye and grinning, both of them remembering how good it felt to just be stupid kids together.

Marcus was curled up against Aiden on the floor by the tree, still processing that this was his first real Christmas in years. Aiden kept his arm around him, sensing when Marcus's thoughts drifted to Phoenix and gently bringing him back to the present.

"Mom?"

"Yes, honey?"

"Maybe Lily and Marcus should be Santa this year? I mean..." Noah suddenly got shy, but Lily smiled encouragingly. "Maybe they've never done this tradition before. I dunno, just thinking..."

"Oh, can I please?" Marcus sat up, excitement replacing the melancholy that had been creeping in. This would be his first Christmas celebration since... well, since everything fell apart with his real family. He felt Aiden's hand squeeze his, grounding him in the present, in love, in belonging.

"Well, I think we know Marcus's answer," Elena smiled, watching her son instinctively comfort his boyfriend. It still broke her heart a little, thinking about what Marcus had lost, but seeing what he'd found here... that helped.

"What about you, Lily?" David asked.

Lily looked up at her mom for permission, getting an encouraging nod. She and Elena had spent weeks planning this Christmas, discussing traditions and gift ideas. They'd all agreed to play Santa collectively—each package simply saying "Love, Santa" to take the pressure off who spent what.

"I'd love to," Lily said, her face lighting up.

For the next several minutes, Marcus and Lily distributed gifts with the seriousness of official Christmas elves. Marcus made everyone laugh by announcing each gift in an increasingly ridiculous Santa voice, while Lily tried to keep track of who got what.

"Who has the gift with the gold star on the bottom?" Elena called over the chatter.

Everyone began examining their presents until David held up a small, elegantly wrapped box.

"I do!"

The room focused on him as Elena explained their family tradition—the gold star gift was always opened first, on Christmas Eve night, by whoever found it under their pile.

David held the box carefully, something about its weight and shape triggering a memory he couldn't quite place. The teenagers all watched eagerly as he slowly unwrapped the red foil paper and green ribbons.

"Come on, Uncle David!" Noah called out. "The suspense is killing us!"

David laughed and opened the lid, pushing aside tissue paper. Then he stopped. His expression shifted completely—the playful anticipation replaced by something deeper, more reverent. His hands trembled slightly as he stared into the box.

"David?" Elena said softly.

He couldn't speak. A tear rolled down his cheek as he reached into the box and carefully lifted out a simple wooden frame.

The room fell silent as he held up the photograph: a younger David sitting beside Michael, both of them radiant with happiness. Three-year-old Aiden sat on Michael's lap, grinning at the camera, while infant Noah slept peacefully in David's arms. Behind them stood the very same Christmas tree that now towered over their current gathering.

"Oh my God," Aiden whispered, recognizing himself and his brother.

Noah's eyes widened. "Is that... is that us?"

David nodded, still unable to find words. Elena had kept this photo all these years, waiting for the right moment to give it back to him.

"Michael made it home," David finally managed, his voice thick with emotion.

The words hung in the air, sacred and true. Everyone understood they were witnessing something profound—the completion of a circle that had been broken years ago when Michael died, now somehow made whole again through the family that had grown up around his memory.

David looked around the room at these people who had become his chosen family: Elena, his anchor through every storm; Aiden and Noah, the boys he'd helped raise and who'd taught him what it meant to be needed; Marcus, the son he'd never expected but couldn't imagine living without; Lily, with her infectious laugh and generous heart; Diana, who'd become a true friend.

And Michael, present in every moment of love they shared, every tradition they honored, every time David chose connection over solitude.

Outside, snow continued to fall on the house where two broken families had somehow become whole, where love had found new ways to grow and flourish, where the past and present had merged into something beautiful and eternal.

David wasn't alone anymore. He never had been, really. Love didn't end when people died—it just found new forms, new expressions, new ways to create family where none had existed before.

This was what home looked like: not a place, but the people who made space for your whole heart, who caught you when you fell, who celebrated your joy and shared your sorrows, who showed up again and again, choosing to be family in all the ways that mattered most.

about the author

Michael Manosca first pursued a career in the arts, studying in Chicago, but storytelling has always been at the heart of his creative expression. His travels across the world have shaped his perspective, infusing his writing with the depth and nuance of the people and cultures he has encountered.

Michael writes in a deeply personal format, inspired by the relationships and experiences that shaped his upbringing. He explores the intricacies of friendship, the search for identity, and the quiet moments that define us. Through vivid characters and emotional depth, he hopes to craft stories that linger in readers' minds long after the final page.

When not writing, he can be found wandering the northern woods, exploring new cities, or enjoying a lively conversation in a tucked-away café. He currently resides along the western coast of the United States and is already working on his next story.

also by michael manosca

Beyond Ties that Bind

Treffen

Bloodlines

Prism

Almost Always

Flickering

A Language of Water